A CERTAIN ENEMY

A Nathan Monsarrat Thriller

by

Michael A. Richards

For my parents, reunited

Special thanks to Sam Gibson and Joyce Lit, good friends and careful
readers, and to John Atkins for his dental expertise.
Any errors, omissions, and inaccuracies belong to the author alone.

A doubtful friend is worse than a certain enemy.

Aesop, *Aesopica*

Never interrupt your enemy when he is making a mistake.

Napoleon Bonaparte

Copyright @ 2020 by Michael A. Richards

ISBN: 9798652665142

Also by Michael A. Richards

CHOICE OF ENEMIES

A THOUSAND ENEMIES

SETTING THE BOARD

Each Chessboard Square is Identified by a Letter and Number

At dawn, Nathan Monsarrat laced his running shoes and assaulted the back roads of Greylock, a college town in the Berkshire hills of western Massachusetts. Following the crest of the yellow lines, he ran smoothly, encountering few cars so early on the Saturday morning of the Columbus Day weekend. Seven miles into the run, he reached a cairn marking the trailhead to the logging roads that laced the rolling hills. A mile further, he turned onto a serpentine hiking trail. He swatted branches and hurdled roots, climbing steadily higher. Breaking through the tree line, he sprinted to the summit.

A former deep cover operative with the Central Intelligence Agency, midway between forty and fifty years of age, Monsarrat carried two hundred pounds of muscle on his six feet, one inch frame. Tendrils of gray crept through his unruly brown hair. His final mission for the Agency had ended badly. Betrayed by a Langley rival to Nigerian terrorists, he endured eighteen weeks of physical and psychological torture before the Agency bought his freedom with a quarter million dollar ransom.

During the long recuperation at a private Virginia clinic, his physical injuries healed, but his emotional wounds festered. The day following his release from the clinic, he submitted his retirement file, receiving from Langley a medical disability settlement, a non-disclosure payment, and a full pension. The Agency helped him secure a position with Greylock College, and at the start of the next semester, he began his new life as Dean of Undergraduate Studies. His tenure with the college soon ended, but he chose to remain in

Greylock. He enjoyed the languid pace of the town, the kindness of its residents, and the beauty of the Berkshires.

He also fell in love with Sylvie Epstein, associate professor in the Department of English. She taught a freshman survey course in American and British Literature in the fall and a senior seminar on Woolf, Thoreau, Lawrence, and Dos Passos in the spring. Outside the classroom, she collected socialist realism art from the Soviet Union and trained for the annual Boston marathon. Each morning, they ran the back roads together, but she had driven to Cambridge the day prior to conduct research for her autobiography of John Dos Passos, a chapter on his years at Harvard.

Alone with his thoughts atop the summit, Monsarrat rehearsed his proposal of marriage. He considered a Hollywood approach, taking a knee and offering his engagement ring, a band of white gold holding a pear shaped diamond, like a magic trick. He contemplated a fairy tale surprise, placing it beneath her pillow. He mulled a casual advance, serving it like a biscotto accompanying an espresso. During his career with the Agency, he had seduced the innocent, blackmailed the corrupt, and eliminated the treacherous. Proposing marriage fell outside his comfort zone.

He descended the summit, reached the logging road, and followed it to the trailhead. Running hard, he covered the seven mile return trip, turned onto Cartwright Road, and sprinted toward his two-story colonial home. His breathing steady, he walked up the driveway, past green lawns and the medley of oak, birch, and maple trees that shaded the house. At the end of the driveway, a Jeep Wrangler was parked before a detached garage.

The Agency had honed his paranoia, and he installed a robust security system to protect the property. On a chain around his neck, he wore the keys to the titanium locks that secured the doors of the house and garage. Motion sensors and alarms safeguarded the interiors. LED spotlights illuminated the exteriors and the lawns. Digital cameras recorded at all times and in every condition. An arsenal of forty-five caliber pistols and .38 revolvers provided a final line of defense against enemies accumulated during his years as a deep cover operative.

He unlocked the door to the garage and entered a ten digit code into a security node, disabling the alarm. He scanned the whorls of his right index finger against the optical reader, the diodes flashed green, and he stepped into his home gym. Barbells and dumbbells filled metal racks next to an inclined bench. Mats covered the cement floor, and a canvas heavy bag hung by a chain from a steel beam. An elastic cord tethered a round speed bag, and a jump rope looped around a wall hook.

He drank a bottle of cold water from a dormitory refrigerator. A regimen of weights preceded sessions on the heavy bag and speed bag. He removed the gloves and applied ointment onto his knuckles. Lifting the rope from the hook, he skipped fast-slow intervals, finishing the workout with five hundred sit-ups and an equal number of push-ups. He secured the garage and followed a gravel path leading to the house.

Minutes before noon, he unlocked the front door, and repeated the security procedures. He climbed the staircase to the second floor. He shaved carefully, showered quickly, and dressed in jeans and a tee shirt. In the kitchen, he brewed a cup of black coffee and ate a ham and cheese sandwich. After cleaning the dishes, he spread a towel onto the counter and stripped a Beretta Px4 Storm .45 caliber pistol. He swabbed, cleaned, and reassembled the weapon before placing it into a shooting case. Three magazines, a dozen boxes of ammunition, and ear protection filled a second case.

He stepped into work boots, shrugged on a hooded sweatshirt, and secured the house. Backing the Jeep down the driveway, he turned onto Cartwright Road. He drove through the town, past the college campus, reaching an outdoor shooting range twenty minutes later. Parking the Jeep, he retrieved his cases and mounted the steps of the firing platform. Twice retired, wealthy with time, he possessed excellent shooting skills.

Downrange, wooden targets were secured to dirt berms, and metal plates were wired to iron stakes of varying height. He secured the ear protection, zeroed the sights of the Beretta, and fired the weapon, left leg forward, knees slightly bent. He placed ten rounds into the bull's-eye of a wooden target, dropped the magazine, and inserted a loaded clip. He switched positions, firing right leg forward into the center of a metal plate. Intent on his task, he ignored the cell phone vibrating in his back pocket.

He continued to shoot until expending the ammunition. The sun slipped below the rounded Berkshire hills as he departed the range. He retraced his route, stopping in town to fill the gas tank of the Jeep, and pulled into his driveway beneath an explosion of spotlights. He parked before the garage. Carrying the two cases, he crossed the gravel path to the house, disabled the security system, and walked into the kitchen.

He scrubbed his hands with soap and lemons to remove the smell of the range. He sliced vegetables for a Mediterranean salad, adding

Kalamata olives and feta cheese. Opening a bottle of Fat Tire Amber Ale, he ate standing at the counter as the outside temperatures dipped and the old house groaned. He washed and dried the dishes before again spreading a towel onto the counter. He brushed, wiped, and reloaded the magazines before stripping, cleaning, and reassembling the Beretta. He inserted a clip and chambered a round. The motion reminded him of the range and the ignored cell phone call.

Opening the cell phone, he expected to find a voicemail from Sylvie but discovered a message from a Maryland area code. Pressing the play icon, he heard a long forgotten voice.

"Hey, man, your old friend the kickoff artist here. Long time, man, way too long. I know, I dropped outta touch, but I'm at the Saint James Hotel in Boston for a dental conference, and it would be great to see you again. I'm off to Cape Cod soon for the last of the holiday weekend with a new lady friend I just met, but I want to talk with you, face to face, half catching up, half your old line of work, before I return to Bethesda. It's important that you meet this woman, give me your opinion. How about lunch tomorrow in Hyannis? On me. Sparks? At noon? I know it's a long drive from the Berkshires, man, but please come. Call me as soon as you can."

Monsarrat had not spoken to Dan Westbrook since graduating from the University of Iowa, where they had played Hawkeye football together, Westbrook the star placekicker to his own role as a reserve linebacker. He did not know how his former teammate learned of his Agency career, his Berkshire home, or his cell phone number. He also did not understand why he had initiated contact after two decades of silence. Replaying the message, he noted its lack of names.

An online search revealed that Westbrook was a naval medical officer, a captain assigned to Walter Reed National Military Medical Center in Bethesda, Maryland. He returned the call, but a bland voice requested that he leave a message. Like Westbrook, he omitted names. "Good to hear from you. Lunch is a go. Get back to me tonight if you can."

A biography of Harry Truman occupied his evening. Thirty minutes before midnight, he checked the cell phone for the last time. Brushing his teeth, he stared at his reflection in the bathroom mirror, wondering why a former teammate estranged for so many years wanted his opinion of a woman he had just met at a dental conference.

OPENING GAMBIT

A Struggle for Expansion by a Standard Pattern of Moves

Pawns Carry High Risks

Nathan Monsarrat woke the next morning to the chirping of his cell phone. He tapped the screen, and a text from Sylvie appeared. *Finishing research late afternoon. Returning home this evening. Dinner? Takeout? My place?*

He calculated the time needed to drive to Hyannis and return to Greylock, added the duration of a lunch, and typed a reply with a pecking finger. *Of course. Drive safely.*

No other messages had arrived during the night. He called the Maryland number, leaving a second voicemail. He remembered Westbrook as dependable, but people changed, although military officers tended to act responsibly. Despite the lack of a response, he dressed in a white Oxford shirt, a pair of linen slacks, and a blue blazer. A Tag Heuer watch adorned his left wrist, and sunglasses protected his eyes. The Beretta rested in a leather paddle holster on the small of his back.

He drove the Jeep across the state, reaching Sparks, a restaurant set on a bluff overlooking Lewis Bay, five minutes before noon. He searched the dining room before again dialing Westbrook. Impatience laced his words. "I'm here. Where are you?"

A waitress wearing a blue polo shirt sporting the restaurant name guided him to a table for two on the empty patio. Her eyes were jade, her ponytail blond, and her smile white. She spoke with a flat Cape accent. "You prefer to order now or wait for your friend?"

He wanted to ask if she had seen Westbrook, but a college memory formed a weak basis for a description. "I'll have a Sam Adams now."

Thirty minutes after entering the restaurant, he signaled for the waitress. "Another Sam, please."

Plovers, terns, and herons pecked the mud flats of Lewis Bay. Beyond the shoreline, a stand-up paddler glided across the smooth surface of the water. A Steamship Authority ferry rounded Dunbar Point toward Nantucket Sound. Hyannis radiated serenity, but his paranoia whistled for attention, like steam escaping a kettle.

He accepted the second beer from the waitress. Flashing a smile as cold as the bottle, he said, "If my friend doesn't arrive in ten minutes, bring the bill."

In his final season at Iowa, Westbrook gained fame as the last player chosen in the NFL draft and the only one to decline an offer, choosing to pursue a career as a Navy medical officer. Monsarrat never considered a football career, hoping to earn a doctorate in economics and secure a faculty position with an Ivy League university. Toward the end of the fall term of his senior year, prior to the start of exam week, he received a summons from his academic adviser.

Piles of student essays obstructed a window and covered a gunmetal desk in an office on the third floor of Schaeffer Hall. Bookshelves sagged beneath the weight of textbooks. The adviser sported wisps of white hair, fingers stained with nicotine, sharp eyes, and a generous nose lined with red veins. Cigarette smoke leached from his cardigan sweater. He gestured at a folding chair. His opening remark was a modest gambit. "You have a very sharp mind, Nathan."

Monsarrat braced for a worrisome follow-up announcement. "Thank you, sir."

"You carry a 4.0 GPA. You speak fluent French and Russian. You possess outstanding physical attributes, a photographic memory, and a clean police record. Your psych eval topped the chart."

Monsarrat did not remember taking a psychological examination. "I didn't speak with a shrink."

"Correct," the adviser replied. "We've been watching you."

"Who is we? Why are you watching me?"

"The we is the Central Intelligence Agency. I'm a talent scout," the adviser explained. "The why is that you check our boxes, intellectually, physically, and socially. Not only do you possess brains and brawn, men respect you and women desire you."

Monsarrat had expected to discuss his graduate school recommendation. "You work for the CIA?"

The adviser opened a desk drawer, retrieved an envelope, and placed it onto the desk. "Fifty years from now, do you want to look back on your life as an endless pursuit of bigger paychecks, larger houses, and faster cars, or do you want to bask in the realization of a job well done keeping your country safe from foreign enemies?"

Monsarrat pointed to the envelope. "Should I open it now?"

"You're flying to Virginia to speak with my Agency colleagues. The envelope contains a round-trip ticket and cash for your hotel room, meals, and taxis. I suggest you collect receipts."

"I have an interview at the CIA?"

"Introductory assessments are held in the Ames Building on Fort Myer Drive in Rosslyn, Virginia. Details are in the envelope."

"I have to study for my Advanced Economics exam in two days."

"It's been pushed back," the adviser promised. "Pack a dark suit, a white shirt, and a blue striped tie. Shine your shoes. Speak politely and keep your answers brief. Ask one intelligent question at the end of the interview, about the Soviet menace or the Chinese peril."

The following January, Monsarrat received a call from an unlisted number. It lasted ten seconds and offered four words. "You've been medically cleared."

A second call arrived in late February, the voice offering only three words. "Security clearances granted."

The final call arrived on April Fool's Day. It began with congratulations and ended with a warning. "You are now a member of the Clandestine Service. Don't tell anyone."

A week after his graduation, Monsarrat flew to Virginia to began his Agency training at Camp Peary, known to recruits as The Farm. He emerged from the program as a deep cover operative with skills in firearms and knives,

electronics and explosives, boxing and jujitsu. He added Arabic to his repertoire of languages, excelled in HALO jumps, and mastered fast roping. He digested an encyclopedic knowledge of the petroleum industry, the basis of his cover as an oil production consultant.

Felix Sanhedrin welcomed him to Langley. Ten years older, five inches shorter, and fifty pounds lighter than Monsarrat, his bald skull glistened like a cue ball. Blue veins pulsed beneath his skin, giving him the appearance of aged Stilton cheese. Standing on the granite seal in the lobby of the Old Headquarters Building, Sanhedrin proclaimed, "Greetings, Nathan. I'm your new boss. You're going to love working for me. Everyone does."

Monsarrat despised him immediately, the feeling reciprocated in full by Sanhedrin. They were oil and water, each destined to repel the other. In the tradition of Langley, the deeper their animosity rooted, the more nuanced their masks of bonhomie shone. They circled each other like a cobra and a mongoose, engaged in the subterfuge of bureaucratic battle. Promotions and power welcomed the victor. A series of deep cover assignments to overseas locales where potable water was rarer than goodwill and life was cheaper than the cost of a bullet awaited the vanquished. Sanhedrin won and claimed the power corridors of the White House as his prize. Monsarrat lost and suffered banishment to the academic towers of Greylock College.

In Sparks, Monsarrat opened his cell phone and left a final message for Westbrook. "I'm heading home."

The waitress appeared with a plastic lobster, the bill secured between its meaty claws. "Your friend stood you up?"

He placed a fifty dollar bill on the table. "He's not really a friend, more like an acquaintance."

He left the restaurant, reaching his home as the sun set beyond the Berkshire hills. He showered and dressed for dinner. Unsure of his approach, he placed the engagement ring into the pocket of his blazer. Before departing, he called hospitals in Boston and Hyannis, but each refused to discuss patient admissions.

He placed the leather paddle holster onto the small of his back and called Westbrook a final time but disconnected as soon as the familiar message played.

An Advanced Pawn is an Ideal Target

In a wine shop on Main Street, Monsarrat purchased a bottle of Shiraz. He drove to the converted red brick factory in Greylock's old industrial section, where Sylvie owned a loft apartment. By the entrance, he pressed her buzzer and stared into the camera until the lock clicked. He chose the stairwell over the elevator. On the top floor, he pushed a crash bar and stepped into a hallway illuminated by dim sconces. At the far end, a plaque identified unit 4A.

The first time he visited the loft, she had shown him the prize of her art collection, a poster of Joesph Stalin and Kliment Voroshilov, the first Marshal of the Soviet Union, before the Kremlin, the ruby star atop the Vodovzvodnaya Tower a beacon of communism. "The work depicts the determination of the civilian and military leaders of the Soviet Union to create a just society, in order to end the economic and political exploitation of the working class."

Monsarrat loathed everything Russian, from the smell of its vodka to the brutality of its intelligence operatives. He pointed to the opposite wall, a poster depicting a somber couple holding Mosin rifles and mowing scythes beneath a blue sky, their boots atop black earth. A second poster displayed a bronzed athlete astride the Kremlin walls, like a colossus in white shorts and singlet, proudly waving the hammer and sickle flag. "A commie sympathizer lives amongst us?"

"Do you mean an intelligent, beautiful, and exotic yet dangerous spy type of commie sympathizer?"

His reply caught in his throat. "Something like that."

Her fingertips stroked his cheek. "There's only one spook in this room, Nathan, and you're him."

He understood his past bothered her, a legacy from her parents, career diplomats with the Department of State. Like his own parents, they had raised only one child. Her father, Hiram, He understood his past bothered her, a legacy from her parents, career diplomats with the Department of State. Like his own parents, they had raised only one child. Her father, Hiram, concluded his career as ambassador to the Kingdom of Morocco. Her mother, Ruth, retired as Under Secretary for Political Affairs. They left Washington, bought a Cape Cod cottage in Osterville overlooking Cotuit Bay, and remodeled it into a four season home.

Monsarrat understood sensitivities. He never discussed his own parents with her. An only child, his mother had died in the spring semester of his sophomore year at the university, killed in a crosswalk of their Iowa town by a teenager driving sixty miles per hour. Two months later, his father succumbed to a full bottle of sleeping pills. "You don't approve of the Agency?"

She attempted an explanation. "Langley and State are the dogs and cats of Washington, but you're unlike the Agency people I knew, living abroad with my parents. You don't use people and discard them. You care about them."

He didn't know how to respond, so he remained quiet.

"I admire you on many levels," she continued. "I respect that you believed in the work you did for Langley, but your distance worries me. You're not emotionally cold. You just seem masked. I'm not sure that I know how to connect with you."

She held up a finger before he could respond. "Tell me it's not my business, I'll understand, but if you can open up, I'll listen."

He viewed his future stillborn, unless he buried his past. "Be patient. I'm working on it."

Approaching the end of the hallway, he saw her door was ajar. Her disregard for the most basic security measures disturbed him, but he had learned to step carefully around her autonomy. He entered the loft and secured the lock.

"Sylvie, I'm here."

Sylvie Epstein crossed the floor in her bare feet. Five feet, six inches tall with the lean muscles of a runner, she wore jeans and a white silk blouse. A gold chain circled her throat, a watch with a rubber strap sat upon her left wrist, and her lustrous Titian hair was piled in a loose beehive. Her eyes were chestnut, her cheekbones pronounced. Standing on her tiptoes, she kissed him and took the bottle of wine from his hand. "Good choice. I ordered dinner, Peking duck, beef with asparagus, and eggplant with garlic sauce for delivery."

He thought her beautiful, bursting with intelligence and grace. "Did you enjoy your time in Cambridge?"

"The research was tedious, and there was an accident on the Pike."

He placed ceramic trivets and serving spoons onto the table, laid chopsticks upon napkins, and set plates on bamboo mats. Uncorking the wine, he filled two crystal stem glasses with Shiraz and poured water into matching goblets. "I'm glad you're home."

She tapped her wrist. "Dinner arrives in twenty minutes. Would you like to watch the cable news and become depressed or follow me into the bedroom and get happy?"

"If you put it that way."

She pulled off his jacket, dropped it onto the floor, turned and pressed her back against his chest. "Lose the gun and massage my shoulders. My muscles are tense from the drive."

He placed the holstered Beretta onto the table, dropped his shirt to the floor, and slipped each button through its slot until her blouse fell onto his shirt. Her bra followed. "A massage needs skin on skin."

"Squeeze harder," she urged. "Right there, below the clavicle."

He cupped a breast with his left hand as he kneaded her shoulder muscles. His fingers traveled to the small of her back, pressing against the twin dimples on either side of her coccyx. "You are tense."

A low growl erupted from her throat. "Relax me."

He rolled a thick nipple with his thumb, pressed his knee into the meat of her thigh, arched her back, and pulled her shoulders tight against his chest. "Mostly, it's a judo move."

"You going to flip me onto the floor?"

"Yes, but very gently."

She twisted to face him, gripped his shoulders, and scissored her legs around his waist. "How's that move?"

Horses whinnied in the bedroom. She dropped to the floor and grabbed his shirt. "My cell phone!"

As she pulled the bedroom door shut, the intercom buzzed. Activating the video screen of the security system, Monsarrat saw a teenager holding a brown paper bag. He buzzed him into the lobby. He hung the clothes on the back of a chair, pulled on his blazer, and removed a fifty dollar bill from his wallet.

He opened the door at the approach of the teenager. Trading money for food, he said, "Keep the change."

He carried the food to the table, placing the warm containers onto the trivets. Murmurs of conversation from the bedroom. A scream exploded, and he drew the Beretta, his mind analyzing the force needed to burst open the door, the configuration of the room, and the angles of fire. He listened for breathing and footfalls that did not belong to Sylvie, sniffed to discern sweat and cologne. He feared that the enemies of his past sought vengeance in the present.

Twisting the knob with his left hand, he felt the latch release. He threw open the door and scanned the room but saw only the woman he loved perched on the edge of the bed, his shirt hanging from her, a cell phone pressed to her ear. Her skin was pale, and tears flowed from her eyes. He sat by her on the bed, the Beretta against his thigh. "What's wrong?"

Sobs interrupted her words. "My dad was talking to me, then I heard a loud thud, and he groaned."

"The line disconnected?"

"The connection's strong, but he won't talk to me. Or he can't. I don't know what's happening but it's very wrong."

"What did he say?"

"He said pirates boarded the boat. He said they'll kill him and my mom unless I deliver a ransom."

Poor Pawn Defense Often Leads to Mate

Monsarrat took the cell phone from her hand. Pressing the speaker icon, he heard the tinny echoes and delayed clicks that marked a connection to a satellite phone. "Where are they, Sylvie?"

"The Gulf of Sidra."

A male voice burst from the speaker, issuing orders in the guttural Arabic before switching to stilted English, as if reading a script. "*Ya kuffar*, oh infidel, worthless female child of a Jew monkey father and a Jewess dog mother, know that I, Caliph Bin Nafe, will remove the heads of the two Jew devils and hurl them into the eternal hellfire of *an-Naar* if you fail my commands."

The transmission faded, static hissed, and the voice of Hiram Epstein issued from the speaker. "Sylvie? Listen to me carefully, darling. I have instructions. Write them down and follow them exactly. Tell me you understand."

Monsarrat tapped his head to indicate he would remember the words. Covering the mic with his thumb, he whispered, "Go ahead. Talk to him."

Her voice wavered. "I understand, Dad. Are you and Mom okay?"

A deep thud reverberated through the speaker, followed by a groan. After a moment, the elder Epstein answered, his voice strained. "Your mother was fine, but no more questions, honey."

Monsarrat noted the past tense. He again covered the mic. "Do as he says."

"Do not involve the police or the FBI. Do not speak with the media or your friends. Bring ten million dollars in one hundred dollar bills to the Hotel Paradise in Sirte, Libya this Friday at noon, local time. Tell me you understand, Sylvie."

"I understand, Dad."

"You have to deliver the ransom. Caliph Bin Nafe has your picture. He knows your face. If anyone else comes to the hotel, he'll kill me."

Monsarrat noted the specific me, not us, and understood that Ruth Epstein was dead. He glanced at Sylvie, but she appeared confused by the words. "Let him hear your voice, Sylvie."

Bin Nafe did not allow her the opportunity. "*Ya kuffar*, heed the words of Caliph Bin Nafe!"

A concert of echoes and clicks marked the end of call. Beyond the fact of the kidnapping, the demands troubled Monsarrat. He knew Bin Nafe as a sadistic former commander in the Jamahiriya Guard, the bodyguards who had protected Muammar Gaddafi, the Libyan dictator, until the fall of his regime. He suspected the terrorist either believed the Epsteins possessed a fortune or that the objective of the kidnapping was not money, but Bin Nafe also believed in miracles if he expected Sylvie to receive a Libyan visa quickly enough to reach Sirte by noon Friday, and if he believed she could smuggle ten million dollars into the country.

Carrying the cell phone and pistol in one hand, he led her from the bedroom. At the table, he helped her change from his shirt into her own clothes and guided her onto a chair. He removed his blazer, slipped on his shirt, and filled her glass with wine. "Drink this."

She drained the Shiraz. "I'm glad you're here, Nathan."

He needed to question her, but her expression was as fragile as glass. He opened the food containers and spooned small portions onto two plates. "You have to eat. You're in shock. Food will help you sharpen your focus and maintain your strength."

"I have to find ten million dollars. I don't know how to start."

He pointed his chopsticks at the plates. "Eat first. Later, we'll talk."

"You'll help me, won't you, Nathan? I mean, this is your world. You know these type of people."

He had been a deep cover operative, manipulating assets to betray their own countries, not a hostage rescue negotiator, but he did not correct her. "Of course, I'll help, but I'll need to ask you questions, and you'll need to be sharp to answer them, so eat the food."

She picked at the plate, dabbing the tears that slipped from her eyes with a napkin. "I need wine more than food."

Monsarrat refilled her glass. "Remember Kipling? Keep your head and trust yourself? Meet triumph and disaster? Hold on when there is nothing in you?"

"An erudite spy who quotes sexist poetry. It's what I love about you," she said. "At least you didn't recite Plath's *Daddy*."

"It's good to hear you laugh."

He wanted to accustom her to the gentle give and take of his interrogation. He began simply. "How do your parents spend their time on Cape Cod?"

"They bought a sixteen foot catboat. When they're not sailing, Dad paints watercolors and Mom works with pottery. They write books together on North African politics, and they tag teach seminars at the community college on arcane aspects of foreign policy."

Monsarrat believed in coincidences as much as in Santa Claus and the Easter Bunny but could not connect Westbrook's failure to meet for lunch in Hyannis and the kidnapping of two retired diplomats from the neighboring town of Osterville. "Are your parents traveling alone or with friends?"

"They met another retired couple from State in Tangiers. Their friends won the grand prize in a contest, a voyage for four on a sloop, the *Joppa*, sailing to Alexandria, and invited them."

He trusted serendipity less than coincidences. Calculating the distance of the route, two thousand nautical miles along the dangerous coast of North Africa, he felt as if he was watching a horror film, certain carnage was imminent but unsure how it would be delivered. "Was tonight their first contact?"

"They called twice, once each from Algiers and from Tunis. Tonight was the third time."

"What do you know anything about their friends?"

"They've known them since forever."

"What about and the captain of the *Joppa*?"

"Not a thing," she replied. "What do you know Bin Nafe?"

Replying vaguely felt like a lie of omission. "I've heard the name."

She slapped the table. "How can I find ten million dollars?"

"Did your parents buy a kidnapping policy for the trip?"

"I asked them. They told me to stop worrying."

Monsarrat once watched a video of Bin Nafe hack at the neck of a hostage with a *flyssa* sword until the head fell to the ground. He feared Sylvie would be unable to bury her parents intact. Despite his concerns, he spoke reassuringly. "Bin Nafe must know that your parents were ambassadors. In his world, only the rich and powerful receive an embassy, and they use their positions to stuff their bank accounts. He probably assumes your parents are wealthy."

"He's wrong," she replied. "My dad warned me not to do it, but I have to call the FBI."

"Be realistic, Sylvie. The feds have no assets in Libya."

"Diplomatic Security protected my parents at their embassies."

His Agency experiences had left Monsarrat with little faith in the Department of State's security officers. "I know a former special operator, an expert on Libya. He's very good. I'll contact him."

"If he saves my parents, I'll find the money to pay him."

The ring in his pocket was a sorrow. "If it works out as I hope, you won't owe him anything. He'll pay you."

Sacrifice Pawns for Superior Positions

Monsarrat drove quickly through the empty streets of Greylock. Pulling into his driveway, he noted in the glare of the security lights the raised flag on the RFD box. He parked the Jeep, walked to the box, removed an express delivery envelope, and dropped the flag. Inside the house, he placed the engagement ring, holstered Beretta, and envelope onto the kitchen counter. His memory provided the number and, despite the late hour, he tapped the screen of his cell phone. When the call connected, he didn't wait for the usual greeting. "It's Monsarrat. Can you talk?"

Early in his career with the Agency, operating under the cover of a consultant to Sonangol, the state-owned oil company of Angola, Monsarrat had collaborated with Harper Enderby, at the time the embassy's Defense Attaché, to smuggle out of the country a disgruntled deputy minister in the Ministry of Petroleum with access to important economic and military intelligence. Their paths intersected as they conducted joint operations in Africa and the Middle East, strengthening the mutual respect first formed in Angola.

A full colonel after twenty-five years in uniform, Enderby retired from the 1st Special Forces Operational Detachment - Delta to his home in the Tidewater region of Virginia. He grew tired of fishing and hunting, smoking cigars and drinking bourbon, and had applied to join the Central Intelligence Agency. Following the path blazed by previous military special operators, he joined Langley's Special Operations Group as a Paramilitary Operations Officer. His country of specialty was Libya, his subject matter expertise the dispersed fighters of the disbanded Jamahiriya Guard.

In his smooth drawl, the Virginian replied, "Go ahead, Nathan."

"I have a proposition concerning your least favorite city in North Africa and the bad guy who robbed you of valuable items."

"We should continue this conversation offline," Enderby suggested.

"My proposition has a shelf life. Fly to me tomorrow. I'll pay for your travel."

"I have meetings that will last all morning and afternoon."

"How about dinner tomorrow? I'll come to you."

"I head downrange after work for a strategy session with my brothers in khaki. I won't return until late Wednesday afternoon but I can meet you at eighteen hundred hours at the Cantina in Dupont Circle, corner of Florida and Connecticut. Since you're traveling, I'll pay for dinner."

"Agreed."

"What can you tell me now?"

Monsarrat provided his intelligence circumspectly. "The bad guy kidnapped the parents of a friend. He wants ten million dollars. My friend doesn't have that kind of money. I want to help her."

"You want to pay the ransom?"

"I want to kill the bad guy and rescue her parents."

"What's my role?"

"I need back-up, someone who knows the bad guy and his environs. He wants to be paid Friday at noon, local time. We'll need to go wheels up soonest. We won't have much prep time."

"You're cutting it very close," Enderby agreed.

"See you Wednesday at eighteen hundred."

Setting the cell phone onto the counter, he glanced at the express envelope. Originating in Boston, the return label displayed a simple level of encryption. Reversed, the sender's name, S. I. Kwah, offered Hawkeyes, the name of the University of Iowa football team. The street, Kicker Lane, referred to the position Westbrook played, and the house number, two, had adorned his jersey. Kinnick, the return city, was the name of the university's stadium. MD reflected the abbreviation for doctor and the state code for Maryland. The zip code revealed Bethesda, home to Walter Reed.

The date and time on the upper left corner of the first sheet of legal paper indicated the letter was composed immediately after Westbrook left his voicemail message. It also lacked names.

Apologies for dropping into your life so suddenly, we've been out of touch too long. If this letter is a surprise, we didn't meet in Hyannis, which means I am worm food. You must understand the severity of the situation. I know it sounds crazy, but the security of our government – hell, of our nation – has been compromised. The danger is existential, and you are responsible for saving us.

Monsarrat reread the paragraph. If Westbrook hoped to secure his attention, he had succeeded. The words offered the carnival pitch of a carny wielding a shiv. He smoothed the sheets of paper and continued reading.

I am an endodontist in the Medical Corps of the U.S. Navy. My rank is captain. My current posting is Chief of the Directorate of Dental Services at the Walter Reed National Military Medical Center in Bethesda, Maryland. I administer the dental clinic of the Medical

Unit in the White House Military Office. I treat the President, VP, their families, and certain high level members of their staffs.

I learned of the IED ambush in Georgetown on the morning of January first from the news, a moment before I received an emergency text that the National Security Adviser was en route to Walter Reed. Calling him severely injured was like saying King Kong was a cute little monkey. I don't know who blew up his vehicle, or why he was assassinated. At the time, I didn't care. I thought the knowledge was outside my wheelhouse.

In my area of operations, the patient required a series of procedures to restore soft tissue mass and hard tissue infrastructure, repair and replace damaged and missing teeth, and address jawbone damage, injuries commensurate with a powerful blast. Not exactly a routine cavity filling at the office but nothing extraordinary for my team.

I assigned Commander Tatyana Zeigarnik, my best maxillofacial reconstructive surgeon, to the patient. Tanya was a naturalized American citizen, born in Murmansk. She was fifteen years old when her family emigrated from the Soviet Union, one of the first refusenik families to benefit from the Jackson–Vanik amendment. She was a decorated officer married to her career. She was squared away, and she was my friend.

Not long after Tanya began her work, a pair of gray suits ordered each member of my team to sign a section of a national security law. The details were hard to understand – too much legal gibberish – but they warned us not to discuss the patient. We signed the paperwork.

Soon after Tanya completed her initial examination, the gray suits returned. They collected her notes, photos, and x-rays. They also confiscated the hard drives from our computers, and shortly after they departed, the VIP disappeared. Later that day, President Augustus Haverhill announced the death of the National Security Adviser. The next day, the White House announced the cremation of his remains.

If the people who planted the IED were arrested, I missed the story, too busy administrating the Medical Unit. We all returned to our hectic jobs, but last week I arrived at Walter Reed to find Tanya waiting in my office. She appeared pale, and she was sweating. I asked if she felt ill. She surprised me by closing the door. You know how sensitive the military is about maintaining propriety.

Tanya reminded me that we had never seen the results of the DNA tests for the National Security Adviser. She then handed me a folder of x-rays, medical photographs, personal notes that she had retained after the second visit of the gray suits. The contents of the folder highlighted abnormalities in the mouth of the patient. She also added her conclusions. I told her the folder was an act of insubordination, but she argued it was our duty to launch a formal investigation.

I studied her evidence and agreed to draft a memo. I signed it. Tanya made two copies of the file, one for each of our classified office safes, and personally delivered the original folder and my memo to *I studied her evidence and agreed to draft a memo. I signed it. Tanya made two copies of the file, one for each of our classified office safes, and personally delivered the original folder and my memo to our rear admiral, the head of the Dental Corps. At the time, I feared for our careers. I should have worried about our lives.*

Two days passed without a response, which surprised me, but flag officers entertain many demands. After the third day without an answer, I spoke with the executive assistant of the rear admiral. She said no folder had been hand delivered by Commander Zeigarnik.

I called Tanya, but both her work line and cell phone routed me to voicemail. In her office, no one had yet seen or heard from her. Tanya would not miss duty call without informing me. Neither would she route calls to voicemail. I created a story for the staff about a plumbing emergency at my house. I left the office and drove to Tanya's home. She didn't answer the door, and drapes covered the windows, so I couldn't see inside. The doors to the house and garage were locked.

Back in my office at Walter Reed, I unlocked my safe. The folder was missing. Following Navy regs, I had never written the combination to the safe on a piece of paper or stored it on a computer. The sole person other than myself who possessed the combination was the Master at Arms, but he could only open the safe in my presence, which left theft as the only explanation. I'm sure you can appreciate that burgling a classified Navy safe inside a secure military installation demands a very specific skill set. So does pilfering a folder from the office of a rear admiral.

At home that night, I watched the local news. A video showed emergency personnel removing a body from the wreckage of a single car accident on the Beltway. A front tire of a blue Audi A3 ruptured, the car flipped, and the driver died. Tanya owned the same model and color car. The next morning, I received official notice of Tanya's death. As her supervisor, I oversaw the inventory of her office. When the Master at Arms opened her safe, I cataloged the contents. The folder was missing.

I accessed her personal C: drive on her work station but couldn't discover any data pertaining to the patient. In my own office, I searched the master F: drive for his records but found no mention of his admission. I left the office to attend Tanya's funeral. Her next of kin, a sister living in Miami, held a shiva *at Tanya's home following the burial. I searched for Tanya's laptop but failed to find it. It may have been inside the Audi, or it could have been removed by whoever stole the folders.*

The invitation to attend the Boston conference was long on my calendar. After my talk on combat dental trauma, an administrator from a hospital in Cambridge approached me, an absolutely stunning woman with red hair, blue eyes, and a centerfold body. Her hands, though, belonged to a stone mason. She introduced herself as Victoria Charing. Then she asked me to travel with her to Hyannis.

I'm not handsome or rich. I'm also not a fool. I sensed she worked for the people who stole the files and killed Tanya, but I accepted her invite. I'd rather run at them than wait for them to come for me.

You have the ball. Use your skills to find the address of my home. A key to the front door is beneath the seeds in the bird feeder. The code to the alarm is the superstitious street number of our team's favorite Iowa City bar, where we drank beer in the off-season. You have three attempts to input the sequence before the monitoring company calls me. Since I won't answer, their next call will be to the cops.

A safe is bolted to the floor in the closet of the master bedroom. The combination is the scores of the first and last games of our final season. Inside the safe is an envelope with information about the folder. I couldn't recreate the x-rays and photographs, but I reconstructed the facts.

Remember what Coach said each game as we took the field: stomp 'em and toss flowers on 'em!

Monsarrat remembered their coach, a phlegmatic leader with a genius for defensive innovation, but his exhortation had been for each player to do his job. Returning the pages to the envelope, he wondered what the endodontists had discovered in the mouth of the National Security Adviser that had frightened them so thoroughly.

Extended Pauses between Moves Frustrate an Opponent

The apartment Harper Enderby rented on North Nash Street in Arlington offered views of the Iwo Jima Memorial, the Netherlands Carillon, and Arlington National Cemetery. Across the Potomac River, spotlights illuminated the Lincoln Memorial. He sat on a padded bench adjacent to a bay window, cell phone in hand, contemplating his conversation with Monsarrat. He typed a two word text, contact initiated, and pressed the send icon.

A moment later, his cell phone rang. He accepted the call with a curt greeting. "We're good."

A woman's voice demanded, "I want a full brief on your conversation with Boy Scout."

Enderby knew neither her face nor her name, but her voice irritated him, as did her moniker for Monsarrat, a man he respected professionally. She had cold contacted him, introducing herself with a recitation of his professional and personal resumes. He considered terminating the call, but the depth of her intelligence impressed him, and her introduction hooked him.

"Open your bank account" she had instructed. "You'll see a deposit for a dollar less than ten thousand. Consider it reimbursement for the time spent listening to my proposal. If you're interested, we'll progress to operational logistics and payment details. If not, keep the ten thousand dollars, and I won't contact you again."

"Wait one," he replied. His fingers tapped the keyboard of his laptop, accessing the website of his bank.

After a moment, she asked, "Shall I continue?"

His account showed the deposit. "How do you know about me?"

"I know you're a mercenary with a hard-on for money," she replied. "If you agree to my terms, I expect you to execute my orders with speed, thoroughness, and ruthlessness, but you should be aware that attempting to fuck with me will result in me ending your life with as much remorse as I would crush a cockroach."

"Do you have a name? So I can check out your bona fides?"

"Of course, I do," she replied. "It's fuck you, pay attention, and don't ask stupid questions."

"Good to know."

She allowed another moment to pass. "Shall I proceed?"

He admired her confidence. "Go on."

She spoke for ten minutes. "Are my conditions acceptable?"

He agreed with caveats. "First, triple the fee. Second, deposit eighty percent into my account now, the final twenty percent upon completion of the mission. Third, provide one hundred thousand dollars immediately for expenses. On trust, no receipts."

The two deposits arrived minutes later. Enderby admired her alacrity, but her eagerness to accept his demands redlined his suspicions. Like a rug merchant in a Middle East souk, he expected negotiations. "I'll be in touch after he calls."

"You know Monsarrat. Underestimating his abilities is a serious mistake," she had warned before closing the connection.

His instincts had screamed treachery. He tried but failed to trace the origins of the call and the cash transfers. He appreciated her professionalism. He liked Monsarrat, even admired him, but a seven figure contract trumped warm feelings. "Roger that," he had replied into the dead connection.

Gazing out the bay window, he provided a summary of his arrangements with Monsarrat, ending his briefing with a question. "Will the parents be a problem?"

"They're retired diplomats," she scoffed. "I want to know why you put off your meeting with Boy Scout. If you give him too much leash, he'll find a way to bite you."

"Don't worry about his teeth. I'll muzzle him," Enderby promised. "Wednesday evening, he walks into the restaurant, he has no time and no options."

"Others have thought so, but they're dead, and he's still alive."

"I am not others."

"Neither is he."

Enderby breathed deeply, counted to ten, and exhaled. "Is everything in place on your end?"

"Don't question me. Worry about your objectives," she snapped. "Most of all, don't fuck up."

"I have never fucked up an operation."

"Not for me, you haven't," she agreed, "but during the aborted Arab Spring, you shit the bed in Sirte. I'm bankrolling this op. It will be fuck up free."

Her mention of the disaster in Libya angered him. "Why the convolutions? I can wrap Monsarrat in chains and drop his body into the Potomac River."

"I'm going to kill him slowly as he begs and cries and screams. Eyeballing his death will be better than sex, and his body will never be found. Do you really want to deprive me of the pleasure?" she asked before ending the call.

He stood and walked slowly from the bay window into the kitchen.

Opening the refrigerator, he removed a bottle of water, cracked the cap, and pondered the more likely reward for delivering Monsarrat, the deposit of her second payment into his bank account or her bullet fired into the back of his head. He opened his cell phone, the call connected, and he donned the persona of a commanding officer. "Tuna, you and the boys lock and load."

His former executive officer, Charlie Anderson, asked, "When do we go wheels up, boss?"

"Meet me at zero six hundred at the patisserie at Chain Bridge and Old Dominion in Maclean. Bring your kits."

"We're off to an exotic Asian land filled with hot, busty babes lusting for hard, handsome Rangers?"

"Fuck no," Enderby replied. "We're landing hot in a sandbox filled with syphilitic goat herders with hard-ons for fucking America and her wayward Ranger children."

Passed Pawns Increase in Value

In his bedroom, Monsarrat spun the electromechanical dial of a thousand pound Class 5 safe. Deadbolts retracted, and the heavy steel door swung open. He placed the engagement ring and Westbrook's letter on the top shelf. From the second shelf, he withdrew a shoebox containing packets of cash and documents for Mark Sanger, a Canadian travel writer from Halifax, Nova Scotia. For deep rooted cover identities, he chose the cultural similarities of the Maritimes.

Sanger's blue and gold, bilingual passport featured visas, entry stamps, and exit notations for dozens of countries. A wallet held a driver's license, credit and ATM cards from Halifax banks, a medical insurance card, a library card, and two membership cards for shopping clubs. Automatic withdrawals from a well funded bank account paid the charges for a cell phone, purchases made with the credit cards, and other bills.

He plugged the Canadian cell phone into a fast charger. While the battery indicator light blinked, he dialed the Sanger number with his own cell phone. For the first test, he listened to three rings before closing the connection. For the second test, he sent a text message, receiving the quick confirmation of chiming bells. For the final test, he left a voice message. A moment passed before trumpets blared. He listened to the recording, deleted it and the text, cleared the call logs, muted the announcements, and closed the phone.

From the bottom of the shoebox, he removed a pair of blue and white Nova Scotia license plates adorned with a current registration sticker, a sailing ship, and the motto, Canada's Ocean Playground. A cellophane envelope held a valid safety inspection sticker from

Halifax, a current registration, an up-to-date insurance card, and an engraved metal VIN plate with an adhesive strip. He returned the empty box to the safe and spun the dial to engage the lock.

He gathered the Canadian automobile items and secured the house. Opening the garage, he drove the Jeep inside. He closed the doors, turned on the lights, pulled on work gloves, and removed the Massachusetts license plates, replacing them with the pair from Nova Scotia. He peeled the safety inspection sticker from the windshield, pressing it flat with a barbell plate. Ammonia removed glue from the glass. He placed the Massachusetts identity into a manila envelope.

He pried loose the original VIN plate at the junction of the windshield and dashboard, peeled the wax paper from its Canadian counterpart, and pressed the adhesive against the hard plastic. He attached the Halifax safety inspection sticker to the windshield, propped open the hood with a rod, inserted a plastic tube into the nozzle of a can, and covered the engine block VIN with black paint. He repeated the act on the side panel of the driver's door before disconnecting the interior lights.

He replaced the prop rod, fastened the hood clamps, turned off the lights, secured the garage, and returned to the house. Sleep proved elusive, strafed by dreams of violent deaths. He woke before dawn, shaved, showered, and dressed in a blue Oxford shirt, blue jeans, and cordovan loafers. He filled a leather shoulder bag with clothes, toiletries, packets of cash, his Canadian identity, the fast charger, and the Sanger cell phone, its battery full. He opened the Class 5 safe and placed his wallet, laptop, and envelope containing the Massachusetts identity of the Jeep onto a shelf.

Using his own cell phone, he called Sylvie. "Did I wake you?"

"I haven't slept," she responded.

He provided an outline of his plans. "I spoke with my friend. We're going to retrieve your package, but you won't be able to contact me while I'm gone."

"I'll be fine," she promised. "When do you leave?"

"Now," he answered.

"Be careful, Nathan. I don't want you to be hurt."

Monsarrat preferred to express his feelings personally, without the screen of a cell phone. "Stay strong, Sylvie. I'll be in touch soon."

He placed the cell phone next to his wallet and secured the safe. He carried the bag to the kitchen, brewed coffee, and ate slices of buttered toast. After cleaning the dishes, he placed the paddle holster and Beretta onto his hip, covering the weapon with his blazer. Extra magazines fit into the pockets. He secured the house and walked to the garage. Inside, he filed the identification from the pistol. He cleaned the finish, holstered the weapon, and placed it into the center console. The bag fit onto the passenger seat.

As Mark Sanger, he backed onto the driveway and secured the garage, only his house keys connecting him to Nathan Monsarrat. Outside Greylock, he filled the gas tank, paying cash for the purchases. He trusted the Canadian identity, but he was loathe to use a Sanger credit card so close to home. Alert for a tail, he drove to the Mass Pike and entered the eastbound lanes. The Columbus Day traffic was light, and he reached Boston without interference.

He parked in the Boston Common Garage, retrieved the Beretta, and slung the bag over his shoulder. He walked through the Public Garden, the autumn colors a rich urban palette. Swan Boats dotted the lagoon, and children scampered around bronze ducklings in the warmth of the late morning sun. He passed the statue of Paul Revere and exited onto Arlington Street. At Park Plaza, Old Glory and the flag of the Commonwealth flew above the brown brick entrance to the Saint James Hotel.

The lobby offered Bauhaus chrome, De Stijl furniture, and an Italian marble floor. Behind a desk, a concierge with chocolate skin and hair like a black shadow wearing a gray suit, white cotton shirt, and red silk tie patterned with the crest of the hotel sat in an executive chair. A tag pinned above the breast pocket declared him Reimond.

Monsarrat placed his bag onto the floor. He offered a warm smile, topped with a fifty dollar bill. "Can you help me, Reimond?"

The concierge took the cash with practiced ease. In the rounded accent of the Caribbean, he replied, "I will do my best, sir."

"A friend stayed at the hotel for the recent dental conference. I want to know if he checked out."

"Could tell me his name, sir?"

"Dan Westbrook."

The concierge consulted his computer screen before offering the palm of his hand. "Doctor Westbrook departed the hotel shortly after the conclusion of the conference on Saturday. Would you like his home address?"

Monsarrat supplied a second fifty dollar bill. "Write it for me."

One hand pocketed the money. The other scribbled information onto a piece of hotel notepaper. "Here you go, sir. Is there anything else I can do for you?"

Monsarrat memorized the information before folding the notepaper into a blazer pocket. "Was Westbrook alone when he checked out?"

"He may have departed with a woman from the conference."

Monsarrat placed a third bill landed in the palm of his hand. "Can you describe her?"

"She was a rare beauty, perhaps thirty-five, forty years old, six feet tall, approximately 125 pounds, red hair and blue eyes, cold and clear like arctic ice. She had the pout of a model, and a slightly crooked nose that added to her allure. She looked strong, especially her hands, and she walked like old money Her complexion was creamy. She wore lipstick but minimal make-up, gold bracelets and rings on her wrists and fingers, and she painted her nails white."

Monsarrat fired questions, as if his money had purchased a quickly ticking clock. "Do you have her name? Address and phone number?"

The concierge equated negative answers with the loss of income. "I am sorry, but she was not a guest of the hotel. You might ask the conference organizers for that information."

"Was she a professional?"

"I do not understand your question."

Monsarrat flashed the Beretta. "Was she a hooker?"

The concierge exchanged his Caribbean accent for the tones of Roxbury. "You a cop?"

"Don't worry about my credentials. Just answer my questions."

"She didn't have the eyes for paid sex," Reimond offered. "More like a cat stalking a canary too stupid to fly away."

"Did they leave in a taxi?"

"She drove a four door silver Lexus LS. Looked new. Another hundred bucks, return in an hour, I'll have the plate info for you."

Monsarrat passed him two hundred dollars. "Get it now."

The concierge tapped the keypad of a house phone. "Luther, you remember a red haired looker? Last Saturday? Silver Lexus? Get me the plate number in five minutes, I'll give you ten bucks."

The phone rang sixty seconds later. The concierge wrote the information onto a second piece of notepaper. Handing it to Monsarrat, he said, "She parked the Lexus with Luther just the one day, not for the entire conference."

Monsarrat again memorized the information before tucking the paper into his pocket. "If Luther made up the number, he'll need the rest of your cash as a down payment on his doctor bills."

Berlin Defense Attacks the King's Pawn

On the sidewalk outside the hotel, Monsarrat tore the two pieces of notepaper into shreds and dropped them into a trash can. He opened the Canadian cell phone and tapped the number onto the screen. The call connected, and he offered a nameless greeting. "Are you working on the holiday? I ask because I'm heading your way. Can I buy you a cup of coffee?"

Jason Datura recognized his voice. "I'm about to eat lunch, sir. Would you like to join me?"

Monsarrat declined. "I'll need another hour to reach Maynard."

"I'll wait inside Kona Koffee at the corner of River and Walnut, down the street from the office."

"When do you have to return to work?"

"No rush, sir. I'm on my own dime today."

Monsarrat drove across the Charles River at the Boston University Bridge, following Memorial Drive to the parkways and Route Two. At the outskirts of Concord, he turned onto a two-lane road leading into Maynard. The old mill town had transitioned from the grimy brick factories of the industrial revolution to the antiseptic computer assembly lines of the digital age. After the collapse of its mainframe industries, Maynard slipped into recession. The September 11th terror attacks presented the town with its third act, host to the Commonwealth Fusion Center, the headquarters of the state's counter-terrorism operations.

He parked the Jeep on Walnut Street, across from Kona Koffee. In its window, a neon hula dancer wore a yellow skirt of *kapa* cloth, a

purple and white *lei* necklace, and crimson *kupe`e* bracelets. An *`ili`ili*
pebble in one hand and a coffee cherry in the other welcomed
customers. The aroma of freshly roasted beans infused the cafe. At a
table for two in the rear, facing the entrance, Datura drummed his
fingers atop a leather valise.

Rail thin, six feet tall, the young analyst wore his brown hair short
and sported a timid moustache of the same color. His pallor indicated
too many hours spent beneath strip lighting, and his suits bore the
hang of a discount warehouse. Black plastic frames carved a welt
against the bridge of his nose, but beneath the thick lenses a quick
intelligence shone in his blue eyes. The valedictorian of the most
recent class to graduate from Greylock College, he owned a dual
degree in Economics and Middle East Studies. On the strength of a
recommendation from Monsarrat, the Commonwealth Fusion
Center hired him as a terror finance analyst, tasked with following the
activities of *jihadi* groups and *al-hawala* funding networks.

Datura stood, his hand extended. His lungs labored to keep pace
with his words. "Good to see you, sir! How are you? You look well.
What would you like to drink? I'm buying."

Monsarrat placed the bag onto the floor, shook the hand of the
young analyst, and pressed a bill into his palm. "Espresso with lemon
rind, but I'm paying. I need a favor."

A barista stood behind the rail, serving Kona coffee in tiki mugs.
Leiomano clubs studded with tiger shark teeth, ten foot ironwood
pololū pikes, and koa *ihe* spears covered the walls. Ukulele, slack key,
and steel guitar music played from recessed speakers. Datura weaved
between tables, his hands cradling a wood tray bearing two espressos
with lemon rinds, two shot glasses of seltzer water, and a dish of

chocolate covered coffee beans.

He set the tray on the table. "You called on a Canadian number. By your posture as you walked toward the table, you're carrying a weapon. Are you in trouble, sir?"

In lieu of an answer, Monsarrat offered the description of Victoria Charing purchased from the hotel concierge. He did not mention Westbrook. "I suspect her name is an alias, but run it against your databases. See if alternate identities pop up. If you get a hit, check for known associates. Search flight manifests, major hubs and regional airports for an itinerary. Also, access Department of State lists, in case she's working under diplomatic cover."

"If she's not a diplomat, is she a member of a terror cell? Al-Qaeda or Da'ish? Maybe one of the South American narco-terror groups?"

Monsarrat suspected she worked for an intelligence service. The death of Zeigarnik and the disappearance of Westbrook indicated secrecy and tradecraft. A *jihadi* group would have posted gruesome videos online. "I wish I had answers, Jason."

He provided the license plate number from the Lexus. "It may be fake, but if it's real, give me the owner's name, contact details, and a photo ID. If the car was stolen, I want the police report."

Datura rubbed his head, as if pressing the requests into memory. "Maybe it's a local rental?"

"Lexus usually isn't a fleet vehicle, but if it is a rental, they'll be a contract, so get me a copy."

"Any chance you have the VIN, sir?"

Monsarrat played the lemon rind around the rim of the cup. "I wish, but no such luck."

"Can you tell me what you're doing, sir?"

Expert at reading the tea leaves of intelligence, Datura lacked the skills of a deep cover operative, to move like a silent shadow through gray playing fields, to sow seeds tainted with deception, to harvest the poisoned crop with the cruel tools of blackmail, bribery, and brutality. Asking him to assume an operative's role would be akin to tasking a plumber to conduct open heart surgery.

Monsarrat again avoided an answer, instead offering additional instructions. "Create a cover story for your supervisors and bundle the requests with others you routinely submit. For your own health, don't mention my name."

Opening the clips on the leather valise, Datura withdrew a tablet and a cell phone. "Both belong to the Fusion Center. They're secure. I can connect directly to the office server and look for the Lexus from here, sir. I'll instruct the program to search for the license plate inside a specific radius with the hotel as my locus, within a pair of two hour windows, prior to the start and after the end of the final day of the conference. You can see the raw intel for yourself."

Connecting the tablet to the secure server was a glacial *pas de deux*. Datura rubbed his jaw with his right hand and tugged his earlobe with his left. "C'mon, c'mon, hurry up."

Monsarrat empathized. "It's a long game. Remember to breathe."

Ten minutes passed before the tablet secured the linkage. Another five minutes passed before Datura turned the screen to Monsarrat. "Got it, sir! The video is black and white, and the resolution is poor, but it shows our Lexus entering the garage of the Saint James Hotel. The woman in the driver's seat fits your description."

Monsarrat watched the car approach the garage. The driver braked before the boom, the window retracted, and a strong hand adorned with rings and bracelets snatched a ticket from the dispenser. The boom lifted, and the Lexus passed beyond the range of the camera. "Back it up and freeze the picture."

Working the controls, Datura said, "The image doesn't hold enough distinct data points for facial recognition, but I may be able to identify her if I enhance the clarity with the software in the Center. I can't do it remotely. The data demands of the graphic manipulation will clog the connection."

"Before you go, can you access the hotel cameras?"

"The geeks in the Center can walk through the back door of the security system, but the radius of your need-to-know will expand. If I enter through the front door, I'll need a warrant, and that would take time and your role could become public."

Monsarrat suspected a healthy bribe to Reimond would provide faster and more private results. "Can you can locate the car as it leaves the hotel?"

Another ten minutes passed before Datura again offered the tablet. "Got it, sir! Look at the passenger seat. Now there's a man sitting next to the driver."

Watching the grainy video, Monsarrat saw his former teammate for the first time since leaving the university. Westbrook sat erect in the passenger seat, his bearing military, skull bald, skin firm, and muscles taut. His eyes swept the street as Charing steered the car with her left hand, her right hand pressing his thigh. "Can you follow them?"

"Can do, sir. Camera coverage around the Common is extensive."

At the corner of Boylston and Tremont Streets, the Lexus stopped in the right lane. Two men wearing baggy suits and rictal expressions stepped from the sidewalk. One weighed two hundred and fifty pounds. The other was four inches taller but carried thirty fewer pounds. A crew cut covered the shorter man's head, and acne scars pitted his face. His nose was flattened, his lips fleshy, his jaw rounded and covered by a heavy stubble. The taller man wore his lank hair over his ears. His skin was sallow, his eyes watery, his lips slivers between a beaked nose and pointed jaw. They entered the car through the rear doors. The taller man removed a .44 Magnum Taurus from a shoulder holster, pressing the hard edge of the six inch barrel into Westbrook's cheek.

Monsarrat swore. "She set him up."

"Do you know the man in the passenger seat, sir?"

"From a long time ago."

The cameras followed the Lexus toward the Inner Harbor. Inside the Callahan Tunnel, the video dimmed. The car soon emerged into East Boston, a war zone of gangs, drugs, and prostitutes. At the Border Streets docks, the feed stopped. "We keep losing cameras to the punks," Datura said.

Monsarrat pitied Westbrook. The derelict streets of East Boston were a far cry from the wooded groves of Bethesda. "Keep looking,."

Datura ran ten more minutes of video, covering the roads leading from East Boston, before powering off the tablet. "I'll continue to search in the Center, and I'll run the facial recognition. As soon as I'm done, I'll text you."

Monsarrat demurred. "We initiate cell phone contact only in emergencies. We'll meet tonight, twenty-two hundred hours, at Longo's in Harvard Square."

Datura placed the tablet and cell phone inside the leather valise. "Will do, sir."

Monsarrat wrote Westbrook's number on a napkin square. "I need one more favor. Can you locate this cell phone?"

Datura put the paper into his pocket. "May I ask a question, sir?"

"Of course."

"I'll still help you, sir. I just need to understand my exposure. Are we inside or outside the law?"

As a deep cover operative, the legalities of his actions had never been a consideration, but Monsarrat sympathized with the young analyst's hesitation. "You know the saying? Better to beg forgiveness than to request permission?"

"It's never applied to me, sir."

"Welcome to the sharp point of the stick, Jason."

Leningrad Variation Attempts Control via Fianchetto

On River Street, Datura climbed into a cherry red Shelby GT500 with broad white racing stripes. The window slid down, and his hand waved in farewell, like a young Spitfire pilot brimming with enthusiasm. "See you later, sir!"

Watching the Mustang speed around a curve, Monsarrat experienced an unfamiliar sense of guilt, as if he had treated Datura as an asset, not a friend. He returned to the Jeep, placed the bag onto the passenger seat, and slipped the holstered Beretta beneath it. He retraced his earlier route, his back clean, and drove through the Callahan Tunnel into East Boston. The afternoon light faded as he reached the Condor Street Overlook, a wasteland of deserted strip malls, empty warehouses, and junk strewn lots. Streetlights, like the security cameras, were broken or missing.

The ringing of the Sanger cell phone jarred him. He knew Datura was too smart to forget his instructions and too conscientious to flaunt them. He accepted the call. "Do we have a problem?"

Panic laced the words of the young analyst. "Sir, I have intel for you. I'm in my car, but a panel van is tailing me."

Monsarrat pulled the Jeep to the side of the road, issuing commands to calm the young analyst. "Tell me your location."

"I'm on Fresh Pond Parkway approaching Mount Auburn Cemetery. I wanted to eat dinner near our rendezvous and eyeball the neighborhood before you arrived, but if I can change direction and make it to the Pike, the Mustang can outrun the van."

Fearing the young analyst harbored fantasies of action, Monsarrat spoke forcefully. "Car chases only work in movies. Drive normally. Describe the tail."

"It's a panel van, a windshield and front windows only, light colored. I can't see the make or how many people are inside."

Monsarrat reached for the Beretta. "Drive to our rendezvous site. Don't worry about finding a space to park you car. Leave it anywhere on the street."

"Where will you be, sir?"

Lying to an asset was like deceiving a lover. Once was difficult, twice was easy, three times was routine. Lying to Datura filled him with remorse. "I'll be with you soon, very soon."

The young analyst craved assurance. "How soon?"

"The same time as you arrive."

"How do I lose the panel van, sir?"

Monsarrat switched on the headlights of the Jeep, driving fast toward the tunnel. "Get to the rendezvous. I'll take care of the tail."

"What do you mean, sir?"

Monsarrat swerved around a slower car. "You know what I mean."

"Am I your rabbit, sir?" Datura asked. "Am I your lure to catch the woman in the Lexus?"

"You're not a rabbit. Concentrate on your driving."

Before the entrance to the Sumner Tunnel, Monsarrat reduced his speed. "I'm entering a dead zone. If we're disconnected, hang up. I'll call you when I'm clear."

Inside the tunnel, the road dipped downward, and the call dropped. Traffic advanced in fits and jerks. He examined the cars behind him in the mirrors of the Jeep, wondering if his operational skills had so degraded that he failed to notice a tail, or a series of tails over the past two days. He prayed that he had not led the people who killed Zeigarnik and disappeared Westbrook to Datura.

He emerged from the tunnel and followed the interstate north to Storrow Drive. He crossed Craigie Bridge, driving fast toward Cambridge. Approaching Harvard Square, he sped through a red light, flashing high beams against oncoming traffic, and looped around the bus access lane at the Cambridge Street underpass onto Massachusetts Avenue. Across from MacArthur Square, he stopped before a trio of black and white squad cars, their lights flashing.

Beyond the picket, a barrier of police tape surrounded a cherry red Mustang, its front end and left side crushed, its rear wheels resting on the sidewalk. Restrained by the seat belt, Datura slumped forward, his forehead above the steering wheel. Blood from a jagged hole in his temple matted his hair and streaked his face.

A Cambridge cop hollered, "Move it! Go home, watch the news!"

Monsarrat drove from the accident, his emotions seething. Honor required that he avenge the blood debt, ending the lives of everyone involved in the killing of Datura. Self-respect demanded he look into the eyes of the killers as they died. He parked before a book store on Church Street, hefted the shoulder bag, and locked the Jeep. The weight of the Beretta was a comfort as he walked back to the damaged Mustang.

An elderly man sporting a clipped gray moustache stood beneath a streetlight near the tape. He wore a herringbone overcoat, a gray trilby, and gold rimmed glasses. His right hand held an ebony walking stick with a knobbed handle. His left hand grasped a leash attached to a Cairn Terrier. The dog growled, and the elderly man shushed him. "Quiet, now, Seamus."

In his brogue, Monsarrat heard traces of Belfast. "It's a horrible accident. Was the driver speeding?"

"Surely, it was not an accident," the elderly man claimed. "It was as cruel and cold an act as I have ever witnessed, and I have seen more than my share of death in the homeland."

"You saw what happened?"

"I saw murder."

Monsarrat prodded him. "A murder? In Cambridge?"

"It was a white panel van, dirty and dented, that swerved across the lines of the pedestrian crossing. Only by the grace of the angels was no one crushed beneath its wheels as it lunged forward, like a bull maddened by the cape, and hit this car so hard that the ground shook as in an earthquake."

Monsarrat matched his cadence. "So it was the crash that killed the unfortunate driver?"

"It was two-headed murder, I say," the elderly man insisted, striking the pavement with his walking stick. "First, the weapon was the panel van itself, but second, a tall man stepped from its passenger seat, a large revolver in his hand. He fired a single bullet into the head of the driver. He removed a wallet from the pocket of the poor lad and a leather bag from the passenger seat before returning to the panel van and speeding away."

Monsarrat recalled the image of the tall man who helped kidnap Westbrook. "The tall man? Were his lips thin?"

"Cruel, also."

"Did he have a strong nose?"

"Like a bird of prey," the elderly man agreed. "Do you know him?"

"I'm looking for him."

"If it's the police you're with, you should know that I never passed information to the constabulary in Belfast, and at my age I'm not about to start cooperating with the authorities in Cambridge."

Monsarrat heard a tremor in his voice. "I'm a friend of the victim."

"So it's a blood feud, is it?" the elderly man asked before wishing him a pleasant evening and leading the Cairn Terrier toward Harvard Square.

"It is now," Monsarrat agreed.

The police stood with their backs to the Mustang. Monsarrat wrapped his handkerchief around his hand, ducked beneath the tape, and opened the passenger door. The dome light did not flash, but the hinges cracked. Probing the body of Datura, he felt a hard edge protruding from the gap between the upper and lower sections of the driver's seat. He tugged and retrieved a cell phone encased in a black rubber cover. He carefully closed the passenger door and walked from the Mustang, silently congratulating the young analyst. Despite his fear, he had possessed the presence of mind to hide his personal cell phone while leaving the Fusion Center devices in plain view.

A Crime Scene Unit vehicle, its lights flashing and sirens wailing, led an ambulance, fire truck, and television news van onto Massachusetts Avenue. Emergency medical technicians removed Datura from the wreckage, placed him onto a flattened bag of thick plastic, pulled shut a zipper, and wheeled the body on a gurney to the waiting ambulance. On the street, a reporter positioned her cameraman. For a flattering angle

Monsarrat scanned the area for a cleaner, a stay behind from the team that killed Datura, but no one exuded the aura of a professional. He returned to Church Street. Inside the Jeep, he placed the Beretta on the passenger seat and removed the protective cover from the cell phone. The napkin square bearing Westbrook's number fluttered onto his lap. If the intel the young analyst discovered was the location of the device, his knowledge had died with him.

Before starting the engine, he apologized. "I'm sorry, Jason. You deserved a better friend."

London System Removes an Opponent's Weakest Piece

Monsarrat drove through Cambridge beneath a drizzling sky. He steered the Jeep into a North Harvard Street strip mall, parking before the entrance to a bodega. In the rear of the store, he found a mailing box, padded envelopes, and packing tape. He paid for the purchases with cash and returned to the Jeep. Exiting the strip mall, he switched on the windshield wipers as the drizzle turned into rain.

He carved a circuitous route toward East Boston until confidant no one followed him. He was less certain the Jeep did not carry a tracking device. Although retired from the Agency, he maintained his faith in the catechism of the deep cover operative, Always Assume the Worst. He believed the team that killed Datura would come for him.

By Chelsea Creek, a motel offered free wifi. In the rear parking lot, he backed the Jeep into an empty slot. He took off his blazer, removed a small flashlight from the center console, and stepped from the Jeep. Rain quickly soaked him. Flat on the pavement, he played the light over the engine block and the chassis, searching for a tracking device or the stray wire that signified a bomb but found no tampering. The lack of visual evidence was not a surprise. An assassin possessed more covert methods for eliminating a target than a Victorian poet could count the ways to profess love.

He returned the flashlight to the center console, placed the blazer and holstered Beretta into the shoulder bag, and sloshed to the entrance of the motel. The scent of lilacs freshened the lobby, a rack offered tourist brochures, and a call bell on the counter invited service. He tapped the plunger, producing a single chime. "Hello?"

A receptionist wearing a blue suit, blue shirt, and blue tie stepped from the office. "Welcome, sir. Looks like the rain caught you."

Monsarrat registered as Mark Sanger, paying cash for one night. He provided a deposit and accepted a receipt. He walked down a hallway with a worn rug and the faint odor of mold. Inside the room, a floor lamp cast a weak light. The single window provided a view of the Jeep in the rear parking lot. He pulled the curtains shut and sat on the floor in his wet clothes, listening for footfalls in the hallway.

While a soldier of Langley, trained to evade and escape, withstand interrogation, resist brainwashing, endure torture, and kill without compunction, he had lived by a binary set of rules. Good versus bad. Us against them. In a seedy Cairo bar, he paid a prostitute to bait a honey trap for the son of the Iranian ambassador. In a filthy Saint Petersburg cafeteria, he bribed the harbor master with an envelope stuffed with dollars to gain intelligence on the cargo of a North Korean freighter. In a fetid Lagos street market, he slipped a knife beneath the fifth rib of a Yoruba politician who sold American military supplies to Boko Haram terrorists.

As a retired academic, he no longer possessed moral certainty but saw the world in shades of gray. Complexities bloomed like wildflowers. Doubts assailed his emotions, worries racked his brain, and failure taunted his confidence. Lacking faith in his skills, he tasted the unfamiliar tang of fear and assessed hip options. Logic urged a return to Greylock, but emotion demanded that his promise to Sylvie was sacrosanct and his vow to avenge Datura a duty.

He stood, stripped off his wet clothes, dried himself with a bath towel, and wrapped it around his waist. He hung the clothes in the bathroom, baking them with the complimentary hair dryer. A hand towel cleaned the Beretta and leather holster. Using the remote, he clicked through television stations until he found a local news channel. A reporter stood before the crushed Mustang, speaking with authority but offering scant information. He switched off the television, spread the towel onto the floor, and executed five hundred sit-ups, followed by an equal amount of push-ups.

After showering, he used the Sanger cell phone to confirm the Westbrook address he purchased from the concierge. He removed the SIM card from Datura's cell phone, placed it inside a padded envelope, and dropped it into the shoulder bag. He slept poorly, woke early, and dressed in dry clothes. He placed a hand towel into his bag, secured the room, and returned to the lobby. "Checking out."

"I just need to inspect your room. It's required when you pay in cash," the receptionist explained.

He returned quickly, offering the deposit with his thanks. "Come back soon, Mr. Sanger."

"I look forward to it," Monsarrat lied.

Outside the entrance to the motel, he dropped Datura's cell phone into a trash can. The rain had stopped, but water filled the potholes in the parking lot. In the budding light, he unlocked the Jeep, placed his shoulder bag and blazer onto the passenger seat, retrieved the flashlight, and conducted a second inspection, the results identical to the prior night. He dried himself with the hand towel, sat in the driver's seat, turned the ignition key, and offered silent thanks as the engine growled.

He drove to the Border Street docks, parking by the loading platform of an abandoned warehouse at the dead end of Decatur Street. He locked the Jeep, secured the Beretta, and swung the bag over his shoulder. Gray clouds blotted the morning light. He followed a ribbon of broken asphalt toward the Inner Harbor. Mud pulled at his shoes as he walked through an abandoned lot filled with rusted vehicles, some perched on cinder blocks, others mired in the ooze.

A broken wharf extended the length of a football field into the Inner Harbor. Frayed strands of nautical hawsers looped around its worn pilings, and in the exposed tidal flats a picket of broken lighters stood like shipwrecked guardians. Wedged between the husks of two lighters, mud covered the axles of a four door silver Lexus LS. The car lacked a trunk cover, hood, and doors. Its windshield, engine, tires, and rear glass panel were missing. The interior was gutted, electronic components and computer chips stolen, and license plates removed. A deburring wheel had erased the VIN from the frame. He blamed neighborhood gangs for the theft and Charing for the removal the VIN stamps.

Gazing at the dried blood that stained the trunk, Monsarrat reconstructed the likely ending to Westbrook's life. Charing and her two assistants had driven the Lexus into one of the abandoned buildings that littered the Border Street docks. After interrogating Westbrook, they stuffed him into the trunk, drove the car to the tidal flats, weighted his body, and tossed him into the Inner Harbor. He hoped the mercy of a bullet had ended his former teammate's life before the water claimed him.

He stood by the trunk of the stripped Lexus, head bowed, observing a moment of respect for Westbrook. He noted the corner of a flattened box protruding from the muck. Lifting it with his thumb and index finger, he retraced his route. Reaching the Jeep, he placed dropped the shoulder bag onto the passenger seat, retrieved the hand towel, and wiped the box clean. An empty cigarette package showed a Romanov eagle and Cyrillic letters of embossed gold against a black background. "Westbrook was right," he said aloud. "Russian killers smoke Russian cigarettes."

He cleaned the mud from his shoes and pants and dropped the towel onto the broken asphalt. Inside the Jeep, he slipped the cigarette box into the pocket of his blazer. Leaving East Boston was a reprieve. He reached the Saint James Hotel before noon, parking the Jeep illegally before the entrance. Crossing the marble floor of the lobby, he waved to the concierge.

Reimond greeted him. "You need more information?"

Monsarrat drew the Beretta and pressed the barrel against his stomach. "Walk outside with me."

"You won't shoot me in the lobby of the hotel, so fuck off."

Monsarrat pressed the muzzle against his crotch. "Like your chances, Ray?"

He moved the Beretta to the pocket of his blazer, stood to the side of the concierge, and led him from the hotel. "Climb inside the Jeep. If you piss me off, I'll put a .45 caliber slug into your center mass."

The concierge followed the instructions. "What do you want?"

"I want you to sit on your hands and stay very still, because if you twitch, you'll die," Monsarrat replied. "I also want you to answer my questions truthfully, because if you lie, you'll die."

He closed the door and took the driver's seat. He secured the passenger seat belt and jerked the strap until it locked tight against the chest of the concierge. He steered the Jeep into traffic. "The red haired looker? Did she speak to you?"

"You kidnapped me to ask about the bimbo?"

Monsarrat drove his right elbow into the concierge's face. "I ask questions. You answer them."

Reimond spat blood onto the windshield. Through swollen lips, he replied, "She didn't say a word to me. She left the hotel with your friend, their faces were pressed together. I told them to have a safe trip. Your friend didn't answer. She just wiggled her fingers in the air. Her hands were fucking huge."

"Did you hear her say anything to Westbrook?"

"My eyes were paying attention, not my ears. She looked good, like a four figure hooker."

"A Russian hooker?"

"She was good looking enough."

"Any Russian guests in the hotel during the conference?"

"Not to my knowledge."

Before reaching the entrance to the Mass Pike, Monsarrat pulled to the side of the road. He stuffed a Benjamin Franklin into the pocket of the concierge, twisted in his seat, and gestured with the Beretta. "What's the deal with your fake accent?"

"Better tips from hotel guests if they think I'm from the islands."

Monsarrat laughed. "Move slowly, Ray. Left hand, unbuckle the strap, open the door. Right hand, on the small of your back. Lean forward, roll outta your seat."

"You fucking crazy? I'll bust my skull!"

"Think of what a .45 caliber slug will do to the back of your head."

Monsarrat secured the door as Reimond fell from the Jeep. He drove away from the curb. Glancing at the rearview mirror, he saw the bloodied concierge stand, his middle finger held high in salute.

EN PRISE

In a Position to be Taken

A Capture Removes an Opposing Player from the Game

Cairstine Fergusson sat in the atrium of her white brick, Federal-style townhouse on Dumbarton Street in Georgetown. The morning sun streamed through the windows, warming her face. The rich perfume of luxury scented the room, a paean to princes and princesses, royal palaces and feudal estates. On the Flemish wall tapestry behind her, a hunter armed with a bow and a quiver of arrows followed his hound in pursuit of a stag through groves of oak trees and across swift streams filled with trout jumping at flies.

The owner of Fergus & Son, an antiquities gallery at the corner of Wisconsin Avenue and Reservoir Road in Georgetown, she wore a silk robe embossed with red and gold Taoist symbols. Sipping café au lait from a bone china cup and saucer set, she scanned the headlines of the local newspaper. With a silver bread knife, she dabbed strawberry preserves onto a croissant. A flake of crust drifted atop a Lladró chess set with burled wood borders, black and tan squares, and porcelain pieces. She wet her index finger, dabbed the flake, and set it onto her tongue.

She played chess matches from memory to improve upon the movements of the Grandmasters. Her board offered Black's sixteenth move, bishop to d5 to capture the White pawn, in the thirteenth match of the 1971 USSR Championship between Vladimir Savon, playing White, and Roman Dzindzichashvili, playing Black. She believed the reticent Georgian lost the game on the decision.

Six feet tall, approaching middle age, her trim weight the same as the day she arrived from Scotland to begin her doctoral studies in the

History of Art at Johns Hopkins University, Fergusson wore her
lustrous black hair in a French bob. Her eyes were hazel, her brows
thick, her lips full, and her nose slanted askew. Her skin was pale, and
her ears pressed against her skull, giving her the sleek, graceful
appearance of a seal in water. Her legs were muscular, her arms
sinewy, and her hands strong with knuckles like gnarled oak knobs.
Her palms were sandpaper, as if they performed the hardest manual
labors, and her nails were tipped the crimson of freshly spilled blood.

She was thrice born, lastly as Cairstine Fergusson in Aberdeen,
second as Daughter Number Forty-Three in Repino, and by birth as
Yulia Lazarevna Belyakova in Leningrad. The only child of two
academics, father Lazar Vladimirovich Belyakov a member of the
faculty of mathematics at Leningrad State Pedagogical Institute and
mother Gesya Andreyevna Belyakova an elementary school teacher,
she loved her doting parents dearly. Until her father returned from
the Afghan War on her twelfth birthday, addicted to opium and *chars*,
the black hashish from Balkh.

Her mother prepared a birthday meal while Yulia sat with her
father in the library of the family's spacious apartment in a building
reserved for honored academic families. She squeezed her eyes shut
as he sang *s dnem rozhden'ya*, happy birthday wishes, and pressed a
gift into her hands. She opened her eyes to find a Vasilisa the
Beautiful doll, a bundle of cotton with a long auburn braid, blue eyes,
and a gown of linen. "Thank you, *Papachka*! I adore her!"

"My sweet, darling Yulechka," he replied, releasing the drawstring
of his pants.

She ripped apart the doll as easily as if it was a piece of paper and
threw the pieces at him. "I hate you! I wish you would die!"

Despite the Order of the Red Star he wore on his jacket, awarded for courage in the battle for Rokha against the *dukhi*, the Afghan peasant fighters, the State Pedagogical Institute could tolerate neither his drug addictions nor his sexual deviations. Blacklisted from the faculty, freed from his academic commitments, he spent his days in pursuit of drugs and prostitutes.

He brought the second humiliation upon the family when the *Komitet Gosudarstvennoy Bezopasnosti*, the KGB, arrested him for violation of the Anti-Parasite Law of 1961. During his trial in the Leningrad People's Court, he stood in a gray prison uniform before the three member collegium. The people's judge and the two people's assessors conferred briefly before extending their unanimous verdict. "Citizen Belyakov, you are guilty of the charge of social parasitism. Your actions have harmed the order of the Soviet Union. You are hereby granted a sentence of resettlement to Kolyma in the Far East, fifteen years atonement in enforced employment, and confiscation of the state provided housing commensurate with your former status."

His wife humbled herself before the people's judge. "I am a mother, a teacher, a holder of the Order of Labor Glory, Third Class. My husband was a good man but returned from the intervention in Afghanistan broken by the cruelty of the *dukhi*. He spends his pension and my salary on his sickness. I have no money to buy food for my daughter and myself. If you take our apartment, we will have no place to sleep. I beg you to grant us Soviet mercy."

The people's judge rendered his decision. "Citizen Belyakova, for your failure as a wife to report the activities of the social parasite Belyakov, and for your failure as a mother to protect your Soviet child from exposure to the anti-social, parasitic lifestyle of your husband, you are barred from teaching for a period of five years. You are stripped of your Order of Labor Glory. Your salary and other assistance granted by the Ministry of Education are revoked. You and your daughter will report immediately to your new domicile on Turbinnaya Street."

Yulia followed her mother to a Khrushchyovka tenement building in Narvsky, a Leningrad neighborhood of prostitutes, drug dealers, thieves, and murderers. On the staircase, she inhaled the stench of sweat, dirt, and human droppings. Rats and roaches commanded the hallway and the filthy *kommunalka*, the communal toilet. She immediately hated the one room, cold water flat on the third floor of the sagging building, its sole window offering a view of a garbage-strewn courtyard.

She slept with her mother on a lumped mattress, a thin bed sheet providing a sham of warmth. If the electricity functioned, a *Mir* radio in a steel case attached to the low ceiling blared news on the All Union First Programme. Noise from domestic quarrels poured through the walls. Violence was her only companion. Cigarette burns from her drunken mother puckered her shoulders. A jagged scar from the leader of the neighborhood *baklany*, a gang of street punks, marked her right forearm. During the White Nights, when the citizens of Narvsky resorted to violence more quickly than usual, Boris Yuryevich Popkov, the butcher, gifted her a third mark.

He arrived at the apartment bearing gifts of stringy meat. His friends, the baker and the dairyman, brought stale bread and gray oleo. Each bartered the ersatz food in exchange for bouts of sex with Gesya. Their bodies stunk and their mouths disgorged insults. *Suka* slut. *Shlyukha* whore. *Pizda* cunt. Yulia wished, her mother, her father, and the people's judge dead, but she hated Popkov most of all.

He stood six feet tall, with a belly like an untreated tumor swelling against his coveralls, stained with blood and grease. He slammed his fist against the door, rattling its rusted hinges. "*Privyet*, Gesya Andreyevna! Greetings! Your lover brings fresh meat to you!"

He pounded against the wood harder. "Gesya Andreyevna! Do you not want my meat?"

Yulia opened the door, her hatred compressed. "Enter our home, Boris Yuryevich."

"Some home," the butcher sneered.

He threw a string of kielbasa and an empty bottle of Zhigulevskoe beer onto the floor. Crossing to the mattress, he pulled aside the sheet to expose the naked woman. "Gesya Andreyevna! Your very own Zhivago is here!"

Yulia's mother smiled weakly. "Welcome, Boryenka. What do you have for me?"

"Meat!" he exclaimed, removing his coveralls.

After his climax, he rolled off the woman to find Yulia standing above him. "Are you also hungry for me, Yulechka?"

"Pick up the kielbasa," she demanded.

Popkov stood, his uncircumcised penis limp against his hairy thigh. "Today I bring you kielbasa, but tomorrow I will give you the tasty beefsteak between my legs."

She noted the darkening bruises on her mother's thighs and buttocks but felt neither love nor pity. She balled her strong right hand into a fist. "You talk like a bull, but I will make you a steer."

He picked up the empty beer bottle and broke it against the steel case of the radio. "I will teach you respect, little *pizda*."

The jagged glass cut through her shirt, slicing her breasts. She pressed her hand against the wound. Blood flowed through her fingers. Before he could again swing the broken bottle, she crushed his penis against his thigh with her fist. "Do you like to receive pain, you *zhopa*, you asshole?"

Popkov dropped the bottle, his breath rattling. "I will tear you apart in another moment."

She reached between his legs for his penis, sticky with fluids. "Not before I will slice off your *khuy*, so you will never fuck anyone again."

She pierced the shaft with a shard of glass, pinning it against his thigh. "It does not look like beefsteak to me, Boris Yuryevich."

On the mattress, Belyakova groaned. "Who will come to me? How will I put food onto the table?"

"*Mamochka*," she replied, "I hope the baker fucks you to death with a loaf of stale bread."

The Nimzowitsch Defense Attacks the White Queen's Pawn

In the atrium, Fergusson considered the Lladró board. She plotted a refinement to the Dzindzichashvili response following Savon's sixteenth move, allowing the White pawn to remain at d5. Instead of capturing the minor piece, she moved the Georgian's bishop to e7 to protect the Black king. The bold choice would spawn major consequences, ultimately altering the outcome of the match in favor of Dzindzichashvili, as her own decision to attack the butcher during the White Nights propelled her from the despair of Narvsky to the wealth of Georgetown.

During the White Nights, residents of Narvsky escaped from the misery of their apartments to the sidewalks of Turbinnaya Street. Throngs gathered around Spidola transistor radios. One group listened to the football match between Zenit Leningrad and its rival, Dynamo Moscow. Cheering the local boys, jeering the Moscow footballers, they drank beer and threw the empty bottles into the overflowing gutters.

Beneath her shirt, twine secured an ersatz bandage of soap and the front page of the *Sovetskaya Rossiya* newspaper to Yulia's chest. She walked along the sidewalk, stopping by a group of pensioners drinking one hundred gram shots of vodka and listening to a radio lecture by a professor from Leningrad Polytechnic Institute on the unique identity disorder affecting the citizens of the city. "On the winter solstice, we receive less than five hours of pale sunlight, but during the White Nights, more than nineteen hours grace us. We lurch from the depths of darkness to the summits of sunlight, suffering

alcoholism and crime. Is it any wonder that our literary giants are
Gogol and Gorky?"

Parading down Turbinnaya Street in uniforms bestowed with Red
Army medals, grizzled veterans of the Great Patriotic War sang
military ballads, sadly for their lost youth, proudly for their wartime
achievements. They sang of their love for the *Rodina*, Mother Russia.
Between ballads, they drank salutes of vodka. Further down the street,
spectators surrounded two pensioners hunched over a plastic chess
pieces set on a card table.

The first pensioner, playing White, advanced a pawn and slapped
the chess clock. "I am sorry to humiliate you."

"You play too cautiously, like Kutuzov fighting the French at
Borodino. I play like Zhukov, scorching the Germans in Berlin," the
second pensioner, playing Black, claimed, moving his knight forward.

Too young to legally enter the State Public Library, Yulia sneaked
into a basement reading room every day after school to study the
matches of the Soviet Grandmasters. She recognized the opening
moves of the game as a variation of the 1923 USSR Championship
match between Levenfish and Dus-Chotimirsky. Levenfish had
played White, utilized a Sicilian opening, and accepted Black's
surrender on the twenty-sixth move. The first pensioner eyed the
capture of his opponent's knight, a move that initially appeared safer
than taking the Black queen and losing his own piece to retaliation.

Whispering into the old man's ear, she advised, "*Dedushka*, dear
grandfather, if you capture the Black knight, your opponent will mate
your king in exactly six moves."

"What will happen if I do not take it?"

"Capture the Black queen, sacrifice your White queen, and develop your bishops. He will surrender in ten moves."

The second pensioner announced, "Move your piece so I can defeat you."

Eight moves later, he tipped his Black king onto the board, surrendering to a two bishop and single rook skewer. "You won only because the *devushka*, the young girl, saved you."

The pensioner playing White asked, "What is your name, child? Who taught you to play chess?"

"I am Yulia Lazarevna Belyakova, and I taught myself."

He pointed to her blouse. "You are bleeding, Yulia. Do you need medical help?"

She rejected his offer. "It is no longer an issue."

She continued to walk down Turbinnaya Street, her destination the fishermen casting their lines on the banks of the Neva River. She entered an alley before State Education Center Number 261. Lost in thoughts of chess, she noted too late the leader of the *baklany*. "Get out of my way."

He greeted her like an old friend. "*Shlyukha*, now we finish what we started, *dah*?"

Yulia touched the scar on her right forearm, a earlier gift from his switchblade. Turning, she saw that his friends blocked her retreat. She stepped forward, kicked the tall youth in the groin, and shoved him onto his back. Dropping her knees onto his biceps, she slapped her palms against his ears and pummeled his face with her fists. Blood erupted from his nose and mouth, and a broken tooth tore her knuckle. He vomited onto the pavement.

A squat youth with arms as thick as pig hocks and thighs like tree stumps pulled her upright. She smashed the heel of her palm into the bridge between his nostrils and upper lip, breaking the bone and a sending a torrent of blood over his chin. She extended her knuckles and drove them into his throat. She cocked her arm to strike again but collapsed as a fist slammed into her kidney.

Oxygen burst from her lungs. The *baklany* ripped the clothes and the bandage from her body. Blood flowed from the wound as they stretched her arms and spread her legs, as if preparing to snap her limbs like a wishbone. They pressed her against the pavement, and a punk with acne scars placed his boot upon her throat. "We will take turns with the *shlyukha*, comrades, as many as we wish."

A face descended toward her, and she crashed her forehead into its nose. The *baklany* fell upon her again, snapping her bones, splitting her lips, and cracking her ribs. They stomped her ankles, knees, and shoulders. A boot ground into her face. She accepted her death, but voices shouted, and the *baklany* fled. Two men, one tall, the other short, approached her. She inhaled the stench of their sweat and vodka and saw their grease-stained white tunics, mud-caked pant cuffs, and scuff- covered shoes. Pocks scarred their faces. Nicotine stained their fingernails and teeth. She decided they were devils.

The short devil wrapped her naked body in his tunic, exposing a threadbare undershirt over a hairy stomach, and carried her to the end of the alley. He opened the doors to the windowless rear compartment of a *tabletka*, a boxy ambulance, and set her onto a gurney. He rubbed ointment onto a bandage and applied it to her chest. Placing his tunic over her like a blanket, he said, "You are lucky, *devushka*. Not often do you find a *tabletka* in Narvsky."

"Bring me to Turbinnaya Street," she demanded through her split lips before the pressure of the gurney's leather straps caused her to pass out from pain.

The tall devil drove north through the streets of the city to Yelagin Island, in the mouth of the Neva River. Crossing the First Bridge, he entered Kirov Central Park, stopping by the Music Pavilion. Turning to his partner, he said, "It is good work, *nyet*? We find boys no mother loves, girls no father wants. We are paid handsomely."

"We are like talent scouts for *Kino studiya* Lenfilm, but with benefits on a gurney, not a casting couch."

The tall devil opened the rear compartment of the *tabletka*. He woke Yulia with a capsule of ammonia salts, pressed a strip of surgical tape across her mouth and used a second strip to secure her head to the gurney. He tossed the tunic to the short devil. "The *Direktor* will like her. She is a fighter."

He loosened the leather straps, pried apart her legs, and mounted her, grunting at the resistance of the hymen. She again passed out. He woke her with a second capsule of ammonia salts, finished, and surrendered his place to the short devil. In a moment, he climaxed. The tall devil lifted her legs and entered her anally. He finished, and the short devil repeated the violation.

The tall devil wiped blood from her thighs and applied ointment to her damaged areas. He secured the leather straps and removed the strips of surgical tape. "Now we take you now to Repino."

Her virginity stolen, her body broken, Yulia hoped to die, but the desire for vengeance revived her. She vowed to kill the two devils, planning her retribution like a Grandmaster plotting lines of attack across a chessboard.

The Latvian Gambit Arises from the Movement of the King's Pawn

In the atrium, Fergusson chose boldly, a king's side castle that would result in mate in seven moves. She rarely regretted a decision, even when her choices had earned physical pain from the instructors at Special Training Institute Number One in Repino, where her prodigy in chess attracted the attention of the *Direktor*, and during her training at Special Discipline Course Number Four in Novosibirsk. Reborn as Daughter Number Forty-Three, she learned to trust her instincts and intellect, her skills and strength.

Repino, thirty miles northwest of Leningrad, boasted groves of pine trees and a sandy beach along the Gulf of Finland. A granite statue to the artist Ilya Efimovich Repin graced the town square. A mile further, a *dom otdykha*, a rest and recuperation center deep in a coniferous forest, offered workers from the Leningrad Association for Electrical Motors weekend respites from the toils of their daily labor.

Each Friday afternoon, a LAZ-695 bus transported two dozen men and women to the *dom otdykha*, returning them to the factory on Sunday evening. Walks into town, dips into the Gulf, *banya* steam baths with birch switches, matches of *basketbol* and *futbol*, and meals of herring, soups, cabbage rolls, dumplings, buns, and desserts filled their days. Vodka and sex occupied their nights. Forbidden to the workers was hiking in the coniferous forest. No explanation was provided, but ignoring the rule earned a one-way trip to Number 4 Liteyny Avenue, Leningrad headquarters of the KGB.

The *tabletka* turned onto a rutted dirt lane. Two miles beyond the *dom otdykha*, KGB soldiers armed with Kalashnikov rifles and accompanied by Alsatian dogs stopped the ambulance. A sergeant examined the driver's papers before allowing him to approach a large clearing. Twenty foot high masonry walls topped by barbed wire formed a square barrier. From each of the corners rose perimeter watch towers with klieg spotlights and NSV 12.7mm heavy machine guns. A timber gate reinforced with steel plating controlled access to the compound.

The *tabletka* jounced to a halt before the walls. The gate swung open, and the tall devil drove forward, parking next to a formation of six men and women in medical uniforms. A nurse opened the doors to the rear compartment, and two orderlies carried the gurney into a medical clinic. A nurse slipped a needle into Yulia's vein. The sedative took effect immediately.

She opened her eyes the following day in a windowless ward of six beds, each bolted to the floor. Fluorescent ceiling tubes offered pale green light. The ward's only patient, she occupied the bed closest to the door. She ached from the crown of her skull to the soles of her feet. Plaster casts encased her arms and legs. Variegated bruises spotted her exposed skin. A fresh bandage covered the wound on her chest. Her lips stuck together, and metal shackles connected her wrist to the bed's steel railing.

A nurse entered the room carrying a glass of ice chips. "*Privyet*, Daughter Number Forty-Three."

As the first chips melted, Yulia felt her lips float apart. "More."

"How do you feel, Daughter Number Forty-Three?"

The question confused her. "I am Yulia Lazarevna Belyakova. I live on Turbinnaya Street in Leningrad. What is this place?"

"The *Doktor*, the head of our medical clinic, will tell all to you."

A middle-aged man with a smile as white as his uniform strode into the room. Talcum daubed his freshly shaved face, and his hair smelled of lavender. Thin spectacles perched atop his nose, and a gold watch circled his left wrist. "I am glad you are awake, Daughter Number Forty-Three."

She countered with questions. "What is my correct response, comrade *Doktor*? *Dobroy utro*, good morning, *dobryy den'*, good afternoon, *dobryy vecher*, good evening, or *spakoynoy nochi*, good night? Why am I chained to the bed? Who is Daughter Number Forty-Three? My name is Yulia."

"What you were called in your previous life is not important. You have a new life and a new name," he responded. "We set your fractures and repaired your facial, cranial, and epidermal damage. The wound across your breasts and your chipped ribs will heal with rest. We repaired the damage to your perineum and anus. We also conducted a successful hysterectomy, although you have lost the ability to bear children."

"In Narvsky, children are cursed," she replied. "Did you arrest the driver of the *tabletka* and his assistant who raped me?"

He ignored her question. "You begin rehabilitation today. I expect full recovery and your entrance into Special Training Institute Number One in four months."

She ate healthy food. Her bones mended. As her strength increased, she explored the compound, part academic campus, part military garrison. A grid of paved walkways marked its four quadrants. In the northwest sector, low structures housed the classrooms where KGB instructors taught lessons in foreign languages, foreign cultures, and foreign history. In the southeast quadrant, a gymnasium, pool, and range provided training in swimming, strength training, boxing and martial arts, rifle and pistol skills. In the northeast sector, instructors, students, and KGB soldiers ate in segregated dining halls. In the southwest quadrant, barracks housed soldiers. Students slept in a dormitory. Instructors shared a blood red *izba*, a house of rough hewn logs and pale blue latticed trim.

In the center of the compound, a chain-link fence crowned with razor wire surrounded the offices and residences of the *Direktor* of Special Training Institute Number One, the *Doktor*, and the behavioral scientists from Line "S" of the First Chief Directorate administering the *Narodnaya Strategiya*, the secret KGB program to remove select children from their parents. The few students who finished the program graduated into sleeper agents for insertion into enemy nations. Failed students received a bullet in the back of the neck and shallow graves in the coniferous forest.

Her rehabilitation lasted only eight weeks. The morning of her release from the clinic, the *Direktor* summoned her. Walking to his office, she played in her mind the opening moves of the Queen's Pawn formation in the 1952 match between Petrosian and Kotov, the Armenian's bishop capturing the Russian's knight at c4.

The *Direktor*, a slender KGB colonel with bootblack hair, eyes the blue of a Siberian lake, and a face unlined by concerns, wore a tailored suit of merino wool. He sat on a chair of carved Karelian birch behind a matching desk. On its glass top rested a nine millimeter Czech Vz.82 pistol in a leather holster, a pitcher of water, two glasses, and a chess board. He pointed at a spindle chair. "I understand you enjoy chess, Daughter Number Forty-Three."

Yulia had told no one of her love for the game. "How have your come by this information, comrade *Direktor*?"

"Accept that the *Komitet* is all knowing and all powerful, Daughter Number Forty-Three."

"I understand, comrade *Direktor*," she replied. "Will I be punished when I defeat you?"

"Of course not," he replied. "Try your best."

Playing Black, he utilized the Alekhine Defense, opening with his knight to f6. She sipped water, studied the board as if she had never seen the opening, and mated in fourteen moves. "Per your instructions, comrade *Direktor*."

He reset the board. "Who taught you to play chess?"

She provided the same answer she had given the *dedushka*. "I taught myself."

He studied her with his cold eyes. "I have news of your father in Kolyma. Would you like to hear it?"

"I do not, comrade *Direktor*."

"What of your mother in Narvsky? Do wish to hear her news?"

"I do not, comrade *Direktor*," she repeated.

"You are smart," he complimented. "You will do well here, as long as you remember the first rule."

Victory emboldened her. "Remember what, comrade *Direktor*?"

"You will not receive special treatment because we play chess."

She earned top scores in academics and physical education, including the close quarter fighting course. Her fellow students resented her achievements. A month into the program, an older boy asserted the prerogatives of size and age to steal food from her plate during lunch in the dining hall. She split his cheek from temple to jawbone with a fork. A week later, an older girl attempted to force a sausage into her mouth. She beat her unconscious with a chair.

The Line "S" behavioral scientists argued that her behavior required termination from the program, but the *Direktor* saw her potential. The next day, she received her third identity. No longer Daughter Number Forty-Three, she became Cairstine Fergusson of Aberdeen. She studied the history, politics, and culture of Scotland. She read Burns, Scott, and Hume. She ate haggis, bangers and mash, and black pudding, all finer than the fare of Narvsky.

Shortly before graduation, three male classmates one year her junior approached her in the gym. Their leader, a beefy cherub with a broad chest, held a shiv. "It is time for you to learn the danger of playing the teacher's pet."

She threw the cherub to the tile floor, crushed his nose with the heel of her palm, and broke his wrists. She took the shiv from his limp hand and sliced his pants, exposing his flaccid penis. "If I am the teacher's pet, you are now my pet *suka*."

The shiv sliced his foreskin, and her hand stifled his screams. She stood, dropped the slice of flesh onto his chest, and pointed the bloody blade at the friends of the cherub. "Would you like a turn?"

Before an hour passed, she stood before the *Direktor*. "Emotional, physical, even sexual brutality is expected within parameters, but your actions today were unacceptable."

Soldiers escorted her to the medical clinic. Nurses bound her in a straitjacket. The behavioral scientists injected her with psychotropic drugs. The questioning lasted three days before they placed her inside a *kishka*, a windowless cell barely tall and wide enough to hold a naked body. After a week, they concluded their interrogations, released her, and again demanded that the *Direktor* terminate her participation in the *Narodnaya Strategiya.*

She emerged weak but full of anger. The *Direktor* noted her defiance after an ordeal that broke the hardest criminals and political prisoners. He rejected the petition of the behavioral scientists and enrolled her in the elite Special Discipline Course Number Four in Novosibirsk, administrated by Line "V" in the Executive Action Department of the KGB. In addition to her role as a sleeper agent, she would serve as a *mokroye delo,* an assassin.

The Russian Defense Declines a Gambit to Defend a Pawn

In Georgetown, Fergusson lapped the trappings of her wealth like a cat presented with a golden bowl of cream. She lifted a Hungarian crystal bell set upon a swath of Hermès silk. Sweet notes filled the atrium. In contrast, her Aberdeen brogue burst like a cannonade. "Rupert! Once again, a café au lait and a croissant."

Bald, goateed, with fists like war clubs and a beer barrel chest, Rupert Marlowe bore the flattened nose and cauliflower ears of an inadequate pugilist. Having lost his cherubic innocence along with his foreskin to Fergusson in Repino, he possessed a single expression, a malicious smirk. Like his employer, he had progressed from sleeper agent in Repino to *mokroye delo* assassin in Novosibirsk. Retribution served as his holy grail. He submitted detailed monthly reports on her activities to Line "N" in Moscow Centre, as the SVR, the *Sluzhba Vneshney Razvedki*, the successor to the KGB was known, and assumed her reports on his activities were as richly detailed.

Born Arkady Alexeevich Limonov in the Siberian city of Chelyabinsk, Marlowe dressed in an English pearl gray suit and gold pince-nez, and he spoke in a plummy Edwardian accent. Entering the atrium, he collected the used dishes and cutlery, placing clean silverware, a café au lait, and a croissant from a silver tray onto the linen tablecloth. "An additional something, ma'am?"

Fergusson enjoyed the deference of the butler, although she still despised him. In the opinion of Moscow Centre, their history ensured that their loyalties remained with their masters, never to each other. "No, Rupert. Carry on."

"Very well, ma'am," he replied before backing from the room, as if taking leave from his liege.

Glancing at the chessboard, Fergusson saw capitulation. She remembered her penultimate chess match with the *Direktor*. Tipping her king onto the board, she had offered a compliment. "You have improved greatly since we first played, comrade *Direktor*."

"You gave me the victory," he replied. "What do you want in exchange for soothing my ego?"

"A respite before I report to Novosibirsk. Seven days only."

He lifted a fountain pen from its blotter. "Even for the class valedictorian, such a request is highly irregular. One day only."

"I will accept no less than five days."

Her temerity did not surprise him. Smoothing a sheet of stationary, he said, "Two days. If you return one moment past forty-eight hours, I will transfer you to a basement cell in Liteyny Avenue."

She accepted the permission and his offer of transportation to Narvsky. In the alley off Turbinnaya Street, she found the leader of the *baklany*. "Where are the others?" she demanded.

He flicked his switchblade. "*Shlyukha*, you are grown up. I will start you now, and when my boys arrive, they will finish you, *dah*?"

She flipped him onto his stomach, pressed her knee into his back, cupped her hands beneath his chin, and pulled his head sharply upward until his spine snapped. "No, *zhopa*. Now I finish you."

Inside the tenement building, the cold water flat was empty. With the stub of a pencil, she scrawled a message across the wall, Dearest *Mamochka*, are you with *Papachka* in Kolyma now? You are both lucky to have missed me.

In the State Public Library, she took a chair in a far corner of the

Main Reading Room, analyzing the Forty-Eighth USSR
Championship match between Balashov and Razuvaev, played to a
draw on the nineteenth move, until the custodian flicked the lights to
announce the closing time. She walked toward the banks of the Neva
River. At the approach of the *tabletka*, she staggered, fell to the
sidewalk, and allowed the two devils to drag her to the ambulance. As
they opened the rear compartment, she announced, "I am offended
that you do not remember me, comrades."

She broke the short devil's nose and crippled the tall devil with a
finger strike to the throat. Tearing strips of surgical tape, she secured
their wrists and ankles, covered their mouths, and bound them back
to back. Inside one of the medical drawers, she found syringes and
vials of haloperidol. "Tell me, comrades, are we inside a *tabletka* or a
psikhushka, a psychiatric hospital?"

She injected each with 60mg of the drug, fifty percent above the
recommended dosage. Their heads lolled, and she removed the tape
covering their mouths, to prevent them from drowning in their own
saliva. The gears of the ambulance ground, but she soon mastered the
shifting. Crossing onto Yelagin Island, she entered Kirov Central
Park, stopping by the Music Pavilion.

In the rear compartment, the two devils stared vacantly, snot and
spittle dribbling over their chins. She removed a fresh roll of tape and
a scalpel from the drawer, released the short devil, and threw him
from the *tabletka*. With the tape, she secured his throat to a door
handle. "Patience, comrade! Your turn comes soon!"

The scalpel freed the ankles of the tall devil. She stripped off his
trousers and hoisted his legs. "You will desire lubricant, but there is
only your blood, so you will feel great pain, but as the Old Believers

say, suffering is good for the soul."

The blade sliced a gash from his coccyx to perineum. Blood flowed like water cresting a dam. His expression slack, he neither resisted nor screamed as she violated him with the scalpel, but his eyes reflected the intensity of his suffering. She freed the short devil from his restraints, repeated the punishment, and returned to the *tabletka*. Slapping the face of the tall devil, she demanded, "Pay attention! It is time to die!"

She plunged the scalpel into his jugular. The life faded from his eyes, and she kicked the corpse onto the ground. She sliced the throat of the short devil, sanitized her hands with antiseptic solution, and dried them with a towel. She cleaned their blood from her clothes, and secured the rear compartment. Shifting the *tabletka* into reverse, she backed over the two bodies.

At the entrance to the *dom otdykha*, she abandoned the *tabletka*. Following the dirt lane deep into the coniferous forest, she buried her clothes, reaching the gate as naked as upon her arrival a lifetime ago. A KGB soldier wrapped her in his tunic. In the medical clinic, the *Doktor* injected her with a sedative.

She awoke again manacled to the ward bed nearest the door. Her eyes focused on the silent man sitting by her side. "Is this necessary, comrade *Direktor*? I returned before forty-eight hours passed."

A chessboard balanced on his knees. "Is your unusual arrival related to the abandoned *tabletka* and the two orderlies found in Kirov Central Park missing their anal cavities?"

"Is this a *provokatsiya*, a provocation, comrade *Direktor*?"

He removed the manacles. "I must warn you. My colleague in Novosibirsk does not enjoy chess."

She played their final match full of fury, utilizing the Kan variation of the Sicilian Defense to defeat him in a dozen moves. The following morning, carrying only the chessboard, a farewell gift from the *Direktor*, she slid onto the rear bench of a Chaika limousine for the trip to a KGB aerodrome, where she boarded an Ilyushin Il-14 for the flight to Novosibirsk.

Daughter Number Forty-Three graduated with top honors in the *mokroye delo* course at Special Discipline Course Number Four. In Lubyanka, the Moscow headquarters of the KGB, she received travel documents for Tatyana Alekseyevna Feofanova, a junior secretary at the Soviet Embassy in Nigeria. Landing at Murtala Muhammed International Airport in Lagos, she joined a KGB snatch team for the drive to Ile-Ife, where Mr. and Mrs. Aonghus Fergusson of Aberdeen, expatriate Scottish academics at Obafemi Awolowo University, had died prior to her arrival in a KGB staged car accident.

Posing as representatives of the British High Commission, the team reached the university in a Peugeot 504, followed by a Renault ambulance. While the diplomats processed paperwork and the doctors attended to the daughter, the black haired, hazel eyed Cairstine familiarized herself with the surroundings. The team departed the city. Thirty miles onward, they entered a dense rain forest. Beneath the dripping canopy, the doctors sedated the daughter.

The ambulance drove to the airport, but the Peugeot continued to the Soviet embassy. An hour before midnight, holding a false British passport, Cairstine Fergusson, born Yulia Lazarevna Belyakova and resurrected as Daughter Number Forty-Three, boarded the British Airways flight to London, accompanied by two caskets in the belly of the plane. From London, she flew to Aberdeen and buried her temporary Scottish parents in the cemetery of the local parish church.

In Lagos, the daughter of the expatriate academics, carrying the documents of Tatyana Alekseyevna Feofanova, a newly arrived Soviet embassy employee stricken with a deadly jungle disease, was rushed onto a medical evacuation plane for an emergency flight to Moscow. The next day, a press release from the Ministry of Foreign Affairs announced the death of the beloved junior secretary. The funeral was attended by family, colleagues, and friends, each as false as the departed.

In Aberdeen, Cairstine lived in the family's semi-detached home on Belvidere Street. A quiet student, she made friends slowly, as expected of a young woman who recently experienced a tragic loss, but took top grades in the Higher and Advanced Highers in Classical Studies. She enrolled in the University of Saint Andrews. She studied, hiked glens, swam lochs, and bagged Munros, the thousand meter high mountains of Scotland. The Faculty of Arts awarded her First Class Honours with specializations in Art History and Archaeology.

She sold the semi-detached house, flew to Baltimore, and enrolled in the Department of Near Eastern Studies at Johns Hopkins University, receiving a Ph.D. in Assyriology. With funds provided by Moscow Centre, she opened her antiquities gallery. On the same day, she received U.S. citizenship and her assignment, to service the product of Moscow Centre's newest asset, Pavlik, a rising star in the Directorate of Operations of the Central Intelligence Agency.

In the atrium, Fergusson altered history. Savon, playing Black, mated Dzindzichashvili, playing White. She always won. She needed new challenges. She needed an intellect sharp enough to stimulate her. She needed a body strong enough to arouse her. She needed a desire hot enough to excite her. She needed Pavlik, her lover extraordinaire, for whom she had defied the immutable rules of Moscow Centre forbidding liaisons between a sleeper agent and her asset, upon pain of death. She ached for him, but Pavlik had died on the first day of the new year when his car exploded.

Winning the Exchange Trades the Pawn for Any Other Piece

Fergusson loved the flamboyance of Georgetown, dressing each day like an actress strolling the red carpet. A sleeveless black plunging sheath dress and a platinum necklace set with brilliant cut sapphires accentuated her cleavage. A pearl bracelet in pink gold circled her right wrist, and a 24 karat bangle rested on her left wrist. She wore a quill cloche hat and leather pumps. Her clutch bag held a Walther Q4. She believed in capitalism, detested communism, and executed her directives pitilessly, fearing the red-toothed wrath of Moscow Centre. She hated the prospect of one day returning to Russia. When she thought of the *Rodina*, she saw Narvsky.

Walking along Wisconsin Avenue in the early morning sun, she inspected her surroundings for agents of the *sluzhba*, the American security services, but the interest she attracted was sexual, not professional. She enjoyed her cover as a successful gallery owner, and her prized acquisitions, a Byzantine mosaic from the Church of the Lions at Umm er-Rasas, a basalt carving from the palace of King Sargon II at Dur-Sharrukin, a stele of Persephone from Wadi Bel Gadir in Cyrene, were valued in the millions of dollars. She also enjoyed her *mokroye delo* assignments, eliminating threats from the American security services, often assisted by Rupert.

The successes had earned commendations from Line "N," but since the death of Pavlik, praise from Moscow Centre had been as rare as a newly discovered antiquity. She dreaded a recall message or, worse, a garrote around her throat, if Rupert's fervid reports to Line "N" convinced their masters that she had become a liability or, worse, a *predatel'*, a traitor who had denounced Pavlik to his killers.

Opening the gallery, she evaluated her situation as she would a match between Grandmasters. Arranging a fatal accident for Rupert would remove the threat of the butler, and convincing Moscow Centre that he was the *predatel'* responsible for the death of Pavlik would remove suspicion from her, but to sustain her cover in Georgetown, she needed to recruit a replacement for her dead lover. Her cell phone vibrated, and she glanced at the screen, spitting three times onto the floor, a Russian response to potential calamity.

The coded message from the butler, Father arrives tonight, demanded her immediate return home. She secured the gallery, again inspecting her surroundings, and walked to the townhouse. She stepped inside and accepted a tray of koa wood bearing a sheet of paper from the butler. Using their code name for Moscow Center, she demanded, "Why did Father contact you and not me?"

He dropped his servile pretenses. "I'm sure all will be known soon, Yulia Lazarevna Belyakova."

His condescending use of her full birth name confirmed her fears. She walked into the study. An ebony mantle crowned a hearth of Italian marble. Books and antiquities filled mahogany wall shelves. A crystal ship decanter offered an eighteen year old single malt from Islay. Mail rose in a mound from the glass top of a rosewood desk. A stereo system provided entertainment, and an Inness painting in a scrolled birch frame hung above a rosewood cadenza.

She pressed a corner of the frame, and the painting swung forward. She spun the dual dials of the wall safe and withdrew a one-time pad. At the rosewood desk, she deciphered the message and read the order, "Return Moscow Centre immediately for reassignment," twice before striking a wooden matchstick. The flame dissolved the paper like a sorcerer's spell.

Since the time of Stalin, a recall to Moscow meant death in the cellars of Lubyanka. She dropped the ember into an ashtray, poured four fingers of single malt into a crystal tumbler, and swallowed it in a gulp. She poured a second serving before examining the mail, bills she would not need to pay, invitations to dinners she would not attend, charities she would no longer support.

The final envelope, an invitation from a travel agency, bore the stamps of an express courier. The name of the firm, Tours of Dumfries, provided the first recognition signal, a town in Scotland. The location of the tour, in the Southern Uplands, met the second prerequisite, a geographic area of the country. The signature at the bottom of the announcement, John Micklewrath, a character from a Scottish novel, completed the trifecta of requirements. The remainder of the invitation provided the date, time, and place for the meeting.

She fed the invitation into the shredder. From a drawer in the cadenza, she withdrew a handheld vacuum, a blackened box of sturdy mesh with a simple latch, dark safety goggles, a metal vial with a screw top, a butane cigar lighter, and a pair of thick asbestos gloves. She carried the items to the fireplace, shook the scraps of paper into the wire box, and closed the latch.

She sprinkled magnesium shavings from the metal vial onto the paper, donned the goggles, and pulled on the gloves. After opening the flue, she clicked the butane lighter. The magnesium incinerated the paper scraps in a brilliant white light. She vacuumed the residue, leaving the chicken mesh box to cool on the hearth. She locked the safe and pressed the birch frame against the wall.

The peaty flavor of the single malt played on her tongue. Her brogue full of warm emotion, she declared aloud her good fortune. "I have doubted and feared for naught, for Pavlik, like Lazarus before him, has risen from the dead."

MIDDLE GAME

Upon Completion of the Opening, Tactical Moves Predominate

A Support Point is Protected by a Single Pawn

At a service plaza on the Mass Pike, Nathan Monsarrat refueled the
Jeep and cleaned the concierge's blood from the windshield. He
entered Connecticut without spotting a tail. The black ribbon of the
interstate dulled his concentration. He crossed into New York,
reaching Manhattan as the sun slipped low beyond the Hudson River.
Exiting onto West 56th Street, he drove to a garage on Seventh
Avenue. He left the Jeep with the attendant, retrieved his bag, and
accepted the claim stub.

He walked toward the Diamond District. On West 47th Street,
midway between Sixth and Seventh Avenues, a discrete bronze
plaque announced the diamond exchange of Solomon Grinnell,
hours by appointment. A forced entry door, blast resistant windows,
security cameras, and an alarm system protected the store. Grinnell, a
former yeshiva *bocher* from Brooklyn, boasted the physique of a
fullback. He dressed in black Armani suits like a Russian *mafiya* chief
and wore a silk *yarmulke* atop his brilliantined black hair. The fringes
of a *tallis* hung beneath the hem of his jacket. His beard was trimmed.
He offered wisdom like a Talmudic sage, and mixed Yiddish, Hebrew,
Arabic, and Russian like a chef stirring bouillabaisse. He specialized
in turning blunt handguns into bejeweled collectibles.

Monsarrat looked into a security camera as he pressed the intercom
buzzer. He had first worked with Grinnell while a soldier of Langley,
collaborating on a honey trap for a senior member of the Libyan
General People's Committee with an appetite for young Jewish boys.
Grinnell costumed a teenage cousin as a Satmar Hasid, the bait to

burn the Libyan during a visit to the United Nations. In the years since, the partnership morphed into a friendship.

The forced entry door swung open, and he stepped into the showroom. A display case offered an empty tray lined with purple velvet, a loupe, and a soft cloth. Framed posters from the Ministry of Tourism in Jerusalem covered one wall. A forced entry door in the rear wall led into a vault room. He watched a similar door in the third wall open and offered a traditional greeting in Hebrew. "*Shalom aleichem*, Solomon."

Grinnell squeezed him with a hug. "*Aleichem shalom*, Nathan. Why the surprise visit? Not that I am unhappy to see you."

Monsarrat appreciated his direct approach. "I need a favor."

"Let's talk inside my office, *habibi*."

Planks of red oak lined the floor, and chrome and glass furniture filled the windowless room. A framed parchment *ketubbah*, a marriage certificate, in Hebrew and Mandarin from Shanghai hung on a wall behind a desk and ergonomic chair. A Hanukkiah from Krakow and a gold Torah crown from Kiev perched upon a pair of stands. Atop a cadenza, a television showed financial news. In the middle of the room, four chairs surrounded a low table.

"I have a new coffee machine that uses some kind of thimble system, plus cinnamon and almond *rogelekh* I bought this morning from the best pastry shop in Crown Heights."

Monsarrat placed his bag onto the floor. "Black coffee, but no sweets for me."

"None for me, too. My wife says I must diet," Grinnell admitted.

Monsarrat described the voice message and letter from Westbrook, his visits to Hyannis and Boston, and his Canadian identity. "I'm sorry about Westbrook and Zeigarnik, but the death of Datura is on me. I can't walk away."

"Are you sure Russians are involved?"

Monsarrat placed the cigarette box he discovered in East Boston onto the table. "I don't believe Westbrook was hallucinating."

"Do you which sort of Russians? *Mafiya*? Intelligence?"

"Definitely the latter."

Grinnell stepped into the bathroom to wash his hands before preparing the coffee. Returning to the office, he said, "In my opinion, Westbrook dropped you into deep *dreck*. If you want to find the people who killed your young friend, you should use another set of eyes. Use one of my assistants."

Moishe Goldman and Mendel Shackowitz provided Grinnell with personal security. Goldman, the younger of the pair, a scrapper with a flattened nose, scarred knuckles, and a fondness for Ruger pistols, stood an inch shorter than six feet. Charming and energetic, he fluttered from the beds of his lovers like a hummingbird among honeysuckle flowers. Shackowitz, older and philosophic, served as the driver. He read tomes of history late into the night in his Perry Street apartment. They argued like brothers, but their loyalty to Grinnell and to each other was absolute.

Despite his respect for their abilities, Monsarrat declined the offer. "I work better alone."

"When He spoke of a stiff-necked people, the Lord had you in mind, " Grinnell chided as he placed two cups of black coffee on the table. "I felt in the showroom that you're carrying a weapon, which means you didn't fly. Since you enjoy neither buses nor trains, you drove here. Give me your claim stub, and I'll move the vehicle to a safe location. A public garage does not qualify."

Monsarrat handed him the paper. "I suspect that Felix Sanhedrin survived the Georgetown assassination, despite the White House announcement, and hired the Russians to kill anyone who could challenge the story of his death."

Yiddish wrapped curses in the aura of blessings. "*Gai gezunterhait*, he should go in good health, that *farshtinkener*, that rotten person, but only to hell!"

"If I'm right, he wants me dead. You also, by association."

"How did the Georgetown bomb not kill him?"

Monsarrat sipped the coffee. "I don't know yet."

"It killed someone. A body was cremated. Unless it was all a show."

"It's a possibility."

"What agenda could Sanhedrin pursue better from the grave than as the National Security Adviser?"

"A dead Sanhedrin can operate with impunity, without White House interference, public oversight, and media scrutiny."

"Do you have a plan to find him?"

"First, I need to drive to Maryland and locate Westbrook's file."

"If you find it, if it leads you to the *farshtinkener*, do you know what you will do to him?"

Monsarrat spoke with certainty. "I'm done with nice. After I drain his intelligence, I'll kill him."

"A plan I support," Grinnell said. "Now tell me about your favor."

Monsarrat placed five hundred dollars on the table. "I want to borrow your Audi to drive south."

"Why so much money?"

"I suspect Moishe will have to fly into Dulles to retrieve the car. I'm leaving the country."

Grinnell sighed again. "Tell me everything."

Monsarrat explained the call from Sylvie's father, the demands of Bin Nafe, and his conversation with Enderby. "There's a redeye flight from Dulles that arrives in Cairo the following evening. It'll give me enough time to reach Sirte."

"Like you, I distrust coincidences, and the disappearances of Westbrook and the Epsteins at the same time worries me, but not as badly as the fact that Bin Nafe is a very nasty terrorist. When Sanhedrin was indisputably alive, he had a long history of hiring terrorists for his dirty work."

"All true."

"Have you have considered the possibility that Sylvie and her parents are bait to lure you into Libya?"

"I'm not a hard target," Monsarrat objected. "It would be easy to kill me in the Berkshires."

"Except Libya is lawless, and Sanhedrin has evil associates in the worst places."

"I don't have a choice. If there's a chance that the Epsteins are alive I have to go there."

"Even if you believe that you're walking into a trap?"

Monsarrat pointed to the Hanukkiah. "Sometimes, belief isn't enough. We need to have faith."

"I understand faith, *habibi*, and I understand foolishness."

You're not wrong, Solomon," admitted Monsarrat. "Sometimes, though, we need more than belief and faith. Sometimes, we need an ace in the hole."

"This ace is part of your plan?"

"I'm working on it."

"As you work, you can tell me how much confidence you have in the abilities of Harper Enderby."

"When I operated with him, he was very good."

"Good is good. Good provides confidence," Grinnell said, "but what I really want to hear is an answer to my question."

"Ask away, Solomon."

"Can you trust him?"

During a Feint, Subterfuge Achieves the Objective

Monsarrat possessed no reason to doubt Enderby but understood that Langley turned saints into sinners and the righteous into rogues. Inside the Agency, loyalty was a chimera, and trust was a mirage. Before he could answer Grinnell's questions, the buzzer rang. "You have much walk-in traffic these days, Solomon?"

"None at all," Grinnell replied, crossing to the desk.

He turned the laptop and studied the black and white feed from the security cameras. "Do these two look like after hours shoppers?"

A pair of hard men waited on the sidewalk, their expressions cold. The shorter man looked directly at the camera and mouthed an order. *Police. Open the door and let us inside.*

Monsarrat recognized the pair as the men who entered the Lexus at the street corner in Boston. "Recognize them, Solomon?"

"Never seen them before."

His jaw muscles tight, Monsarrat said, "They kidnapped Westbrook, and I believe the tall son of a bitch shot Datura."

Grinnell whistled softly. "What do you want me to do?"

"Buzz them inside. Listen to their spiel. Escort them into the office. I'll ask them a few questions."

"You mean interrogate them?"

"I'll try to be neat."

Grinnell sent a text message to Goldman and Shackowitz, *Come to store now.* He withdrew a snub-nosed .38 Smith & Wesson Special in a leather paddle holster from a desk drawer and clipped it onto his belt at the small of his back. "Our playing field is now more level."

Monsarrat placed a hand on his shoulder. "They're killers, Solomon. Try not to piss them off."

"I only need to stall them until Moishe and Mendel arrive."

The cell phone pressed to his ear, Grinnell entered the showroom. He pressed a switch to unlock the forced entry door and waved the men inside. Speaking into the dead mic, he said, "Yes, I know I'm late, dearest, but I have customers. They have been very patient."

The two men withdrew leather credential cases from their jacket pockets, flashed their badges with practiced motions, and pocketed the cases. The taller man spoke with the harsh consonants and whining vowels of Russian. "Are you Solomon Grinnell?"

Grinnell placed the cell phone on the display case. "How may I help you, gentlemen?"

The shorter man spoke in a similar accent. "Just answer us, asshole. Are you Grinnell?"

"Insults are not necessary. I am Grinnell. Please show me your badges again."

The taller man reached into his jacket pocket, withdrew a photograph, and placed it onto the counter. "Where is he?"

"How can I answer this question? I don't know him."

"His name is Nathan Monsarrat," the shorter man declared. "Tell us where you hid him."

A text message, *Almost there*, flashed onto the screen of Grinnell's cell phone. "You two are cops like I'm Tom Cruise."

"Don't make trouble," the taller man warned.

"Trouble from you two?" Grinnell mocked. "Cameras are filming you. I already tripped the silent alarm. Real cops from Midtown North will arrive in less than a minute. The rest of your miserable lives, you're going to spend in Sing Sing."

The shorter man showed a Smith & Wesson .357 Magnum with a three inch barrel. "We watched Monsarrat enter the store. We didn't see him leave."

The taller man withdrew a .44 Magnum Taurus with a six inch barrel. "Where is he?"

Watching on the office laptop, Monsarrat recognized the weapon from the video of the Lexus. He stepped toward the door. He wanted to interrogate the two men but could not risk losing his friend.

In the showroom, the shorter man cocked the hammer of the revolver. "Do you want to die?"

Grinnell drew his own revolver. "Let me share a Yiddish saying with you two. *A mentsh on glik iz a toyter mentsh.* An unlucky person is a dead person."

The Beretta steady in his hand, Monsarrat stepped through the doorway into the showroom. "Solomon, get down!"

He chose head shots, if the targets wore body armor beneath their clothes. The first .45 caliber bullet disintegrated the face of the shorter man. The second slug exploded the skull of the taller man. His hearing deafened by the blasts, his own voice sounded distant. "You good, Solomon?"

Grinnell stood against the counter, covered with the gore of the two dead men. "I need to close the shutters immediately. The windows are thick, so they absorbed the noise, but if anyone on the street was watching, I don't want to think about it."

Monsarrat gathered the casings in his handkerchief and placed them next to his photograph on the counter. "We need to get their bodies out of your store fast."

As he spoke, Mendel Shackowitz unlocked the front forced entry door and stepped into the showroom. He wore the black garb of a maître d' and carried a Heckler & Koch MP5K with a 30 round clip. "Is it your blood, Solomon?"

"It belongs to them," Grinnell answered as he lowered the shutters.

Moishe Goldman, wearing a gray turtleneck sweater, blue jeans, and work boots, held a suppressed Ruger SR45. He turned on the ceiling lights. "Nathan! Why am I not surprised?"

"It's good to see you, Moishe," Monsarrat replied.

Shackowitz spoke with a European formality. "You look well, Nathan, despite the situation."

"As do you, Mendel."

Grinnell interrupted them. "We have work to do now. Moishe, empty their pockets."

Goldman held the trigger guard of the Taurus between his thumb and index finger, as if it carried a bad smell, and placed it onto the counter. He patted the corpse of the taller man, removing the credential case and a folding knife with a three inch blade from his pockets. He repeated the action on the shorter man, setting the .357 Magnum next to the Taurus. He added a second credential case and a push knife with a two inch grooved blade in a hard plastic case to the collection. "No wallets, no identification beyond fake credentials."

Monsarrat examined the photograph. "It was taken yesterday."

"You didn't know someone was watching you?" Grinnell asked.

"They did more than watch," he responded, cursing his failure to make the tail. "They followed me to Datura, waited until he was alone, and killed him."

Shackowitz stepped into the office, returning with a bucket, towels, sponges, rubber gloves, ammonia, and plastic garbage bags. "Solomon, take Nathan inside. Moishe and I will clean up."

"I'll call the Second Avenue mortician," Goldman offered. "He owes you for your work turning the Makarov used to execute Beria into a showpiece, but we still need to ID these losers and find out what they wanted from you."

In the office, Monsarrat said, "They were my best chance to locate the woman driving the Lexus."

Grinnell washed the gore from his hands and face. He cleaned his shoes and clothes. "They were hard men, Nathan. They wouldn't have talked."

"Everyone talks. It's only a matter of time and technique."

Grinnell poured three fingers of bourbon into a crystal tumbler and handed it to his friend. "Drink it. You'll feel better."

Monsarrat drained the tumbler, shaking his head at the offer of a refill. "I need a clear head."

"Do you have a plan?"

Monsarrat shared his thoughts. "The two corpses should report to their handler, if you gave me up before they killed you."

"Since they won't make that call, will someone come here?"

"Probably sooner than later."

Critical Positions Define the Decisive Moves

Monsarrat sat alone in the darkened office, the remains of a sandwich from an Eighth Avenue deli, a half-full two liter bottle of water, and newspaper sections scattered across the desk. On the laptop, he watched the feed from the security cameras covering West 47th Street. A cabbie flicked the stub of a cigar through the lowered window of his taxi. A sidewalk hooker in stiletto heels greeted the driver of an SUV. A couple walked a Great Dane on a leash festooned with plastic bags.

An hour before midnight, a black Audi S8 pulled to the curb. The passenger door opened, and Shackowitz stepped onto the sidewalk. He wore a herringbone overcoat and a teardrop trilby, its brim pulled low. Tortoiseshell glasses perched on the bridge of his nose. A shopping bag hung from his arm. He opened the padlock, lifted the security shutters as if they were papier mâché, and unlocked the forced entry door. He crossed the showroom and stepped into the office. "Are you ready, Nathan?"

"No time like right now, Mendel," Monsarrat replied.

From the shopping bag, Shackowitz removed a biography of Rabbi Kuk, a two liter bottle of seltzer water, and a bag of kosher potato chips. He laid the overcoat, trilby, and glasses on a chair, reached into the bag a final time, and removed a Beretta Px4 Storm, two extra magazines, a vest of thin Kevlar, a flashlight, and a pair of rubber gloves. "Ammunition is in the trunk of the Audi. I filed the identification from the weapon and cut the labels from the hat and coat. If you give me your own Beretta, I'll make sure it will never be traced to the two dead men."

"Spoken like a true spook," Monsarrat said. He cleared the chamber of his own Px4 and ejected the magazine. He returned the bullet to the clip and handed the pistol to Shackowitz. "Tell Moishe to look in the trunk of the Audi for the weapon and bullets."

"Try on the Kevlar and the clothes. Tell me if the sizes are right."

His shirt buttoned easily over the vest. Monsarrat shrugged on the too large overcoat, followed by the trilby and glasses, and pulled on the gloves. "You have a fine eye, Mendel."

Shackowitz coughed politely. "I know you like to work alone, Nathan, but in my opinion, I should drive the Audi and watch your back. Solomon agrees."

"It'll be a fast trip."

"Bullets also travel fast."

"I'm good, Mendel," Monsarrat promised, removing the spectacles. "Clear glass. A nice touch."

Shackowitz plucked at the overcoat. "It's too big, but the car is only a few steps away."

"Who's driving?"

"Solomon had a prior appointment, so I recruited my cousin Shaina. In her heart, she is an actress, and she understands her role is to act like a displeased date who I made stop at the store so I could take care of business. She will make sure that everyone on the street knows she does not enjoy mixing my work with her pleasure."

"I'll play my role," Monsarrat promised.

"Also, Shaina is a very aggressive driver, so buckle your seat belt."

Shackowitz described the exfiltration route, concluding with an assurance. "Moishe is waiting for you in New Jersey. If you change your mind, he will drive the Audi and watch your back. Solomon approves of this plan, too. If you insist on traveling alone, Moishe will take Shaina home in his car."

Monsarrat again declined the offer. "No worries, Mendel, but tell me about your cousin."

"As a teenager, she acted in the wrong films. She took drugs, too. Moishe and I went to Hollywood, broke a few bones, and took her home. Now she works at a travel agency. She is excited to help us."

"I'm sure she'll make you proud."

Shackowitz handed him two keys. "Square head for the forced entry door, round head for the shutters padlock."

Monsarrat thanked him. He placed the Beretta, extra mags, flashlight, and rubber gloves into his shoulder bag. He locked the forced entry door, dropped the shutters, and secured the padlock. Light from the Audi spilled onto the street as a six foot tall woman stepped from the car. She wore a crimson lace shawl over her shoulders, and her breasts strained against the buttons of her white silk blouse. Black equestrian boots complemented a black skirt. Long lashes fluttered over her blue eyes.

She spoke with a Bronx accent. "Hurry up, Mendel. You promised to take me dancing."

When Monsarrat kissed her full lips, he tasted a medley of fruit. He took her hand, guided her to the car, and whispered into her ear. "Thanks for the ride."

She settled into the driver's seat. "Mendel told me not to ask you personal stuff, like your name."

He took the passenger seat, buckled his seat belt, and tossed his bag onto the rear bench. "He's a smart man."

She reached into the glove box for a pen, tore a sheet of paper from a notebook, wrote her name and cell phone number, and handed it to him. "If you take off those silly glasses, you're a good looking guy, and man, you kiss good. You wanna get to know me better, call me."

He glanced at the paper before returning it to her. "It's a date."

"You don't wanna keep it?"

He repeated the digits. "I have a photographic memory."

"Good looking, great kisser, and smart. A triple play. All you need is a good job and no wife."

His eyes swept the street. "No job, but no wife, either."

"No wife is good news, but why no job?"

"I'm retired."

"You don't look so old."

She drove toward the Hudson River with a abandon, switching lanes without signals and accelerating past slower drivers. At a yellow traffic light, she stomped the gas pedal. From the Lincoln Tunnel, she accessed the New Jersey Turnpike, speeding north. In the Vince Lombardi Service Area, she screeched to a stop next to a Porsche Cayman with New York license plates.

She handed Monsarrat the fob. "Not so bad driving, huh? No matter what Mendel told you."

"Not so bad at all, Shaina," he agreed.

Goldman greeted them. "You're sure you don't want company, Nathan? Shaina can drive herself back to the city."

Monsarrat handed him the store keys and the disguise. "You need to watch Solomon's back."

"We're ready," he promised. "Where do I pick up the car?"

"I'll text you the address and courier the fob and the parking ticket to Solomon. I'll leave the Kevlar and the Beretta in the trunk."

Inside the Audi, Shaina finished reapplying her make-up. She stepped from the car and announced, "Moishe, c'mon already! It's late. I have to be at work in the morning."

Goldman opened the Cayman's passenger door. "Don't fret, darling. We're going now."

Monsarrat adjusted the seats and mirrors of the Audi before accelerating onto the southbound ramp of the Turnpike. Driving the length of the state, he crossed the Delaware Memorial Bridge, stopping at the Delaware House Travel Plaza for gas. In the food court, he bought a large black coffee. He continued south on the Delaware Turnpike, soon entering Maryland. North of Baltimore, construction before the Fort McHenry Tunnel slowed traffic.

An hour passed before he reached the Beltway, a pink dawn spreading across the sky. He thought of the death of Zeigarnik on the same road. Beyond the spires of the Washington Temple, he entered the town of Chevy Chase. He tapped the map icon in the Sanger cell phone to locate Westbrook's home. On a leafy street between Rock Creek and Connecticut Avenue, a driveway led to a windowless, attached garage. Faux gaslight sconces on the porch walls were dark, and plantation shutters over the windows of the house provided privacy. A beech tree grew on a postage stamp lawn.

He drove past the house, parking before a mailbox decorated with dolphins. Harried parents holding briefcases and gym bags bundled children with school backpacks into minivans. He opened the shoulder bag, withdrew the Beretta, holster, flashlight, and gloves. At the Goldilocks time, not too early, not too late, he stepped from the Audi, locked the car, and slipped the holstered pistol onto his belt. He pocketed the flashlight, pulled on the gloves, and carried the overnight bag as if he was returning home from a overnight trip, hoping the neighbors were too busy, too weary, and too indifferent to pay attention.

He mounted the white brick steps onto the porch. The rail held a Swiss chalet bird feeder. He swung open its face and found the key beneath the seeds. Approaching the front door, he saw it listed off the jamb. He dropped the key into his pocket, stepped inside the house, activated the flashlight, and pulled the pistol from the holster. With his foot, he pushed the door shut.

The foyer supplied a mixture of odors, stale air, shifted dirt, and old sweat. He played the light over the alarm panel. The screen remained dark, but if a low current battery maintained a connection to the monitoring company, he pressed 1-3-6-6-6 into the keypad, the superstitious street number of their football team's favorite bar. The system failed to respond, and he wondered if the failure had been reported to the police. More likely, Charing had intercepted the call from the monitoring company and forced Westbrook to provide the false assurances that blunted their concerns.

In the dining room, he flipped a wall rocker, but the room remained dark. The modem and cable boxes in the living room failed to blink, and the television refused to engage. In the kitchen, the microwave and stove clocks showed black. A wall phone offered only silence. Sour smells leaked from the interior of the refrigerator. A door leading into the backyard swung crookedly.

Each moment inside the house increased his risk. He climbed the stairs to the second floor, the steps creaking beneath his weight. The master bedroom offered a gutted mattress and dresser drawers stacked in a corner, their contents piled in heaps. Broken picture frames formed a mound. Upended night tables and the remains of two lamps were scattered across the room.

Clothes, shoes, a broken suitcase, and papers covered the floor of the closet. The empty safe, still bolted to the floor, showed scars from an acetylene torch. In the mess, he found a torn envelope addressed to LB, the initials for linebacker, the position he had played on their football team. Continuing his search, he found a balled sheet of lined legal paper. He stepped into the bedroom, cleared a space on the floor, smoothed the paper, and held the flashlight over a love letter his former teammate had written to him.

In Fingerfehler: Overconfidence Causes a Poor Move

Westbrook had written the love letter in the same coded style as the
message he sent from Boston. Monsarrat's appreciation of his former
teammate increased. Prior to departing his home for the dental
conference, convinced Zeigarnik had been murdered, suspecting his
own life would soon end, he had disguised his intelligence so well the
team that tossed his house found it, read it, and dismissed it.

*Dear LB, Writing to you, I think of our happy times at the old
farm-house, sitting in the dooryard, the lilac-bush flowering, its
perfume strong. I miss you so much, and I am so sorry that I hurt you.
My love forever, your DW.*

Monsarrat opened the Sanger cell phone and typed the odd words
into the search box, *farm-house, dooryard, lilac-bush, perfume strong.*
He scrolled the results, tapped the screen, and the entirety of the Walt
Whitman poem, "When Lilacs Last in the Dooryard Bloom'd,"
appeared. He scanned the sixteen sections before returning to third
stanza of the poem.

*In the dooryard fronting an old farm-house near the white-wash'd
palings,*
*Stands the lilac-bush tall-growing with heart-shaped leaves of rich
green,*
*With many a pointed blossom rising delicate, with the perfume
strong I love,*

With every leaf a miracle—and from this bush in the dooryard,
With delicate-color'd blossoms and heart-shaped leaves of rich
green,
A sprig with its flower I break.

He remembered the final words from Westbrook's letter, their
coach's supposed exhortation, *Stomp 'em and toss flowers on 'em*. He
walked into the bathroom, tore the paper into scraps, and flushed
them down the toilet. Returning to the first floor, he exited the house
through the broken door in the kitchen. Three wooden steps led from
a small porch to the backyard. *The old farm-house*. A white vinyl
fence of pointed stakes enclosed the rear of the property. *White-
wash'd palings*. Fragrant lilac bushes stood in a line along the rear of
the house, their leaves green and flowers shaped like hearts. *Blossom
rising delicate, with the perfume strong*.

He set his bag onto the porch. The fourth bush in the line offered a
single broken stem. *A sprig with its flower I break*. Kneeling, he
inspected the loose earth. He returned to the kitchen. Searching
through the debris, he found a large metal spoon. He returned to the
bush and dug with the utensil until a plastic freezer bag appeared.

He shook dirt from the plastic. Duct tape sealed the bag and
blocked sight of its contents. Discipline prevented him from
immediately opening it. He folded the bag and placed it into the
pocket of his blazer. Repacking the soil, he brushed leaves and dirt
from his clothes, retrieved his bag, and reentered the kitchen. He
cleaned the spoon and returned it to the debris. Departing the house,
he stepped onto the front porch, and pulling the door closed.

On the street, he dropped the key through a storm grate. Inside the

Audi, he placed the overnight bag on the passenger seat, tossed the gloves onto the floor, removed the holstered Beretta from his belt, and shoved it beneath the bag. He drove through the residential neighborhood to the Chevy Case Circle, entered the District of Columbia, and followed Connecticut Avenue toward Dupont Circle, parking on Corcoran Street. He pulled the tape from the freezer bag, revealing sheets of lined legal paper protected by plastic stretch wrap. He removed the papers, peeled off the plastic, and smoothed the sheets of Westbrook's précis of the missing files, dated a week prior.

Subject: Evidence of Soviet Dentistry Exhibited in Endodontic Treatment of Patient Now Deceased: National Security Adviser Felix Sanhedrin

Begin Summary: Endodontic treatment on mandibular left second bicuspid (#20) and maxillary right first bicuspid (#5) of patient now deceased - National Security Adviser Felix Sanhedrin - admitted on 1 January of this year to Walter Reed National Military Medical Center revealed trace elements of arsenic trioxide, N2, and Russian red cement, compounds used extensively in the Soviet Union during the decades of the 1970s and 1980s, beneath standard components and compounds used in American dentistry, indicative of unsuccessful attempts to mask evidence of Soviet dentistry. This discovery bears national security implications. End Summary.

Monsarrat absorbed the enormity of the summary, like an infidelity revealed. Zeigarnik and Westbrook claimed the patient was the National Security Adviser, that Sanhedrin was dead, and that Soviet dentists had treated him, possible only if Sanhedrin had been a citizen of the Soviet Union. He flipped the page and began to read the précis, four paragraphs in length. His right hand slipped beneath the overnight bag, seeking the reassurance of the Beretta.

1) Endodontists in the Soviet Union routinely used arsenic trioxide to devitalize inflamed pulp tissue. Although most arsenic trioxide will be expunged from the body through natural means, traces remain in the mouth throughout the life of the patient. In the case of the National Security Adviser, arsenic trioxide was discovered in both the periodontal tissue and alveolar bone. The use of arsenic trioxide in the United States is virtually unknown.

2) Additionally, N2 – another compound commonly used in the Soviet Union - was discovered in the periodontal tissue of the patient. As with arsenic trioxide, the use of N2 within the United States is virtually unknown.

3) Finally, Russian red cement, a filling material popular in the Soviet Union but never used in the United States, was discovered in the alveolar bone of the patient. The resorcinol-formaldehyde resin when joined with a ten percent sodium hydroxide solution results in a polymerization which forms a brick-hard red material that is resistant to all known solvents. Hence, its presence in the mouth of the patient provides incontrovertible evidence of Soviet dentistry.

4) Conclusion: Given the preponderance of evidence of compounds used extensively in the Soviet Union in the periodontal tissue and alveolar bone of the patient (specifically arsenic trioxide, N2, and Russian red cement) HIDDEN BENEATH standard components and compounds used in American dentistry, an investigation must be conducted to determine the reason(s) for these compounds to be present in the mouth of the patient. Our discovery bears national security implications. The probability that the patient was treated by Soviet dentists inside the Soviet Union is 100%.

Reading the précis again, he considered the importance of Westbrook's claim that neither he nor Zeigarnik had seen the results of a DNA test from the man they believed to be the National Security Adviser. Their empirical evidence proved the victim of the roadside bomb, perhaps Sanhedrin, perhaps someone posing as him, had been treated by Soviet dentists. The connection between the former National Security Adviser and Moscow Centre flashed dangerously.

He placed the pages into his bag, removed the envelope with Datura's SIM card, and dropped it into a pocket. He attached the holstered Beretta to his belt, stepped from the Audi, and activated its locks. Walking toward Brenda Carlyle, digital security genius and former Agency colleague, he hoped she still maintained her morning caffeine rituals.

In Zugzwang All Moves Result in Capture

Brenda Carlyle spent her mornings drinking espressos inside Bread and Freedom, a coffee shop at the corner of New Hampshire Avenue and Riggs Place, composing inflammatory missives against the assault on civil liberties by the federal government. She wrote under the pseudonym Henri Gravelle, posting the pieces to her blog, The Natural State. Her knowledge of routing protocols, learned at Langley, ensured anonymity.

During her afternoons, she donned the business suit of a successful cyber security consultant, charging her lobbyist, NGO, and political action committee clients significant fees to protect their computer systems against hackers. The sessions provided much more money in far fewer hours than her former position as a Cyber Threat Analyst with the Central Intelligence Agency responsible for neutering threats from the *Federal'naya Sluzhba Bezopasnosti*, the FSB, and the *Glavnoye Razvedyvatel'noye Upravleniye*, the GRU, against the CIA stations in Russia.

Monsarrat had met her in Moscow after performing an in-and-out job to service an intel drop on a Saturday evening in late September. Dressed as a bearded factory worker with silver hair beneath a cap sporting the red and white badge of the Crvena Zvezda basketball team, he haggled prices for a *matryoshka*, a nesting doll featuring *Snegurochka*, the Snow Maiden, with a vendor in an alley behind Red Square. He provided the recognition code, *I want Polkhov Maidan style with pink roses*.

The vendor, an Agency deep cover operative working under the guise of a pensioner, wore an oversized denim jacket laden with medals from the Great Patriotic War. He provided the counter signal, *I suggest you buy Sergiev Posad design for better value.*

Monsarrat passed him a stack of 100 ruble notes in exchange for the doll, wrapped in the previous day's *Kommersant* newspaper, and slouched away wearing a scowl of defeat. He trudged down the alley. At its end, a black Mercedes S500 with darkened windows and Moscow license plates idled by the curb. He opened the rear door and slid onto the bench.

As the driver eased the car into traffic, the man occupying the front passenger seat turned and handed him a package wrapped in butcher paper and secured with twine. "Any hiccups, Nathan?"

Monsarrat handed the Deputy Chief of Station, the second highest ranking American spy in Russia, the doll. "Not yet."

He removed the wig and beard, plucked cotton balls from his nostrils, and cleaned makeup from his skin with cosmetic wipes. He changed into blue jeans, a white tee shirt, a black sweatshirt, and running shoes. He balled the worker's costume and dropped it onto the floor. "Have you found it?"

Unwrapping the newspaper, the Deputy separated the dolls. The third held a single sheet of thin paper. He read the message and offered congratulations. "It's all here. Well done."

Monsarrat relaxed into the leather bench. "Drop me on the Noviy Arbat. I'll make my own way to the airport."

The Deputy passed him an envelope with documents, tickets, and cash. "Watch your six. Leaving Russia these days can be a bitch."

Monsarrat pocketed the envelope. "You can add the *matryoshka* to your collection of Russian folk art."

On Noviy Arbat Street, the driver turned off the headlights and glided to a stop before a darkened storefront. "Go now."

Monsarrat exited the car quickly. He walked in the opposite direction from the Mercedes, turned onto a side street, and made his way through a dark passageway to Novinskiy Boulevard. A single light illuminated the top of the crumbling steps leading to the entrance of a *perekhod*, an underground tunnel used by pedestrians to cross beneath the boulevard. At the bottom of the steps, a second bulb lit the opening of the dank underpass.

He paused at the top of the stairs, sniffing the air for unseen dangers. A young woman passed through the pool of light and descended toward the *perekhod*. Two inches shy of six feet tall, weighing one hundred and twenty pounds, she wore blue jeans, sneakers, and a white sweatshirt with the logo of the University of New Hampshire. Beneath a Red Sox cap spilled chestnut hair. Her eyes were intelligent and brown, her lips determined and full beneath a freckled nose.

At the bottom of the steps, three thugs stepped from the dark underpass into the pool of light. The leader drew a Grach 433 pistol from his jeans. "*Dvai, krysa, yest' krasavetz!* Come suck me, girl. I have a big dick for you!"

"*Yob tvoiu mat.* Fuck your mother," the young woman responded.

Monsarrat ran down the steps. He threw the leader against the tunnel entrance, plucked the Grach from his hand, and struck his temple with the butt, dropping him to the pavement. Covering the two remaining thugs with the pistol, he asked the young woman, "Do you speak English?"

"I've got this," she replied.

Handing her the pistol, he said, "Make sure you don't shoot me."

He broke the knee of the second attacker and greeted the third thug with a head butt, followed by four fingers thrust into his trachea. He surveyed them with a grim satisfaction before turning to the young woman. "You okay?"

She handed him the Grach. "I didn't need your help."

He dropped the full magazine into the pouch of his sweatshirt, disassembled the weapon, and tossed the pieces into the tunnel. "You're very welcome."

"I would have handled them," she insisted.

They crossed through the tunnel and climbed the crumbling stairs on the other side of the boulevard. Fifty feet distant, the Stars and Stripe hung above the entrance to a Second Empire building protected by rows of bollards and security cameras. She stopped and apologized. "I spoke badly."

His flight did not depart for hours. "I'll accept your apology, if you let me buy you a drink."

"I don't drink with a man if I don't know his name."

He introduced himself. "I'm Nathan Monsarrat."

"Prove it."

The demand confused him. "You want to see my identification? Are you with the *politsiya*?"

"I want to be sure you're really Monsarrat," she explained, pointing at the flag. "I work in the embassy. I have to be careful when men I don't know rescue me on the streets of Moscow."

He offered his passport. "Your turn. Who are you?"

She flashed her diplomatic ID. "I'm Brenda Carlyle. I sent the country clearance reply to your request for entry cable."

He offered his hand. "It's a pleasure to meet a colleague, Brenda."

She shook it. "The pleasure is all mine, Nathan."

"Let's get that drink. I know a quiet place by Park Presnenskiy."

"I've had enough of Moscow for tonight," she replied. "We'll go to my apartment."

Monsarrat smiled at the memory as he pushed open a door and stepped inside Bread and Freedom. Named for the anarchist Pyotr Kropotkin, the coffee shop offered chrome and steel furniture, reproduction artwork, and mounted cube speakers that whispered piano sonatas. An Italian espresso machine gleamed. A line of patrons waited to order carry-out coffee. Others sat at the tables, engrossed in tablets or laptops. The few conversations were muted.

In the rear, beneath a framed portrait of Kropotkin, Carlyle hunched over a laptop, stained saucers and demitasse cups spread across a table for four. She wore jeans, a New England Patriots sweatshirt, and sneakers. At his approach, she closed the laptop, stood, and hugged him. "You look tired, Nathan, you're filthy, and you need a shower, but what really concerns me is you're wearing a vest and carrying a weapon."

He kissed her. "It's good to see you, Brenda. Not working for Langley agrees with you."

"Quitting the Agency was the best decision I ever made."

He sat next to her, placed the bag on the floor, and repeated his now familiar refrain. "I have to ask a favor."

"Before you prostrate yourself, I need another shot of caffeine. You still drink espresso with a twist of lemon?"

He reached for his wallet. "I'd love a double."

She held up her right hand. "I've got this."

Monsarrat smiled again at the words. He noted the patrons of the coffee shop, more bourgeoisie than Bolshevik, their designer handbags and Swiss watches, latest model laptops and cell phones. Only the framed portrait of Kropotkin hinted at radical thought within the walls of Bread and Freedom.

She returned with two demitasse cups. "Tell me what you need."

He removed the envelope from his blazer and handed her the SIM card from the cell phone of Datura. "Incoming and outgoing calls for the past forty-eight hours. Same for texts and emails."

She unsealed the flap. "I'll give you phone numbers and IP addresses, plus email and text messages, voicemails incoming and outgoing, plus the duration of the calls, but identifying originators and recipients by name will take time."

He pressed the lemon rind around the rim of the cup. "Is it safe to work in a coffee shop?"

"The connection is bulletproof. I pay hackers each month to breach the security, and every time they fail."

"The owners hired you to test the security of their wifi system?"

She pointed to the empty cups on the table. "I am the owner, Nathan. I drink so many espressos, it made sense to buy the place."

He whistled softly. "Well done, Brenda."

From her backpack, she took a mobile reader, connected it to the laptop, and slipped the SIM card into the slot. Fingers dancing upon the keyboard, she said, "It wants a password. I'll need a minute."

"Take your time."

"Just how deep in the shit are you, Nathan?"

"Somewhere between my chin and my eyeballs," he replied.

The Overworked Pawn Undertakes Too Many Tasks

Carlyle turned the laptop toward Monsarrat. Data from the SIM card, as esoteric as hieroglyphics, filled the screen. "This far and no further, Nathan. It's not that I don't want to help you. I just have two businesses, a dozen employees, and my health to consider. Who owns the cell phone?"

"It's safer if you're dark on the details," Monsarrat replied.

She closed the laptop and folded her arms atop her sweatshirt. "You want my help, you play by my rules."

He responded with a sanitized version of the death of Datura, excluding Westbrook, Zeigarnik, Sanhedrin, and the two thugs in Manhattan. Nor did he mention Enderby, Sylvie, or Bin Nafe. "It may have been a random act of violence, but the SIM card could tell me who killed my friend."

She flipped open the lid of the laptop. "That's all?"

"I'm trying keep you whole."

"Saint Nate," she sighed, "always searching for a damsel in distress. If your intentions weren't so virtuous, you'd be another chauvinist."

"I don't have much time, Brenda."

She summarized the data from the SIM. "Your friend was very private. I found four incoming and four outgoing calls. Of the outgoing calls, three went to landlines, one to a cell phone. Of the incoming calls, three were from the same cell phone. The fourth is a riddle, wrapped in a mystery, inside an enigma. There may be a key, but I haven't found it yet."

"Are you teasing me?"

"I'm dead serious."

"Did he have texts or emails? Incoming? Outgoing?"

"None within the past two days."

He swore. "What about audio? Could you extract it?"

"We're not in the movies. Listening to a call in the real world requires real time access."

"Do you have names for the people he called?"

"Identification was easy," she admitted. "Of the three outgoing calls to landlines, the shortest duration was placed to Mr. Hong, the owner of a Chinese restaurant in Maynard, Massachusetts. The longest duration call was placed to Mrs. Walter Datura."

He hoped whoever conveyed the news of her son's death had delivered it gently. "It's my bad. I should have told her."

"You do the necessary, Nathan. It's how you stay alive."

"Except my friend is dead."

She stroked his face. "It's good that you retired. Killing bad guys doesn't faze you, but if a kid loses her balloon, your heart breaks."

He didn't want to discuss his emotions. "What can you tell me about the third call from the landline?"

"It went to the desk of a Mrs. Beth Foxx at the Massachusetts Registry of Motor Vehicles."

"I know why he called her."

"Care to share?"

"Just keeping you safe," he repeated.

"Same old, same old," she sighed. "Which leaves the sole outgoing call to the cell phone owned by Mark Sanger of Halifax, Nova Scotia."

"I'm Sanger," he admitted.

"Is there a Canadian citizen you haven't played, Nathan?"

He first recognized her brilliance in Moscow, but since leaving the Agency, her barbs had sharpened. "What can you tell me about the four incoming calls?"

"Three originated in Boston, from the Sanger cell phone," she explained. "The first lasted two minutes. The second didn't connect. The third wasn't answered. You didn't leave a message."

Monsarrat again heard the echoing rings. "The fourth call?"

"Soon after your final attempt, the last call arrived. It was also ignored, and no message was left."

"He couldn't answer. He was dead by that time," he explained. "Anything more? Cell phone? Landline? Phone number? Name of the caller? Location of the call?"

"The device was secure, and the data was encrypted."

"If a secure phone calls an open line, can the data be encrypted?"

"When you left the game, technology used a rock as a hammer."

"What do your instincts tell you?"

"I don't have instincts," she answered. "I work with facts, two in particular. First, the encryption is government level technology. It's too sophisticated to be sold commercially or by a hacker."

"Which government?"

"Maybe ours. Maybe the Russians, the Chinese, or the North Koreans. Could be the Iranians or the Israelis. I can't know for sure without the source codes."

"You're supposed to narrow the options, not expand them."

"You forgot my second fact," she admonished. "The call came from somewhere in Georgetown."

"Are you sure?"

"I found a vulnerability in the encryption," she replied. "At first, I thought I could insert a pinhole incursion and siphon the data, but it was actually a worm trap. I avoided it, conducted a second reconnaissance, then tried a different approach. Instead of probing, I vacuumed. It was the right choice."

Monsarrat rubbed his forehead. "I don't speak geek, Brenda."

"I used a proprietary program I developed that siphons data without leaving a trace of its actions. The target remains unknowing. It's the ultimate steal."

"Small words, Brenda. Tell me what you learned."

"I need another hour or two, maybe three, before I can give you specific origination of the call, the number of the phone, and the name of the owner, but now I have to shower and dress for work.

You need to shower, full stop. Grab your bag. We'll go to my condo in Adams Morgan. It's a quick walk."

"Call in sick. Bill me for your lost hours."

She handed him the SIM card and closed the laptop. "No can do, Nathan. You'll have to wait until I finish with my clients."

"I'm wheels up tonight, Brenda."

"Where are you flying?"

"Same answer as before."

"Same bullshit."

He stood and hoisted his bag. "Once you have the intel, send it to the Sanger cell phone. You have the number."

"Should I transmit it clear or test your cryptographic skills?"

"Unless it's radioactive, hide it in plain sight."

"How will I know if it's radioactive?"

"It will sear your eyeballs," he replied.

She stood and kissed him on the lips. "Be careful, Nathan. You were damn good in your day, but you're retired now, and whoever encrypted the call isn't a drunk thug in a Moscow *perekhod*."

He dropped the SIM card into his pocket. "I don't want trouble."

"No, you want payback, but a Kevlar vest won't stop a sniper round to your head," she warned. "The data in your pocket won't keep you safe, either. I've already copied its contents to my laptop. You should destroy it."

Removing the SIM, he broke it and placed the pieces onto a saucer. "Thank you, Brenda."

"An adorable combination, deadly, saintly, and polite," she remarked. "Where are you going now?"

He debated how much information to share with her, finally settling on an anemic response. "To see a contact who owns a gentleman's club named Luxor. He owes me a favor."

"A whorehouse for the District's rich and powerful."

"The nastiest people are often the most valuable assets," he replied.

She walked him to the door of the coffee shop. "I'm glad you're here, Nathan, even if it is for business reasons."

He kissed her and pushed open the door. Returning to the Audi, he opened the Canadian cell phone, entered a number, listened to the curt instructions, and left a voicemail. "I visited your home on Ogbuma Close in Warri. I brought Johnnie Walker Blue Label. You served pepper soup with goat meat and Mbongo spice. You clapped when I finished. I'm on my way. See you in twenty minutes."

He drove to a garage on 16th Street, parked the car, and walked toward Luxor. In the triangle formed by Lafayette, Farragut, and McPherson Squares, a gilded statue of Tutankhamen sat astride the

Great Sphinx. Next to the statue stood a bouncer the size of an offensive tackle costumed as a harem guard. Monsarrat approached him warily. "The Prince is expecting me."

"No bags inside Luxor."

The ringing of the cell phone prevented his reply. He listened for a moment before responding, "I'm at the entrance now. Tell your castrato to let me and my bag inside."

He pressed the speaker icon, and the booming voice of Prince Jasper Adumu erupted. "George, allow this man to enter Luxor."

"You got it, Prince Jasper."

Monsarrat pulled open a door marked with a cyclopean eye. Purple curtains of crushed velvet lined the hallway. He offered a fifty dollar bill to a buxom Cleopatra perched on a stool behind a cage of thick bars. "Busy morning?"

"Not so much," she replied, waving away the cash. "Prince Jasper says you can go inside for free."

He entered the main room of the club. As his eyes adjusted to the dim light, he saw a stocky middle-aged man with a bald head like a cannonball approach him. He bore the rounded shoulders and barrel chest of a weightlifter and walked with the rolling gait of a sailor recently returned to land. A dual flag pin of the United States and Nigeria adorned the lapel of his brown suit, a red silk handkerchief fluffed in the breast pocket of his jacket, and a diamond studded Rolex watch circled his left wrist. Tribal cicatrices, scars denoting strength, power, and wealth, covered his forehead and cheeks. His feet appeared too small to support his girth.

Prince Jasper's voice fluttered in falsetto. "My dear friend! I welcome you to Luxor, but are you in trouble? You look as if you've been fighting in the dirt!"

Monsarrat clapped his shoulder. "Let's talk in your office."

Climbing the staircase to the second floor, Adumu paused frequently, his lungs wheezing. In Nigeria, along with his twin brother, Prince Joshua, he had organized nationwide protests against the government's human rights violations. Monsarrat had whisked them out of their country moments before a government goon squad arrived in Warri to forever silence their criticisms. Since arriving in the United States, Prince Joshua had padded his physique, as well as his bank account.

In his luxurious office, Adumu dropped onto an ebony sofa with stout legs and a pyramid of pillows. He motioned Monsarrat to join him. "Would you like a drink, Nathan?"

Monsarrat declined. "I need you to secure a Libyan entry visa, an invitation from the Ministry of Foreign Affairs, and a reservation at Hotel Paradise in Sirte for Mark Sanger, a Canadian journalist."

"I can have everything for you in six weeks."

"I need them today by four o'clock."

Adumu laughed, his thick fat rolling. "Request the possible, Nathan. Do you want a hostess? I have white girls, black girls, Asian girls. My Russian girls are voluptuous. As many as you desire, at no charge."

Monsarrat wanted the documents before meeting Enderby. "Four o'clock, Prince Jasper. Today."

"You ask the impossible! A Canadian citizen must apply in person for a visa at the Libyan embassy in Ottawa. Issuance takes weeks."

Monsarrat pressed the Sanger passport into his hands. "You extort diplomats and politicians after filming them *in flagrante* in your private rooms with your hostesses. If you don't own a Libyan outright, you own someone who does. Either way, I need everything by four o'clock today."

"Your request is not only impossible, Nathan, it is a violation of the trust my clients place in me."

"They don't trust you, Prince Jasper, they fear you, as you should fear me. Also, you owe me, and it's time to repay your debt. Remember how you and your brother escaped Warri."

Adumu seized the mention of his sibling. "My brother thrives in London. He often asks of you."

"Send him my regards, right after you give me the visa, invitation, and hotel reservation."

The Nigerian attempted a new tack. "Libyans do not enjoy blackmail. They enjoy hanging men by their ankles, puncturing holes in their veins, and making bet on how long until they bleed out."

"The government goons weren't friendly types, either."

"At least, allow me a week. With the help of the Almighty, I will deliver the package to you."

"Tell the Almighty you need to deliver by four o'clock today."

"The task is impossible, Nathan!"

"Make it happen, Prince Jasper," Monsarrat warned, "or you'll learn that the Libyans aren't the only bastards in this city."

Russian System Preempts a Counterstrike

Monsarrat expected trouble from the guard, but only the boy pharaoh astride the Great Sphinx waited outside Luxor. A red minivan with the black lettering of a livery company pulled to the curb, facing traffic, its front windows retracted. Sunglasses covered the eyes of the driver. His black hair was slick, his skin pale, and his complexion pitted. A plump nose rose above a thick moustache. He held a cell phone in his hand, his eyes flicking between its screen and Monsarrat, comparing the man against a photograph.

The driver yelled, "Bud, you called for a ride?"

His accent triggered memories of the two dead men in Manhattan. Paranoia flaring brightly, Monsarrat replied, "Not me."

"You're the only one here. Get in the van."

Monsarrat fingered the Beretta. Certain times called for disengagement. Others, like daylight snatch attempts, reeked of desperation and demanded confrontation. "You're mistaken."

The panel door of the minivan slid open, and two thugs who could have been cloned from the driver jumped onto the sidewalk. "You're the one who made the mistake, bud."

Monsarrat dropped his bag. With his index finger, he rubbed the skin above his upper lip. "You boys share the same barber?"

The driver ordered, "Teach him some manners."

Monsarrat tensed his thumb and curled the fingertips of his right hand. He scythed the hardened ridge of his outer palm toward the first thug, crushing the stiff edge of the windpipe and dropping him onto the sidewalk, struggling to breathe. He broke the jaw of the second thug with his elbow, held him in a choke hold until his body slackened, and dropped him onto the ground.

Opening the driver's door, he noted small groups had gathered on both sides of the street, most filming the encounter with their cell phones. He pointed the Beretta at his forehead. "Get out of the van."

The driver stepped onto the sidewalk. "You're making a big mistake, bud."

"Lace your fingers behind your head and spread your legs," Monsarrat ordered. He bent the driver over the hood and patted him. He removed his cell phone and wallet, placing the items into his own pockets. "What's the code to unlock the cell phone?"

"2-8-4-6," the driver replied, his voice muffled.

The wail of approaching sirens added urgency to his questioning. "Who hired you?"

"*Idi nah hooy*, fuck you!"

He wanted to ask more questions, but did not want to speak with the police. He swung the butt of the Beretta into the driver's skull and threw him onto the sidewalk. Hoisting his bag, he walked from the scene. He retrieved the Audi and drove to Dupont Circle. On Connecticut Avenue, he pulled to the curb, opened the Canadian cell phone, and accessed the website of a local hotel. As Mark Sanger, he reserved a room. Minutes later, he passed the fob to the valet, received a claim stub, and registered at the hotel reception desk.

The room offered a view of Columbia Road. He closed the drapes, dropped the bag onto the bed, and unclipped the holster from his belt. Examining the driver's wallet, he found fifty dollars, a pair of credit cards, and a Virginia license for Oleg Zentsov of Edsall Road in Alexandria. He removed the money and opened the cell phone, examining emails, texts, and call logs. He listened to voicemails but did not learn who had hired the moustached thugs.

He launched an internet search of Zentso, exploring public records, including the property tax office and the motor vehicle office, and criminal complaints. In cyberspace, Zentsov did not exist. He sought photographs and social media postings. Instinct led him to the website of the Russian Embassy. A photograph showed the driver standing in a crowd listening to an address of the ambassador. He closed the browser, adding more Russians to his growing tally.

From the hallway dispenser, he filled a plastic bag with ice. In the bathroom, he buried his hands beneath the cubes. When the ice melted, he stripped off his clothes and the Kevlar, brushed his teeth, and shaved. Beneath the hot spray of the shower, he scrubbed his skin. Toweling dry, he set the alarm on the Sanger cell phone, collapsed onto the bed, and immediately fell asleep.

He woke an hour later more groggy than refreshed. In the bathroom, he splashed cold water onto to his face. He shrugged on the Kevlar, dressed, checked the load of the Beretta, and called for the car. In the lobby of the hotel, he dropped Zentsov's cell phone and wallet into a trash can. He tipped the valet with the driver's cash and tossed the bag onto the rear bench of the Audi. Driving across the city, his anger mounting, he approached Luxor.

Parking in the same spot the red minivan had occupied, he saw that the guard again stood before the entrance. He opened the Sanger cell phone. He counted three rings before the call connected. "Come outside, Prince Jasper, tell your castrato to sit, and walk to the Audi."

Ten minutes passed before Adumu waved off the guard. He signaled for the window to be lowered. Offering an envelope, he explained, "I won't join you. I'll never hoist myself from the car seat."

Monsarrat lifted the flap to inspect the visa, letter of invitation, and hotel reservation. "For your sake, Prince Jasper, I hope they're good."

"My dear friend, the documents are genuine but obtaining them exhausted me. The Libyan was difficult. I was forced to utilize the most base methods of persuasion."

"I'm sure you'll recover."

Adumu offered a declaration. "My debt to you is now paid in full."

"We are nowhere near even, Prince Jasper, but you can pay down your debt by telling me who you called. I want to know who sent the thugs to Luxor."

"What are you talking about, Nathan?"

"You instructed your castrato to walk when I left your office, so he wouldn't try to help me."

"Try to help you how?"

Drawing the Beretta, Monsarrat warned, "I saved your life in Warri. I can cancel it here."

The Nigerian recoiled at the sight of the weapon. "Please, Nathan. I do not understand."

"You set three Russians to snatch me."

"Do you mean the violence outside Luxor today? You were involved? Russians, also?"

"You play the innocent poorly, Prince Jasper."

His falsetto sharp, Adumu protested, "I did not turn on you. My brother and I owe you our lives!"

"Who did you call? A customer in the Russian Embassy?"

"I called not a soul!"

"Tell me you didn't betray me for money."

"I swear on the graves of my ancestors, I am not disloyal!"

"You contacted someone, Prince Jasper," Monsarrat explained. "If you hadn't made the call, the Russians wouldn't have known I was here. They wouldn't have thrown me the party on the sidewalk."

The Nigerian raised his hand. "If you doubt me, Nathan, shoot me now, but I will die in despair."

Monsarrat holstered the Beretta. "Don't die yet, Prince Jasper. We'll talk again when I return."

Classical Play Emphasizes Swift Development

Monsarrat drove to Dupont Circle, parking in a space across from the Cantina. He entered the restaurant thirty minutes prior to his meeting with Enderby. Talavera tiles lined the floors and walls of the restaurant, and leaded glass windows offered scenes of an idyllic Mexico. A collection of *Día de Muertos* masks lined the walls. From the embossed tin ceiling, the wooden blades of fans spun lazily. He sat at the bar, sipping a bottle of Dos Equis, the bag beneath his feet, and examined the patrons.

Enderby arrived five minutes late. The eyes of the former Special Forces colonel were cobalt, his jaw dimpled, his cheekbones sharp, and his nose firm. Streaks of gray seared his short black hair, and a small scar hung like a teardrop from the corner of his lips. He wore a white turtleneck, gray slacks, and cordovan loafers. A watch with a large circular face rested on his left wrist. The bulge of a .50 caliber Desert Eagle in a leather shoulder holster broke the smooth drape of his houndstooth jacket.

Monsarrat extended his hand. "You look well, Harper."

Enderby's grip was a moray eel attacking its prey, but his drawl was a soothing cat's purr. "You look poorly, Nathan. Did you walk all the way from the Berkshires?"

Monsarrat smiled. "Are you hungry, or are drinks good for you?"

"Beer's fine. I'm wheels up on the redeye Lufthansa from Dulles tonight, and I don't eat before I fly," Enderby replied. "Brief me first, and I'll bring you up to speed on my end."

"Do you track Caliph Bin Nafe for the Agency?"

Hatred thickening his voice, the former Special Forces colonel summarized the Libyan's rise to power and wealth. "The bastard graduated from protecting Qaddafi to running narcotics, cigarettes, and sex slaves along the caravansary route from the Gulf of Guinea through North Africa and onward to Italy, but his forte is kidnapping businessmen and diplomats. Once the money's delivered, he beheads the hostages with his *flyssa* sword."

"You still want him dead?"

"More than anything. I lost two of my team in Sirte to Bin Nafe."

Monsarrat ordered two more bottles of Dos Equis. He shared his knowledge of the Epsteins and the demands of Bin Nafe, but omitting his relationship with Sylvie. "Securing the ransom is a non-starter. Neither my friend nor I have access to that kind of money. I suspect Bin Nafe has already killed her mother and plans to kill the father and my friend, once she delivers the ransom."

"I hate to bear bad news, Nathan, but odds are good that the Libyan has already killed both Epsteins. He'll try to kill you, too, when you show up, with or without the money," Enderby said. "My boys and I will keep you alive and put down Bin Nafe. If we can rescue the old couple, all the better."

"Tell me how it plays out."

"We use three teams. Blue prepares ingress into Sirte from Cairo, Red preps the hotel site, Green facilitate egress from Libya into Europe," Enderby explained. "If you haven't already, book a seat on tonight's Lufthansa flight from Dulles to Cairo. We'll rendezvous with Blue at the airport and cross the border into Libya by private plane. Red will meet us at wheels down in Sirte. Go time, we do what we do, Green takes us home."

"Good work on short notice," Monsarrat complimented.

Enderby presented his caveat. "We'll secure the Epsteins, if they're alive. They're one half of the mission. The second half is eliminating Bin Nafe. I'm grateful to you for setting him up, but if you hit a wall somewhere, I'll complete the mission without you."

"We're not competing, Harper. We're complementing. If the Epsteins are alive, we bring them home. If they're dead, we'll bury them at sea. Either way, Bin Nafe dies."

They discussed strategies and tactics, objectives and logistics. Before departing the restaurant, Monsarrat provided Enderby with the Sanger cell phone information. "We won't speak again until Cairo, but if you need to contact me, send a text to this number."

He departed the Cantina and retrieved the Audi. Inside the car, he dialed the number for Lufthansa reservations, purchasing a one-way ticket to Cairo International Airport on the redeye flight. He drove the the hotel and parked before the entrance, passing twenty dollars and instructions to the valet. "I'll be back in a few minutes. Keep the car close, and I'll double the tip."

Inside the business center, he purchased two boxes and a flat envelope for overnight delivery, addressed them, and specified signature requirements. In his room, he tore the heading from a sheet of hotel stationary. Writing an unsigned note to Sylvie, he experienced a sour feeling of regret. False hope shrouded the words, and he felt like a coward, writing not calling, but speaking with her demanded an honesty of his expectations for the rescue of her parents that he was ill prepared to offer. *"En route to retrieve your valuables. Will contact when they are in my possession. Stay strong."*

Before leaving the room, he sealed the envelope and placed it, the two boxes, and the hand towels into his bag. He checked out, found the valet, and handed him a second twenty dollar bill. Driving toward Dulles International Airport, he opened the Sanger cell phone and dialed the number of Amos Chaggai, a former assassin who retired from Mossad to grow grapes in the north of Israel. He first encountered Chaggai in a Beirut hotel, both vying to kidnap the same target. The Israeli ended the stalemate by firing two bullets into the target's chest and a maraschino cherry into his forehead. An improbable friendship had developed between them, based on a mutual respect and a shared questioning of the acts they committed to protect the security of their countries.

The call connected, and Monsarrat heard an accented *Hallo*. "I apologize for the hour."

"Apologies are not necessary, my friend," Chaggai replied. "Tell me. Are you in trouble?"

"I could use your help."

"Of course. Whatever you ask."

"Do you still have friends in your old office in Jerusalem?"

"Mossad friends are forever," replied Chaggai.

Sharing intelligence over a cell phone was as secure as listing secrets on a Jumbotron, but Monsarrat possessed no other option. He explained the mission and provided his itinerary. "Can your former office friends make sure I'm not tossed into a Mukhabarat prison in Egypt and Libya?"

"Do you have specific worries about their security services?"

"More like vague fears."

Chaggai did not request details. "Egypt is easy. We are secret allies. It is in our yard."

Monsarrat remembered the Israeli's fondness for American slang. "We say, in our backyard."

Chaggai accepted the correction. "Libya is difficult. We own few assets. Also, the Mukhabarat is the least of your concerns. Worry more about al-Qaeda and Da'ish affiliates. Local warlords, also."

"Any help you can provide will be appreciated. Send a text. I'll check for messages," he instructed, supplying the Sanger number.

Chaggai noted the information. "Your passport is Canadian, also? In case I need to arrange consular assistance for you?"

Monsarrat laughed and ended the call. Gaining the Dulles Access Road, he sped toward the airport. Aviation Road led to a national chain hotel. He parked in the lot beyond the entrance, unzipped the bag, and placed the keys to his Greylock house and the Westbrook file into the first box. He stepped from the Audi, stripped off his shirt, removed the Kevlar, and placed it and the Beretta, wrapped in the hand towels, next to the box of ammunition inside the trunk. He dressed, closed the lid, and took the gloves from the Audi. He locked the car and placed the fob into the second box. Before entering the hotel, he dropped the gloves into a garbage bin.

He followed signs in the lobby to the business center. Greeting the clerk, he sealed the boxes and dropped the envelope next to them. "Am I good to go?"

"Prepaid, sealed, and ready for pick-up," the clerk agreed.

He sent a text to Grinnell with the location of the Audi and the tracking number of the package, read his confirmation, and deleted the messages. He boarded the airport shuttle bus, departed at the Main Passenger Terminal, and followed an airline crew to the Lufthansa check-in area at Counter Three. He passed the agent the

Sanger passport, open to its Egyptian visa, receiving in return First
Class boarding passes and a warning to proceed directly to the gate.

At the East Checkpoint, he cleared security, passport, and
immigration controls. The pedestrian walkway led to Terminal B. He
arrived at Gate 45 at the final boarding call. Inside the cabin, he
placed his bag into an overhead bin and set his watch to match the
time in Cairo. When the steward offered the drink cart, he chose a
bottle of water.

He closed his eyes as the big plane lumbered down the runway,
waking after seven hours to the jolt of tires bumping along the tarmac
of Munich's Franz Josef Strauss International Airport. He retrieved
his bag and walked to the First Class Lounge, drinking black coffee
and checking the cell phone for messages until boarding for his
onward flight was announced. Returning to the gate, he saw Enderby
sitting on a bar stool, eyes intent on the German news, a full glass of
dark beer by his hand.

On the plane to Cairo, he again placed his bag into an overhead
bin. Settling into his seat, his thoughts bounced from Sylvie Epstein to
Brenda Carlyle before settling upon Abby Houghton, the Special
Assistant to President Augustus Haverhill. Once colleagues at
Langley, later lovers, before retiring from the Agency, he proposed
marriage and new lives, far from Langley. She responded by
betraying him with Felix Sanhedrin, a wound slow to heal. He did
not want to speak with her again, but if anyone knew the location of
Sanhedrin, it would be Abby.

He slept until the steward woke him for the descent into Cairo.
Lifting the shutter, he glanced through the porthole onto the sprawl
of the city. The afternoon heat shimmered, sand painted the sky a

sickly gray, and a dun landscape stretched to the horizon. The plane bumped onto the tarmac, and he retrieved the Sanger cell phone, finding two text messages. The first, from Carlyle, assumed the persona of a real estate agent. "Have info on 4th unit. Call me to discuss." The second, from Chaggai, offered facts. "(1) Target killed offshore Sirte. No evidence hostages. (2) Friends both places."

He deleted the texts, buoyed by Carlyle's tease but worried by Chaggai's report. In an arrivals hall as cheerful as a warehouse, two muscular men, each over six feet tall, stood beneath a *Qibla*, a prayer arrow pointed toward Mecca. They wore white linen slacks and white cotton guayaberas. Scrolled Ranger tattoos braided their corded forearms. The first man sported short brown hair and a trimmed moustache and beard. Sunglasses sat atop his head, exposing his brown eyes. He held a handwritten sign, Mr. Blue. The second man could have been his twin, save for his blond hair and blue eyes. Monsarrat approached them. "I'm Nathan Monsarrat."

"Charlie Anderson," the bearded ranger said. "My friend is Arnie Hollinger. He'll wait for Harper, but we can get this party started."

Hollinger spoke in deep tones. "The sooner we begin, the faster we all get happy."

Shaking their hands, Monsarrat felt their strength. "I get happy when the party's over."

EN PASSANT

A Method of Capture Specific to the Pawn

Sacrifice a Pawn in Return for Quick Development

Cairstine Fergusson waited for Pavlik at a table for two in Café Wien, a Viennese *mélange* coffee and an untouched slice of *gugelhupf* sponge cake before her. Her location afforded a clear view of the entrance at the busy corner of 19th and "Q" Streets. She had followed tradecraft and arrived early for the meeting, choosing her lines of sight carefully. In all aspects of espionage, she valued the role of the senses, especially the visual recognition signals inviolable since Rahab hung a red cord from the window of her Jericho home.

A curly blond wig, blue contact lenses, and clear glasses in black plastic frames disguised her. To honor the Scottish occasion, she wore a tucked tartan jacket over a linen blouse and a matching waistcoat, adorned with the gold chain of a watch fob. A tweed deerstalker, Inverness cape, beige slacks, and leather pumps completed the outfit. A gold necklace circled her throat, gold bracelets hung from her wrists, and gold hoops accented her ears. Her crocodile purse contained the Walther Q4.

The cell phone chimes of Big Ben marked the noon hour. Sipping the *mélange*, she worried about Pavlik, his emotional and physical health after the long months spent living as a dead man. She placed the deerstalker upon the hardcover edition of *Waverley*, the spine of the Sir Walter Scott book toward the door. Without the dual visual recognition signals, Pavlik would continue past the table.

At three minutes past the hour, the door to Café Wien opened, and the gust of an unseasonably warm breeze heralded the arrival of her deceased lover, but a woman stepped through the doorway. Between thirty-five and forty years of age, of medium height and with the lean muscles of a tennis player, she wore a silk blouse beneath a pink cashmere jacket, designer jeans, and cork espadrilles. No rings adorned her crimson-tipped fingers, but a double strand of Mikimoto pearls circled her throat. A peaches and cream complexion, sharp cheekbones, cornflower blue eyes, dimples, and soft red lips defined her face. Her blond ponytail bounced as she approached the table.

She examined Fergusson, lifted the deerstalker, and smiled brilliantly. "I haven't seen one in ages! Who's your favorite Sherlock? It's old Basil for me."

Fergusson rarely found herself at a loss for words, but the woman's beauty and enthusiasm stunned her. Her reply sounded like the dull thud of a dropped exchange. "Of course, Rathbone was the best, although Richardson shone in *The Hound of the Baskervilles*."

The woman placed the deerstalker on the empty chair. "Oh, I do appreciate a literary sister, but I must run now. The game's afoot!"

Fergusson watched her order a takeout cup of coffee from the barista, feeling a stab of disappointment when she exited the café. She reached for the deerstalker to replace it upon the hardcover novel, and an exquisite origami swan fluttered to the table, like a paper Zeus fleeing the bed of Leda. She thought the woman's tradecraft extraordinary, the passing of the message a combination of elegance and verve. She slipped the swan into her purse.

The *mélange* had turned cold and the *gugelhupf* sodden. The failure of Pavlik to appear frustrated her, as did the invitation's lack of a fallback contingency. Her lover extraordinaire may have suffered a heart attack, died at the hands of an assassin, or simply changed his mind, but she suspected the origami swan would provide an explanation. She gathered her purse and hardcover novel, placed the deerstalker upon her head, and called for the check.

She followed "P" Street into Georgetown, walking beneath the autumn foliage of oak and poplar trees, the sidewalks filled with shoppers. Inside her townhouse, she shouted for the butler, but only silence answered. In her bedroom, she discarded the Café Wien disguise, changing into a navy blue jacket and skirt, white Oxford shirt, and blue leather pumps. Her jewelry was muted. She packed an overnight bag and carried it into the study.

Locking the door, she pressed a remote control, and the opulent notes of Rachmaninoff's Piano Concerto Number Three in D Minor, Opus Thirty, filled the room. From the wall safe, she withdrew a Meisterstück fountain pen, a leather case holding sheets of rag paper, and an English translation of *War and Peace* published by the Masters of Russian Literature series. She placed the items in a neat line upon the desk. Smoothed against the glass, the flattened swan revealed a series of digits in vertical columns written by a hand that did not belong to Pavlik, a message that could only be encoded and decoded with the specific edition of the Tolstoy novel.

Thoughts of the blond woman delayed her opening the pages. She slapped the glass with the palm of her hand, unleashing her brogue. "Heid doon, arse up! Get on with it!"

She deciphered steadily, enjoying the precision of the work, the gold nib of the fountain pen spreading ink across the rag paper. Reading the full message, Pavlik demanding a crash meeting, location and time provided, she marveled at the artistry of the blond woman in creating an origami swan from a sheet of one-time paper.

She struck a wooden matchstick, dissolving the message. Returning the items to the safe, she spun the dual dials. She used her home phone to summon a taxi, confident the *Rezidentura* had tapped the landline. "I need a driver to take me to Dulles. I'm flying Aeroflot."

On the other side of the study, she found the butler waiting with a suitcase in his thick hand. "Are you going on vacation, Rupert?"

"I am in charge now. You will obey my orders," he stated. "We travel together to Moscow."

She wanted to snap his bull neck but leaving his corpse in the townhouse would further erode her standing with Moscow Centre. "It's not necessary. I know the way."

"Our masters have made their decision."

She taunted him with their bloody encounter in Repino. "If you choose to obstruct me, I'll finish what I began in Repino, remove the remainder of your tiny *khuy* and mail it to your friends in Line "N" so everyone in Moscow Centre will see the full truth of you."

He bristled at the threat. "I'd promise to piss on your grave, but the gulag will never disclose the location of your corpse."

She dropped the overnight bag to the floor. The speed of her hands was a blur. She drove the heel of her right palm into his chest and arced her left arm in an uppercut. He crashed to the floor, his head bouncing twice. She pressed her fingertips against his throat. "Tatties o'wer the side, Rupert. Disaster has spared you. If I possessed more time, I'd dissect you and no one would ever find the pieces."

She examined her image in the hallway mirror. Leaving the Georgetown townhouse saddened her, as did abandoning the gallery and its priceless antiquities, but she embraced her future, a woman of means freed from Moscow Centre, reunited with her lover extraordinaire. Lifting the bag, she departed the townhouse. Locking the door was a symbolic conclusion to her life as Cairstine Fergusson. From the porch, she saw two Suburbans with darkly tinted windows idle across the street.

A taxi pulled to the curb, and she entered it. She withdrew the Walther and five hundred dollars from her purse and shoved the pistol beneath the rear seat cushion. At Dulles International Airport, she handed the cabbie two hundred dollars and waved the remaining cash. "Three hundred dollars, if you help me."

He responded in an accent from the Punjab. "As long as I don't break any laws."

"I need two favors," she said. "I want you to pick me up at the taxi rank between arrival doors six and seven in one hour exactly."

"If you're late, I'll leave," he warned.

"Fair enough," she agreed. "I also want to use your cell phone. My battery has run down."

Stepping from the taxi, she saw the two Suburbans at the curb fifty feet distant. Ignoring them, she dialed from memory the number of a garage on Potomac Street in Georgetown. When the call connected, she said, "It's Cairstine Fergusson. I want my Ferrari delivered to me in ninety minutes."

"No problem, Ms. Fergusson," the manager replied.

"Look for me in the rear of the commuter lot at the East Falls Church metro station. I understand you don't usually deliver so far from your premises, but I promise to compensate you handsomely."

She returned the cell phone to the cabbie. Before entering the terminal, she turned to watch the driver pull away from the curb. Approaching Counter One, she noted a pair of male watchers, one standing by a flight monitor, the other loitering between security checkpoints. She waited at the front of the First Class line less than a minute before the Aeroflot agent waved her forward. Providing her passport and visa, she said, "I'd like a seat in First Class, on the aisle, on the next flight to Moscow."

"Any luggage to check, Ms. Fergusson?" the agent asked.

"Just my carry-on."

"Would you like to book a return flight?"

"My schedule is a work in progress," she replied.

Departing the counter, she walked toward the West Checkpoint, beyond the sight of the two watchers. She processed through security, passport, and immigration controls. Riding the shuttle to Terminal D, she spotted a second pair of watchers, a man and a woman, at the departure gate, waiting in hard seats with backpacks in their laps as passengers jostled for position in the Coach queue. She stared at them until they glanced away from her.

She walked into the ladies' room across the corridor from the departure gate. A TEMPORARILY OUT OF ORDER signboard leaned against the wall. She set it in the entrance and walked to a row of sinks. Placing her overnight bag onto the floor, she splashed water onto her face. In the mirror, she watched the female watcher from the departure gate approach her, backpack in hand. She bent over, retched, rinsed her mouth, and retched again.

The watcher stood next to her. Partly sympathetic, partially aware of the impending departure of the Aeroflot flight, she whispered in Russian, "Let me help you."

Fergusson slammed the palms of her hands over the woman's ears, dropping her to the floor. She lifted her by the hair and drove her head into the sink. Blood erupted from her nose and a gash in her scalp. She propped the watcher's throat against the edge of the porcelain, plucked the cell phone from her pocket, and opened the backpack. A wallet held cash and a diplomatic identification card of the Embassy of the Russian Federation. A leather case, like a cigar tube, contained a fountain pen.

She removed the cap and pressed the gold nib. A surgical needle ejected, its point moist. She pressed the nib again, and the needle retracted. "It's gaein be awricht ance the pain has gane awa', lassie. Tell me the code to your phone."

The woman supplied the information. "I don't want to die."

"It's too late for false hopes."

She struck the back of the woman's neck with her tensed palm, shattering her trachea against the sink. "It's a sadness, death, but you bungled your mission and so paid for your failure."

She washed and dried her hands, inspecting her face and clothes in the mirror. The sympathy of the woman proved that she was only a watcher equipped with a killing tool, not a trained *mokroye delo* assassin. She departed the ladies' room, bag in her left hand, fountain pen firm in her right hand, and returned to the departure area.

The male watcher sat alone. She removed the cap of the fountain pen and pressed the nib against the vein on the back of his hand. "If I so choose, laddie, you'll die here, so tell me your orders."

"Where is my partner?"

"I only need one *zhopa* to relay my message. I chose you."

He sobbed with fear. "The *Rezident* assigned watchers to the airports. We are to confirm you boarded your flight."

She pressed the nib harder against his hand. "What are your orders after the plane is airborne?"

"We send a text message, *the soup is cooking,* and return to the *Rezidentura* to debrief."

The monitor marked the flight as Departed. With one hand, she entered the code into the dead woman's cell phone. "Tell me the number the *Rezident* is using for this mission."

She tapped the digits as he spoke, typed the message, and pressed Send. She clicked the nib and watched his expression contort from shock to pain. She clicked the nib again, capped the pen, wiped it and the cell phone, and dropped the devices onto his lap. "It's not personal, just your own bad luck."

Zwischenzug is an Intermediate Move

Opposite the shuttle bays, Fergusson entered a ladies' room. She detached the battery from her cell phone and snapped the SIM card, tossing the pieces into a trash can. From the overnight bag, she withdrew a gray wig, a fringed mauve shawl with a paisley imprint, brown contact lenses, and a pair of tortoiseshell sunglasses. She boarded the shuttle, finding a seat on a bench. The machine lurched across the tarmac to the docking bay. She stepped into the midst of the scrum departing the security area. Escalators led to the baggage carousels. Beyond the tumbling luggage, she exited the terminal and walked toward the taxi rank.

Sliding onto the rear bench of the waiting cab, she handed the surprised cabbie the promised money. "Don't worry about my appearance. Just drive."

Pocketing the bills, he examined her in the rearview mirror. "Would you like to return to Georgetown?"

"Stop at Oakwood Cemetery in Falls Church first."

She retrieved the Walther and dropped it into her purse. No Suburbans followed them. Staring out the window as the cabbie sped toward Falls Church, she enjoyed the irony of using the skills she learned in Repino and Novosibirsk against Moscow Centre. Entering the cemetery, she breathed deeply, relaxing her muscles and clearing her mind for the necessary task.

Fergusson directed him to a gravestone in the isolated "E" section, at the rear of the cemetery. Exiting the taxi, she stumbled, dropped to a knee, and gasped in pain. "I've twisted my ankle."

The cabbie stepped from the taxi. Reaching for her arm, his expression changed from concern to agony as the heel of her palm shattered his nose. She slid behind him, placed her knee onto the small of his back, and cupped his chin in her hands. She drove her knee forward and jerked his head upward and twisted it to the side, shattering his spine. Dropping the body onto the pavement, she reached into the taxi and released the lid of the trunk. Before stuffing him inside, she removed his cell phone and wallet, retrieving the cash she paid him. "No fault of yours, laddie. You only saw too much."

Retrieving the overnight bag, she closed the taxi doors and followed a path through the cemetery, exiting onto Tuckahoe Street. The pavement ended at a park, and she followed a gravel path until reaching the Old Dominion Trail. She removed the contact lenses and dropped the disguise, plus the wallet and cell phone of the driver, into a trash can, reaching the commuter lot at the East Falls Church metro station minutes past her promised arrival, the manager of the garage that housed her brilliant silver Ferrari Spider standing by the Italian car like a loyal sentry.

She handed him a hundred dollar bill. "I've listed the Ferrari for sale. Has anyone inquired for it?"

"Not a soul, Ms. Fergusson."

"Just my bad luck," she replied, pleased the car was not under observation by the *Rezidentura*.

She drove west on Route 50 through northern Virginia, confident no one followed her. White picketed paddocks spread across the rolling green hills. In Middleburg, she purchased a bouquet of yellow roses from a florist. Before Ashby Gap, a hamlet in the Virginia horse country, she turned onto a single track road lined with magnolia, white oak, and hickory trees. Revolutionary War era stone walls marked property lines, and a brass plaque on a red brick pillar stated Fermanagh House. In the crisp air, song birds twittered. A winding gravel drive lined with dogwood trees and tulip beds led to an antebellum Greek Revival manor. She parked the car before a stone staircase leading to a wide portico. From habit, she locked the doors and set the alarm.

At the top of the staircase, Corinthian columns buttressed a flared cornice, and arched bay windows flanked a doorway. She walked to the end of the portico, the bouquet of yellow roses held like an offering, absorbing the views of the Shenandoah Valley, the Blue Ridge Mountains, and the blond woman from Café Wien cresting a hillock, the double strand of Mikimoto pearls bobbing against her throat. Her hair loose, she wore a silk tee shirt, blue jeans, and sandals. In her hand, she carried a tennis ball. A Golden Retriever puppy waddled by her side.

She rolled the ball across the grass. The puppy scooped its mouth, shook it, and waited. She wrestled the ball away and called, "Welcome, Cairstine. How was your drive?"

Fergusson waved the bouquet. "I hope I'm not too tardy."

The woman mounted the stairs, the puppy straining to follow. "You're no longer a blue eyed, curly blond. You've returned to your natural state. I approve."

An unexpected blush heated Fergusson's face. "I'm pleased to meet you again, lassie, only I don't know your name."

Accepting the bouquet, the woman's smile dimpled. "I'm Abby Houghton. I'm sorry we couldn't chat earlier in the café, but I'm glad you're here now."

"As am I," responded Fergusson. "Tell me, Abby. Is Pavlik inside?"

Houghton's expression offered distaste. "He may have been Pavlik to you, but I don't care for the name. Please call him Felix."

The puppy barked and rolled onto his back. Houghton slipped her foot from a sandal. Rubbing his soft stomach, she said, "Felix named him Robespierre, to give him an attitude."

Inside the foyer, Houghton laid the flowers onto a plastic chair. The manor appeared ready for renovation, its furnishings sparse, walls devoid of paintings, and southern pine floors naked. "Don't mind the mess. The work is progressing slowly."

"Apologies are not necessary, but tell me your relation to Felix?"

Her expression bland, Houghton replied, "I don't understand."

"Are you his housekeeper? His cook? His strength trainer? His interior decorator?"

"Felix was my husband."

The announcement shocked Fergusson. "You're wrong, lassie! I would know if Felix married."

Houghton wagged her finger, as if reprimanding the puppy. "We married a year ago next week, Cairstine. We didn't tell anyone. In fact, we never seen together socially, to maintain the facade."

Anger seared Fergusson's reply. "Then it's a pity you can't celebrate the anniversary publicly, not with Felix's pretended death."

"Are you trying to hurt me?" Houghton snapped. "You know Felix died on the first day of the year!"

"How can that be? He sent me the coded invitation to meet at Café Wien. Yourself passed me his instructions to arrive here!"

Her anger passed quickly. "Oh, you poor dear! You think Felix sent you the messages? Come with me into the sun room, Cairstine. We'll have a drink and talk, girl to girl."

Floor to ceiling leaded windows overlooked the darkening hills. A card table and two folding chairs commanded the middle of the room. In the corner, a ladder, cans of paint, turpentine, mason jars, and brushes sat atop a drop cloth. "I'm doing as much of the work as possible. When I'm finished, I'll sell Felix's townhouse in Georgetown and live here. Robespierre needs room to run."

Motioning Fergusson into a chair, she walked into the kitchen, returning with two jam jars, a bowl of shelled peanuts, and a laptop. She passed a jar to her guest and set the bowl onto the floor. "A single cask bourbon with muddled mint and lime. It's a local favorite."

Fergusson sipped the drink. "My compliments."

"The manor owns a fascinating history," Houghton explained. "During the Civil War, Confederate soldiers commandeered it as a hospital. Northerners turned it into a brothel. During Reconstruction, it served as a recruitment center for the Klu Klux Klan."

Fergusson placed her jar onto the table, struggling to suppress her anger. "I have interest in neither history nor bourbon nor real estate. Only tell me who mailed the invitation and encoded the message you carried to me, since you insist that your husband is dead."

"Felix told me you are a chess savant. Can't you read the board?"

Fergusson studied her hostess until the realization dawned. "You have assumed the role of Pavlik!"

"Well done, Cairstine," Houghton complimented, placing her own jar onto the table. "Felix taught me the procedures and the book code, and I used them to contact you."

The enormity of Pavlik's indiscretions shocked Fergusson. "Then you are aware of his activities?"

"If you mean the fact that he spied for Moscow Center, of course, I know," Houghton answered. "Felix kept no secrets from me."

Fergusson struggled to absorb the revelations that Pavlik, her lover extraordinaire, had so thoroughly deceived her. For his love, she had willingly betrayed Moscow Centre, but by marrying Houghton, he had kissed her with the lips of Judas. "Why send me the messages now? Why did you wait so long after his death?"

The puppy waddled into the room, carrying a pair of Bulgari sunglasses in his mouth. He chased his tail before dropping onto a spot of sunlight warming the floor, sharp teeth gnawing the frames.

"No, Robespierre!" Houghton yelled.

Startled, the puppy yelped, dropped the frames, and ran from the room. Houghton picked up the sunglasses and inspected them for teeth marks. "He's a typical male, always demanding attention. If you don't give it to him, he'll take it from you."

Fergusson felt the pressure of time. The dead members of the *Rezidentura* would have been discovered, and new orders would have been issued to capture her by all available methods. "I can stay patient not much longer, lassie, so stop talking about your puppy and come to the point."

"Oh, I do appreciate a forceful sister," Houghton replied, mimicking her persona in the café. "The point, Cairstine, is that I propose to continue Felix's work. With you directly. No one else."

Fergusson laughed. "Felix may have taught you procedures and codes, but how will you reproduce the intelligence he took from the White House?"

"I won't," Houghton replied. "I'll provide better intel. Felix was the National Security Adviser, but I'm the Special Assistant to Augustus Haverhill, the President of the United States."

The statement stunned Fergusson. "You worked with Felix in the White House?"

"Before he arranged for my position in the with Haverhill, we worked together in the Agency."

"He never mentioned you."

"Why would he provide my name to Moscow Centre?" Houghton asked. "He loved me. He wouldn't place me in danger."

Fergusson tried to concentrate on the woman's proposal, but the disclosures had struck her like blows to the head. "You say that you have full access to Haverhill?"

"The President's Daily Brief, his calendar, his conversations. Whatever Augustus Haverhill sees, I see. Wherever Haverhill goes, I go. Whenever he has an original thought, he seeks my approval. I'm not just his Special Assistant, I'm his alter ego. I'm his Rasputin."

Fergusson made the sign of the Old Believer's cross, her index finger straight, middle finger slightly bent. "Without the mad monk's horrible fate, I hope."

In Symmetry, Pieces on Both Sides Mirror the Other

Robespierre returned to the sun room. Rolling onto his back, he offered a plaintive bark. Houghton slipped off her sandal and tickled his stomach. The puppy kicked his hind legs before wriggling free. He propped his muzzle onto a paw, peered at Fergusson with one eye closed, and growled deep in his throat.

"The alpha wolf is eyeing me with nefarious intentions. Place him outside before he attacks."

Houghton stepped into her shoe. "He's just a puppy."

Fergusson offered Robespierre her hand to sniff, but he growled again. She snapped her fingers beneath his nose, and he ran squealing to the far side of the room. "How do you propose to continue your husband's work?"

"Felix said Russians once treated secrets like curses, never to be spoken aloud, but no longer,"

"Does your story end happily?"

"Felix hoped the identity of Pavlik was the most closely guarded secret in all of Moscow Centre but feared that dozens of your bureaucrats had access to his file. His identity was the ultimate lottery ticket. Whoever sold it to the FBI would be rich. Most of all, he dreaded that you would make a mistake and blow his cover."

The words pained Fergusson. "He should have known better."

"Felix was suspicious and careful," Houghton continued. "So am I. He didn't want to end his days in a Guantanamo Bay cage with daily waterboard treatments. Neither do I. Nor do I wish to suffer a horrible death from the Novichok nerve agents created by your

Moscow Centre scientists."

Remembering her own actions at Dulles, Fergusson shared the fear. "Where are you leading me?"

"I'm offering to provide you with the most sensitive intelligence from the Oval Office, by the same communication channel you and Felix utilized. In return, I want Moscow Centre to continue to deposit Felix's payment into his account, with back pay to last January."

"Moscow Centre will insist on a new identity for you, a new communication channel, and a new bank account."

"Don't tell Moscow Centre the money is for a new asset. Tell your masters that Felix is alive."

The irony amused Fergusson, Moscow Centre wanting to end her own life while the secret wife of its most valuable asset hoped to begin a new life as her resurrected husband. "If I say Pavlik is alive, Moscow Centre will demand flesh and blood proof."

"Russians love fairy tales. Offer one and make it convincing," Houghton answered. "Keep in mind that once you pass along my intel, no one in Moscow Centre will question my *bona fides*."

"You underestimate the paranoia of Russians. If I can't produce Felix, Moscow Centre will consider your intelligence *dezinformatsiya* and punish me, not you, with a horrible death."

"Felix would be disappointed in you."

"I can't keep your name secret, but I can present you as a protégé of Felix. Moscow Centre will reward you handsomely."

Houghton removed a nanodrive from the pocket of her jeans. Pressing it into Fergusson's hand, she said, "I applied the same encryption Felix used. We'll talk again, after you read the intel."

Fergusson shivered at the touch of her fingers. "What level of intelligence does the drive contain?"

"An unedited transcript of a recent chat between Haverhill and the Chinese premier. Unless you honor my terms, it'll be the last intel you receive from me."

A plan to regain the graces of Moscow Centre teased Fergusson, using Houghton's intelligence to buy forgiveness for defying her orders and killing of the two watchers. "Open your laptop."

Houghton unlocked the screen and passed it to her guest. "Go to page three, where Haverhill first mentions Russia."

Fergusson inserted the drive and entered the password. When the document opened, she read it intently. "This is simply amazing."

"Do you accept my conditions?"

Fergusson understood that possession of the nanodrive, coupled with threatening to expose her high treason to agents of the American *sluzhba*, granted her ownership of the woman. She removed the nanodrive, stared into the woman's blue eyes, and lied. "We'll give it a fair twirl."

Houghton's laughter chimed like crystal bells. "We're going to be a great team, Cairstine!"

Excited as much as by her cloying scent as her own desire to gain vengeance for Pavlik's betrayal, she agreed, "Aye, I believe it."

Houghton stroked her wrist. "I knew we would be friends."

Fergusson again shivered. "Mixing the professional and the personal is a dangerous game."

"Don't you want to be my very close friend, Cairstine?"

"We will need to be careful."

Houghton placed her finger into her own mouth, removed it, and rubbed saliva onto Fergusson's lips. "Here is neither the place nor the time for careful."

"Moscow Centre will have our heads."

Houghton brushed her lips. "No, they won't, because you'll never tell Moscow Centre about me."

"No one will ever know."

"Not now. Not ever."

"Enough talk, lassie. Why don't you show me the rest of the manor? Start with your bedroom."

Risky Play Increases the Chance for Defeat

Fergusson deactivated the alarm and unlocked the doors of the Ferrari with the fob. The interior lights illuminated a piece of paper on the passenger seat. The familiar Cyrillic cursive and the childhood name penned, **Yulechka**, thrilled her. Only a man as skilled as Pavlik could have defeated the security of the Italian car. Felix Sanhedrin might be dead, as Abby Houghton insisted, but Pavlik lived, and his heart and soul belonged to her, not the woman in the manor who claimed to be his wife.

She opened her purse, placed the nanodrive inside, and withdrew the Walther. Shifting the safety to the off position, she placed the pistol atop the paper. She engaged the Ferrari. The headlights flared, and she drove to the bottom of the winding gravel drive. Passing between the red brick pillars, she entered the dark Virginia countryside. Driving fast, she reached a deserted stretch of road and pulled onto a dirt shoulder. In the glow of an interior light, she read Pavlik's instructions, activated the cigar lighter, and pressed the flash paper against its glowing coil. It disintegrated in a puff of ash.

The thought of her reunion with Pavlik excited her, but her rage toward Houghton burned, and she vowed to destroy her. The smirking demeanor of the woman infuriated her, but not as deeply as the indignity of the high definition recording she had played on her laptop following their bout of bruising sex. On the screen, her arms and legs, spread across the mattress and bound with silk scarves to the bedposts, heaved as Houghton bit her nipples, the pearl necklace around her throat swaying. She smiled into the hidden camera, licked the middle finger of her right hand, and thrust its crimson tip into the soft folds of her wetness. The audio played as sharply as her desire.

"Cairstine Fergusson, have you been naughty or nice?"

Houghton closed the laptop. "I backdated the calendar function, so the video shows that we've been lovers for more than a year. If Moscow Centre was to learn of my relationship with Felix and watch my home movie, they might suspect you killed him to have me for yourself."

The threat of a sexual scandal paled in light of her own actions hours prior at Dulles, but pride formed her reply. "You've made a terrible mistake, lassie. I don't take well to blackmail."

"It's not blackmail, Cairstine. It's my insurance policy, in case you think it's a good idea to share my name with Moscow Centre. We both know how your bosses will react if they learn you're fucking the wife of their former White House asset."

Fergusson struggled to control her anger. "Call it charity if it eases your conscience, but it's a mistake to have me as your enemy."

"Threaten me, Cairstine, if it makes you happy, but we both know you won't kill me, because without my intelligence, you're just an expensive line item on a balance sheet waiting to be erased by the bookkeepers inside Moscow Centre."

"You shouldn't worry about what Moscow Centre will do to me, but what I will do to you should keep you from sleeping at night."

Houghton had bestowed an angelic smile upon her guest. "Indeed, I do worry, Cairstine, and since I have trust issues, while you were showering I emailed a copy of our video tryst to a lawyer with instructions to forward it to the *Rezident* if I fail to send him a text each day with my code word."

Fergusson bumped the wheels of the Ferrari onto the pavement. She drove a mile further, stopping on a bridge straddling the Shenandoah River. Exiting the car, she disassembled her cell phone, leaned over the guardrail, and dropped the case, battery, and SIM card into the muddy waters. "It's a lang road that's no got a turnin'. She will pay dearly for her actions."

Following Pavlik's instructions, she drove west along the back roads, sped through West Virginia, crossed into Maryland, and gained the interstate. Traffic thinned beyond Baltimore. On the Delaware Turnpike, she stopped at the travel plaza. Her back clean of surveillance since, she stripped the Walther and dropped its parts into a trash can. Thirty minutes later, she reached Philadelphia International Airport and entered the long-term Economy Lot. She conducted a quick inspection of the Ferrari. A shuttle bus ferried her to Terminal A-West.

At the British Airways ticket counter, she paid cash for a one-way, First Class ticket to London on the redeye flight. After passing through formalities, she entered a ladies' room near the departure gate, tore the parking ticket into pieces, and flushed them. As a final gesture, she dropped the Ferrari's fob into a trash can. On the plane, she handed her bag to a steward. As gravity pressed her into the seat, she closed her eyes and slept.

Eight hours after departing Philadelphia, the plane landed at Heathrow Airport. She cleared passport control, immigration, and customs, exited the terminal into the late morning sunshine. At the taxi rank, she hailed a black cab, offering her destination in an English dusted with a lilting Parisian accent. "The Lucas Inn on Peckham Road in London, *s'il vous plaît*."

She paid the cabbie before the Inn, waiting until he drove the cab out of sight before walking away from the entrance. She strolled along Peckham Road, seeking signs of surveillance, if Moscow Centre had learned of her destination and activated the London *rezidentura*, its largest in Europe. On Rye Lane, she entered a milliner shop, departing with a hat suitable for Day Three at the Royal Ascot. Outside the shop, her back remained clean.

From a Melon Road greengrocer, she bought fruits, vegetables, bread, and cheese. Her hair and face hidden by the hat, she passed Essex House, a corner pub, and turned onto Crofton Road. Telephone wires sagged over the street. Dented gray trashcans lined the sidewalks. Parked cars narrowed the road. A low concrete wall and a postage stamp yard fronted number fourteen, a whitewashed brick building sporting fresh coats of white paint and black metal shutters. A single flat occupied each of its two floors. Above the roof gutters, a satellite dish pointed toward the sky.

The second floor flat offered a large bay window and a view of the street. She had purchased it at the urging of Pavlik, and beyond herself, only he knew of its existence. She removed a key from her purse, unlocked the deadbolts, secured the alarm system, set her new hat on a cadenza, and kicked off her shoes. The porcelain tiles cooled her bare feet.

In the kitchen, she placed the bread onto the granite counter and the fruits, vegetables, and cheese into the refrigerator. She stripped dust covers from the furniture and opened the windows to release the musky odors of disuse. In the master bedroom, she placed her bag onto the bed. Clothes and shoes wrapped in plastic hung from rods and filled the drawers of a walk-in closet. Surveying her British realm, she declared, "It's a far cry from Dumbarton Street, but as a London safe house, it's bleeding Blenheim Palace."

She lifted a reproduction of *Self-Portrait* by Raeburn from the wall , exposing an embedded safe, and tapped a code into the keypad. The diode blinked yellow, and she pressed the tip of her left index finger against the biometric scanner. The light turned green, the deadbolts retracted, and the door swung open. She removed a Walther Q4, a loaded magazine, and a suppressor identical to the weapon she discarded in Delaware. A laptop, cell phone, and identification package for Fiona Murray, a green eyed beauty with long auburn long hair from Dundee followed. She stripped and cleaned the Walther, inserted the magazine, and attached the suppressor. She plugged the laptop and cell phone into chargers before locking Fergusson's identity and Houghton's nanodrive inside the safe.

She unpacked and stripped off her traveling clothes, dressing in jogging clothes and running shoes. From the drawer of a carved cherry wardrobe, she removed an auburn wig sealed inside a zippered plastic bag. She fitted the piece and inserted green contact lenses flecked with gold into her eyes. A pair of Cartier sunglasses and a large billed cap completed the outfit. As Fiona Murray, she secured the flat, walked to a dry cleaner shop on Peckham Road, and paid for expedited return delivery service. Exhausted, she returned to the flat, showered, and fell into a dreamless sleep.

The dry cleaner delivered her clothes the next morning. She ripped the receipt from the plastic cover, fed the paper into a shredder, and tossed the confetti into the garbage garbage can. She contemplated her new life as Fiona Murray and her reunion later in the day with Pavlik, her very own Lazarus, her lover extraordinaire.

A Poisoned Pawn Often Results in the Loss of the Capturing Piece

Standing inside the entrance of the manor, Robespierre gnawing the tennis ball by her feet, Houghton smiled smugly. The Ferrari disappeared from view, and she turned toward the foyer. "You can come out now, Felix. Cairstine is gone."

Felix Sanhedrin, wearing a white Oxford shirt with the initials *FS* embroidered on the pocket, brown corduroy pants, and cordovan brogues stepped past her onto the portico. Gesturing at the dust churned by the Ferrari, he said, "I don't know what you see in her. She's too masculine for my tastes."

In his voice, Houghton heard jealousy. His expression lacked emotion. Joining him, she chose her words carefully. "I'm only doing what you taught me. I'm taking care of the necessary."

He responded with a rebuke. "I watched your performance, Abby. You enjoyed her."

She reached for his hand. "You haven't briefed me on the Sirte mission. It went well?"

He shook off her hand. "How could I? Your dalliance arrived five minutes after I returned from Libya. I haven't had time to shower, much less brief you."

"Seducing Cairstine was your plan, Felix. So was telling her that I'm your widow."

His anger receded. "It's what we do. We deceive."

"She truly wanted you to be alive. She was terribly disappointed to learn you were still dead."

He answered as if he had never placed his message inside the

Ferrari. "There is no purpose to her life without me. Eventually, Moscow Centre will recall her. She exchange her Georgetown townhouse for a flat in Zvenigorod."

She bent to rub the puppy's ears. "With the intelligence on the nanodrive, she doesn't need to worry. Moscow Centre will keep her in Georgetown as long as I work for Haverhill."

"Haverhill was too eager to step in front of the cameras and tell the world that I bought the farm," Sanhedrin complained. "Our addled president is addicted to watching himself on the news. He sees a cameo in every catastrophe."

"Haverhill genuinely liked you," she protested. "He wanted to mourn your death with the people."

"About as much as he'd mourn the passing of his own gas."

"I respect Haverhill. I feel badly about deceiving him," she said. "You've have him at number two on your enemies list after Nathan."

Her use of Monsarrat's given name elicited a Pavlovian reaction. "Haverhill is a frog, but your boyfriend is a scorpion. I'll celebrate when he's finally and truly dead."

"He's not my boyfriend," she snapped.

The puppy waddled forward, dropping the tennis ball. Sanhedrin kicked it down the steps. "Go fetch, Robespierre."

"Patience, Felix. He'll be dead soon."

"Monsarrat or Robespierre? Both would be best, but the puppy would be much easier to kill. He's slow and stupid."

Houghton issued a stern warning. "Do what you want with Nathan but don't hurt my dog."

"Monsarrat, though, is smart and lucky."

"You're much smarter, and you're luckier," she soothed. "You're

Much more talented, too."

"It's not only Monsarrat. There's also his girlfriend in the Berkshires and the three Jews in Manhattan, which means another trip north. I'll have to leave as soon as you depart for Egypt."

"Wait for me to come home. I'll help you."

"You take care of the Sinai. I'll take care of the others."

Houghton stroked his cheek again. "Will you kill Cairstine, too?"

"I don't see why. She never worked against me. Anyway, she's not important, and she believes I'm dead."

"Do you think she despises you for selling out your country?"

"Frankly, I don't give a damn what Cairstine thinks."

"Lie to the rest of the world, Felix, but not to yourself, and certainly not to me," Houghton replied. "We need her to convince Moscow Centre you're alive, because they'll pay a dollar for intel if they believe you supplied it but only a dime if they think I delivered it."

"The Russians are world class chauvinists," he agreed, "but I really don't understand your desire to work with them. It's not as if we need their money."

His absolute assurance tantalized her, his total absence of empathy aroused her, and his utter ignorance of her motivations mystified her. "Powerful men in the White House want to wear me like a bauble, but I'm not a dumb girl with a great rack. I do it for payback. I do it for the rush. I do it for me."

He kissed her lips. "The betrayal excites you?"

"You understand betrayal, how screwing people gets you off."

"I just didn't know you were so keen to screw Fergusson."

She returned the discussion to Libya. "Tell me about Sirte."

The memory eased his tension. "I first bought Bin Nafe's loyalty when he was a member of Qaddafi's Jamahiriya Guard. He was always difficult, but after the death Qaddafi, he became the leader of his own terror organization, and the son of a bitch grew insufferable."

"How did he die?"

"Too quickly."

"Tell me everything," she urged.

"I reached the *Joppa* by a fast inflatable with a duffel bag stuffed with hundred dollar bills. Bin Nafe and three of his goons had already decapitated everyone on the sloop with *flyssa* swords, save for Epstein père. The Libyan was so eager to count his money and behead his final hostage, he refused to follow the script when he called the daughter in Massachusetts."

Houghton shuddered. "No one deserves that death."

"The Epsteins were bait to lure Monsarrat, and Bin Nafe deserved to die for all the problems he gave me over the years. After the Libyan executed the old man, I terminated him and his three helpers, retrieved my money, scuttled the *Joppa*, and returned to the hotel for a shower and room service, except the water was out again and the last chef had taken a bullet to the forehead months ago. I reached the beach, sliced the inflatable, and made my exfil rendezvous. "

"Such a cost. So many corpses."

"The operation cost me, too. The money I spent to arrange the fake contest for the friends of the Epsteins to win? Airline tickets for four people? Five star hotel rooms in Tangiers? Hiring the captain? Buying the *Joppa?* Will the insurance cover its scuppering? Don't forget Enderby and his merry men cost me, too. Your boyfriend doesn't die easily, and killing him is a very expensive operation."

"You'll feel better when Nathan's dead."

"I'll feel better when you stop using his Christian name."

Her cell phone erupted, preventing her reply. She retrieved it and tapped an icon. "Talk to me."

Static erupted from the speaker, followed by a garbled voice. "We're ready. What is your ETA?"

"Expect me within twenty-four hours."

Static flared again. "Advise of changes."

"One final instruction."

"Go ahead."

"Don't. Fuck. Up," she warned before closing the connection.

Sanhedrin clapped his hands softly. "Well done, Abby."

"He annoys me," she admitted. "Why did you choose him?"

"His ability to do the job, his love of cash, and his lack of morals."

"Can I kill him after I kill Nathan?"

Her use of the name again angered him. "He knows me, so I can't do the job myself, but you can't get rid of him. He's too valuable."

"I'll try to restrain myself."

"You're a star, Abby," he said. "While you're gone, Cerberus and I will become best friends."

"His name is Robespierre."

Sanhedrin laughed at his own joke. "Whatever you call him, he'll always be a son of a bitch."

The puppy waddled close to him, squatted, and loosed a stream of urine onto his shoes. He yelped as Sanhedrin leaped backwards.

"You told me the mutt was housebroken."

Houghton shrugged. "Accidents happen."

"No, they don't," he replied. "They're excuses for losers."

ENDGAME

The Final Phase of the Game, Centered upon the Eighth Rank

Overprotective Play Uses Too Many Pieces to Defend a Position

Nathan Monsarrat followed Anderson across the bustling arrivals hall, pressing the bag to his chest like a running back trailing a lead blocker. The Ranger punched a code into the combination lock of a metal door bearing a sign in Arabic, Private – Authorized Personnel Only. When the door closed behind them, Anderson clapped his back as if he had scored the winning touchdown. "Congrats, Nathan. You've survived the worst of Cairo."

Half-filled coffee cups and crushed cigarettes smoldering in ashtrays sat on gunmetal gray desks. Swivel chairs littered the empty room, as if the occupants had been recently evacuated. Computer monitors blinked, and ceiling fans whirled in slow circles. Anderson spoke over his shoulder. "The bureaucracy responds positively to *baksheesh*."

He led Monsarrat from the room into a hallway. "The Mukhabarat isn't fond of us, but they like our greenbacks, so they make sure the security cameras go down, the computers go offline, and everyone takes a cigarette break at the same time."

"There's no record of our arrival and departure?"

"We're blacker than the devil's soul."

A crash door opened to the tarmac. Across the apron, a Gulfstream 200 sheltered beneath an open ended desert camouflage tarp with hanging sides. Black paint covered its skin, and black casings masked its portholes. Its twin Pratt & Whitney turbofans spooled. Monsarrat hoped Chaggai could track the plane. "Did you borrow the Gulfstream from Langley?"

"Fucked if I know," Anderson replied. "Harper arranged the

logistics, the plane, the teams, the cash to grease the right palms."

Monsarrat followed him into the cabin, retrofitted for the transportation of prisoners. Bolts secured steel benches with welded restraint loops to the floor. The interior portholes were sealed and covered. Storage bins and closets had been removed. In the rear of the cabin, the lavatory had been sealed. A wire security door with a hardened lock and escutcheon separated the cabin from the cockpit.

A third member of Enderby's team stepped forward. Four inches over six feet tall, with a pair of plastic sunglasses atop a crew cut the color of a pale carrot, he wore sandals, jeans, and a gray tee shirt that clung to his torso like an epidermal layer. "Welcome aboard, sir. I'm Nick Parilli, the pilot. Sirte is 1600 klicks distant. At 45,000 feet with a max airspeed of 900 klicks, we'll arrive in less than two hours, but the steel benches will put cramps in your ass cheeks long before we reach cruising altitude."

"Nick wants people to like him, so he paints lipstick on the pig," Anderson interrupted. "We won't come close to the bird's ceiling. We'll fly low and slow over the desert to baffle radar, and the benches won't be the only uncomfortable part of the ride. Expect turbulence the entire time over the sand."

Parilli held out his hand. "I'll stow your bag."

Enderby entered the cabin, followed by Hollinger. He greeted Monsarrat before distributing orders. "Arnie, secure the plug door. Charlie, lash open the wire door. It's just us on this flight. Nathan, the head's by the cockpit. Hit it now, if you need it."

He concluded with a final order to Parilli. "Nick, get us airborne."

Enderby led Monsarrat to the benches. The whine of the twin turbines filled the cabin, and the Gulfstream rolled down the runway.

It lifted off the tarmac, corkscrewed tightly, and accelerated hard. "Hot takeoffs are always fun, but combat landings are the real thrill."

Monsarrat sat facing the cockpit. He rubbed his finger across his forehead, but the skin remained cool and dry, free from the heat he should have felt and the sweat that should have dripped as the Gulfstream flew low into the setting sun. He rubbed the back of his head, his hand warn and moist. He experienced a sense of disorientation, as if his axis had been inverted.

He assessed his situation, Parilli and Anderson in the cockpit, Hollinger and Enderby flanking him on the benches. His chances of killing four special operators were less than zero, and if he did eliminate them, his knowledge of landing the Gulfstream consisted of buckling his belt. "My last trip in a Gulfstream, a steward served drinks and canapés."

Enderby noted his tensed muscles. "I told her you were too smart to ignore the sun on your back, not on your face, flying east not west, but she told me to shut up and follow orders."

"Who did you tell?"

"The woman who hired me."

Monsarrat gripped the bench as turbulence bounced the plane. "Hired you for what?"

"You've always been smart, Nathan. Don't stop now."

"What's her name?"

"I don't know," Enderby admitted, "but the bitch sure as shit hates your sorry ass."

"Did she tell you why?"

"I'm just the hired help. She wasn't keen on sharing personal information with me."

Monsarrat knew only one woman, Abby Houghton, who harbored emotions so strong that she would hire mercenaries to kidnap him, but he suspected that her lover, Felix Sanhedrin, jerked her strings. "How much did she pay you to sell me out?"

"You don't need to worry about my profit margins."

"Tell me our destination. She must have shared that info with you."

"Our destination is a decommissioned Agency rendition site in the Sinai, three hundred-plus klicks from Cairo, a place the locals call the Valley of the Moon."

"It's more like the dark side of the moon," Hollinger offered. "The Mukhabarat won't approach. Even the Bedouin stay away. They say the souls of tortured jihadis haunt the place."

Monsarrat experienced a trickle of hope. The Valley of the Moon was close to the northern border of the Sinai. If he escaped the rendition site, he could cross into Israel. "I've always wanted to visit the Sinai, go to St. Catherine Monastery, follow in the footsteps of Moses to the summit of the mountain."

"Good to know you still have your sense of humor."

Monsarrat held back Chaggai's intel. "What was the promise you made? To kill Bin Nafe so the souls of your dead friends can find peace? You plan to get it for them in the Sinai?"

"The dead are patient. They'll wait a while longer."

"What about my friend's parents? She doesn't deserve to lose them, so you can earn a few bucks."

"It's more than a few bucks, and we both know that war is messy."

"So is treachery."

From the cockpit, Parilli yelled, "Starting approach. Prepare for a hard desert landing."

Enderby spoke to Hollinger as turbulence again rocked the plane. "Buckle up our guest, Arnie."

"You don't need restraints. I'm a go along, get along kinda guy," Monsarrat promised.

The Ranger passed a Desert Eagle to Enderby, removed two sets of shackles from a backpack, and secured Monsarrat's ankles and wrists to steel loops. "He ain't going nowhere, boss."

Flying low over the desert, Parilli put the Gulfstream through a series of evasive maneuvers before leveling the plane. He touched down on a concrete runway laced with drifting sand. The wheels slipped, and the plane slid but remained upright. At the end of the runway, he maneuvered the Gulfstream into a tight turn, positioning the plane for a quick takeoff.

The plug door opened, and a rush of heated air filled the cabin. Hollinger waved a Sig Sauer P226. "It's just a nine millimeter, Nathan, but at this distance I can tap my initials into your forehead."

Unlocking the shackles, Enderby called to Anderson. "Tuna, grab Nathan's bag. Eyes sharp and move fast. The neighborhood is hot."

With the setting of the sun, the desert temperatures dipped. Cirrus clouds floated in the darkening sky, and a dry wind from the south carried grit. The ticking of the engines violated the quiet. Hollinger prodded Monsarrat toward concrete perimeter walls stained the color of the sand. A wooden beam gate as substantial as a drawbridge controlled access to the interior. "Metal security gates warp in the heat," he explained. "Wood dries and cracks but is easier to replace."

Enderby swung the heavy gate open, revealing a grid of solar panels and a windowless concrete building in the center of a square dirt compound. He introduced Monsarrat to three men cradling M-4 rifles. "The Nordic chap on the left is Jake Edberg. The Korean gentleman in the center in Pete Lee, and the black Adonis on the right is Derek Williams. Each is a special operator, and each is a very hard case. I suggest that you do not test them."

Monsarrat radiated a confidence he didn't feel. "You boys feel like grabbing a beer? Fly outta here to Cairo? I'm buying."

Lee ignored him to brief Enderby. "The command center is good to go. Solar batteries are charged and sat comms are live. I rerouted the protocols of our link into the Agency, so our signature appears to be connecting from a remote site in Virginia, but we need to get away from the eyes in the sky. The Egyptians, the Israelis, even the sand jockeys fly drones over the area."

"Secure our guest in the interrogation room, Pete. Treat him with dignity. Don't go Gitmo on his ass until I say so," Enderby instructed. "Nick, grab commo gear, ammo, whatever supplies you need for the plane. Arnie, Jake, same for first shift on perimeter detail. Derek, help Nick set up the netting to cover the plane. Tuna, you're on me."

Escorted by Lee across the compound, Monsarrat asked, "Who built the site?"

"The Egyptians, after the 1956 debacle. The Israelis expanded it when they controlled the Sinai. The Agency requisitioned it after 9/11, when the rendition program ramped up."

"Sounds like a prime R&R destination."

"Hollinger says that ghosts come out at night. I don't doubt him, but dead spooks don't worry me. The living ones, though? They scare the piss outta me."

"Which living spooks?"

"The Mossad," Lee replied. "The locals believe that the Israelis will come over the border one night, kill everyone inside the walls, and reclaim the site."

"Do the locals say when the Israelis will come?"

"On a moonless night when the demons rise from their graves, the Israelis will hide among them."

Monsarrat hoped Chaggai would soon fulfill the prophecy. "One thing I learned, Pete? Always listen to the locals."

An Isolated Pawn Offers an Ideal Targets

The interior of the windowless concrete building offered the comfort of a cardboard box. Battery lanterns cast pools of light. The bare walls bore the scars of firefights lost, and holes in the ceiling marked lights detached. The cover of a gutted electrical panel hung from a hinge. Plastic buckets littered the floor, and screw eyes rose from the concrete. In the center of the room, seam tape secured Mylar blankets to the floor, an array of laptops, communication equipment, and batteries in chargers spread across the silver surfaces. Wires snaked through the door to solar panels in the compound.

Enderby turned to Anderson. "Tuna, let me know if we pick up a blip, no matter how small, land and sky. I don't care if it's a rabbit dropping and plopping behind a sand dune We check everything."

He plucked a sat phone from its charger and stepped into the compound. The call lasted only minutes but pressed a scowl onto his face. Returning to the building, he replaced the sat phone, picked up the overnight bag, and walked into the interrogation room. A single lantern provided illumination. Beneath the steady gaze of Lee, Monsarrat sat in the far corner, stripped of his watch, belt, jacket, and shoes, his eyes closed but muscles taut, like a predator pretending to sleep. A thick padlock hasped to an eye screw secured his shackled wrists and ankles.

Enderby ordered Lee from the room. Sitting across from his prisoner, he opened the bag and sifted through its contents. "My employer truly is a bitch."

"Tell me about it. I once asked her to marry me."

"She turned you down?"

"She betrayed me."

"If she's done with you, why the intense emotions?"

"She thinks I tried to kill her new boyfriend."

"No wonder she hates you," Enderby commiserated as he tossed aside the bag. "The good news is that she arrives soon, so you can try to reason with her. The bad news is that she's going to kill you, no matter what you say."

Monsarrat prayed Chaggai would arrive sooner. "We can make our own arrangement, Harper. I'll double the money she promised you."

"Don't take it personally, Nathan, but I have to honor my contract. If my reputation dives into the shitter, no will hire me again."

"No one hires a dead man, Harper," Monsarrat insisted. "I'm not the only one she'll execute. She'll kill you and your team."

"Do you truly believe a woman can take us down? Even if she brings shooters, they won't be better than my boys, and we'll see them approaching."

Monsarrat pitied Enderby's innocence. The former special operator had never been on the receiving end of a Felix Sanhedrin *coup d'état.* "Your employer is a front for her boyfriend. He's better than you and your boys, and he's allergic to loose ends."

"I'll try to remember."

"How much is he paying you, Harper?"

"Are you confused, Nathan? My employer is a woman."

"She's only your first contract. I'm talking about your second contract with the man who approached you after you accepted the deal with the woman."

"You think I took contracts from two clients to kill you?"

Monsarrat saw surprise flicker in the cold eyes of his captor. "Your first contract is with Abby Houghton. She's paying you to kill me."

"I don't know the name."

"You know it," Monsarrat scolded. "She's the Special Assistant to Augustus Haverhill, and you learned it from the man who gave you the second contract."

"You're more entertaining than the paperback I brought," Enderby admitted. "Who's my second target? Who purchased that contract?"

Monsarrat shook the restraints. "I talk better without shackles."

"Info first, Nathan. We'll discuss your freedom later."

"Your second target is the woman who hired you to kill me."

"Go on. You have my attention."

"The man who purchased the second contract will snuff you and your boys as soon as you provide proof of her death. He's the nastiest piece of work I know. He'll waste you like he's erasing chalk lines from a blackboard."

Enderby settled against the wall. "We aren't chalk lines."

"Maybe the Mukhabarat, or the Bedouins, or the local al-Qaeda or Da'ish terrorists will pull the trigger," Monsarrat continued. "Maybe it'll be a Libyan. The guy loves irony."

"You seem well informed, Nathan. How do you know so much about my supposed second employer?"

The tacit admission increased Monsarrat's confidence. "He's Abby Houghton's new boyfriend."

Enderby clapped his hands in a slow cadence. In his Tidewater drawl, he said, "Good on you, Nathan. I do not know whether to shit or go blind, I am so enthralled. Tell me his name?"

"Felix Sanhedrin, the former National Security Adviser."

"Just so I'm clear, Nathan, is it Sanhedrin who'll kill me or his malevolent ghost?"

"He's not dead. He survived the hit in Georgetown."

"Bless me, you are a delight," Enderby claimed. "Tell me, why would the resurrected Sanhedrin hire me to kill his girlfriend?"

"She's like you. She's a loose end. She knows too much."

Enderby stood and brushed the dirt from his trousers. "I've enjoyed our chat, Nathan, but I need to change into clothes more suitable for the desert. You need to work on your script."

"If not the Mukhabarat, the Bedouins, or the locals, Sanhedrin could send a Russian *Ohotnik* drone armed with high explosive missiles from Hmeimim airbase in Syria," Monsarrat continued.

"You score high on shock and awe but fail badly on realism. How could he order a Russian drone attack against a CIA rendition site on sovereign Egyptian territory?"

"I'm saving the best for last," Monsarrat answered, rattling the shackles. "The knowledge is worth much more money than both your contracts combined. It'll make you rich. Get us outta here before the woman arrives. Once we're home, you can sell my intel and retire."

"Not going to happen."

"Sanhedrin set you up, Harper. You're not freelancing an assassin for hire gig. You're working for the Russians. You want that as your legacy? From Special Forces to Moscow Centre?"

He deepened his Tidewater drawl. "Lord, if that story is not one steaming bucket of shit."

Watching Enderby walk from the room, Monsarrat whispered a mantra, Chaggai Will Come. Because he promised to watch my back. Because Abby will kill me. Because Sanhedrin will win. Chaggai Will

Come. He repeated the words until Enderby reappeared, carrying two pouches and a bottle of water.

"I know how Sanhedrin operates, Harper," he offered. "He was my boss at Langley. Unlock the shackles, get us home, and I'll help you kill him. You'll never have to worry about him."

"Pay attention, Nathan," Enderby said, opening the water and placing it into the floor. "It's potable, from a supermarket in Virginia. The MREs come courtesy of Uncle Sam. You prefer Menu Number 17, beef teriyaki, or Menu Number 12, bean and rice burrito?"

"We'll go to the White House and brief Haverhill. He'll pin medals on us," Monsarrat continued, ignoring the food.

"You'd do that for me? Put in a good word with the president?" Enderby asked. "Screw the medal, though. I want my star, so I can add brigadier general to my business card."

Monsarrat held out the shackles. "Live like a hero, Harper. Don't die as a traitor."

"What about the parents of your friend? Don't you want to fly to Libya and save them?"

He remembered the message from Chaggai. "It's a bitch of a decision, but there's only time for one op, and I'd rather take down Sanhedrin and Houghton than rescue a pair of retired diplomats."

Enderby stood and dropped the MREs onto the floor. "If you'd like my opinion, Nathan, I prefer Number 17."

Monsarrat watched him leave the room. The temperature fell further, and the interrogation room turned frigid. Shivering, he yelled, "Harper! Bring me a blanket!"

Enderby reappeared and tossed him a Mylar blanket. Before leaving the room, he asked, "Anything else?"

"Unlock the shackles."

Monsarrat waited until he judged ten minutes passed and yelled a second demand. "Harper! Take me to the bathroom!"

He yelled until Enderby reentered the room, carrying a bucket and a roll of toilet paper. "Take the shackles off."

Enderby dropped the paper into the bucket and slid it along the floor. "You should have eaten the MRE. It would have stopped you shitting faster than a rubber plug up your ass."

"Unzip me, take it out, and hold it while I piss."

He waited until the former special operator departed, shook the toilet paper from the bucket, contorted his body, and urinated into it. He issued a new demand. "Harper! Empty the bucket!"

He yelled until Enderby again returned to the room. "Empty the bucket, bring it back, and wipe my ass. I crapped my pants. You don't want me covered in shit when Houghton arrives."

Enderby flashed his annoyance. "Why the fuck should I care what she thinks if I'm going to kill her?"

Monsarrat claimed his anger as a victory. "Short term planning will always come back to bite you, Harper."

A Single Move in the Endgame May Cause or Avert Defeat

Monsarrat slept fitfully, dreams of rescue paired with nightmares of execution. Inside the windowless room, the lantern was dark, but he felt the morning heat radiate through the walls. The aroma of brewing coffee drifted toward him. He heard Enderby issue orders as the team prepared their assignments. He found the bottle, swished water in his mouth, and spat it onto the floor. "Harper! I need to piss Hurry up!!"

Entering the room, Enderby placed the bucket onto the floor. "Sleep well, Nathan?"

"The mattress sucked, and I prefer a room with a view."

"You must have done well in your SERE training."

"Top of my class. What about you, Harper? Did you flunk the Code of Conduct test?"

"Truly, I do like you, Nathan," Enderby laughed, "but you know the saying, today's the first day of the rest of your life? It doesn't apply to you. In truth, today's the last day of your life, so enjoy it."

"I have advice for you, too, Harper. You want me to hit the bucket, charge the lantern."

Enderby dropped an orange chem stick onto the floor, the intense light painting the room in a day-glo pastel. He retrieved the lantern and said, "It's a five minute burn."

Monsarrat finished with the bucket. When the orange light faded, he issued new demands. "Harper! Empty the bucket and bring me a cuppa coffee! Black, no cream, no sugar."

He continued to yell until Anderson, wearing desert fatigues and

carrying an MRE coffee bag inside a cardboard carton, stepped into
the room. He tossed a second orange chem stick onto the floor.
"You're a pain in my ass."

Monsarrat noted the sunglasses hanging from the neck of the
Ranger's tee shirt. "Your problem, Tuna, is that you have to deliver
me whole, no cuts, no contusions. I even have to smell nice. You're
not gonna touch me, so stop stalling, gimme the coffee, and empty
my piss from the bucket."

He lunged forward as Anderson lowered the carton to the floor,
grabbing the Ranger' ankle with his left hand. He pressed his right
forearm against his knee until it buckled, collapsing him onto the
concrete floor. The hot liquid scalded him, but he yanked Anderson's
lower lip downward and smashed his exposed teeth with the heel of
his palm. He gouged Anderson's eyes, feeling a grim satisfaction as
his victim screamed in pain.

He pulled the sunglasses from Anderson's tee shirt, snapped the
stem from the frame, shook out the pin, and placed it at the bottom of
his gums. He saw Enderby run into the room, press his fingertips
against the Ranger's jugular, and swing the Desert Eagle in a slow arc.
He felt the butt crash into his forehead. His vision blurred, he
watched Lee and Williams enter the room, lift Anderson, and carry
him away. He recognized the voice of Enderby but couldn't
understand the words. His skull burned, the room spun violently, and
he vomited onto the floor. He reached for the water bottle, rinsed his
mouth. His tongue brushed the pin.

His voice slurred, he said, "I'm concussed."

Enderby viewed him with disgust. "You look like a squashed
eggplant. Your girlfriend will be upset, but fuck her. I'm calling an

audible. She walks in the door, I whack her, I whack you, send proofs of death to my second employer, and go wheels up."

Despite his pain, Monsarrat lisped, "Forget their names already?"

Watching Enderby retreat from the room, he probed his gums, squeezing the pin between his index finger and thumb. In the fading light of the chem stick, he bent toward the screw eye. Pain shot through his head. The stench of vomit hijacked his will. In the dark, he worked the padlock with the pin.

He stopped at the sound of footfalls. Enderby tossed a third chem stick into the room. "You don't take orders, Nathan. You don't follow advice. I suppose I'll just have to kill you."

Anderson, his mouth bloody and eyes reddened, entered the room. He carried a bucket, a strip of cardboard, an entrenching tool, a fresh bottle of water, and a washcloth. Watching him clean the mess, Monsarrat offered slurred encouragement. "Good job, Tuna."

Anderson swung the tool like a driver, striking Monsarrat on the side of his head with the flat of the blade. "You already looked like shit, so now you're just a bit worse."

Enderby ripped the entrenching tool from the Ranger's hand. "Get rid of the puke. Clean yourself up. You look almost as bad as him."

Monsarrat spat blood. "You need better help, Harper."

Enderby opened the bottle of water and passed it and the washcloth to Monsarrat. "No man should die covered in his own vomit."

Alone in the room, the light of the chem stick fading, Monsarrat searched the floor for the pin, dropped when struck by the entrenching tool, but failed to locate it. He rinsed his mouth, spat the water onto the floor, and wiped his face with the cloth. He leaned against the warm wall, his head throbbing, and slept. He awoke to the slamming of a car door. Beneath bis fingers, the wall felt cool, and he guessed that the sun had set.

He whispered his mantra, Chaggai Will Come, as a single set of light footsteps preceded the arrival of Abby Houghton. Graced by neither makeup nor jewelry, she carried a sat phone in her right hand and a lantern in her left hand. She wore a slouch hat, a cotton shirt, cargo pants, and desert boots, but neither her attire nor the Beretta M9 in a holster strapped to her right thigh dampened her radiance.

Despite their history, he experienced a familiar tremor of pleasure. "Hello, Abby."

"Live long enough, you see everything, even Nathan Monsarrat in shackles," she taunted. "You look terrible, and you smell horrible."

"Have you come to beg me to take you back?"

"I'm glad you've kept your sense of humor, but I need a minute."

She placed the lantern on the floor, unlocked the sat phone, and tapped the screen. The call failed to connect. She glared at Monsarrat, as if he had fouled the device. "What happened to my signal?"

He pitied her. She wanted so badly to be the toughest person in the room, but her instincts were hopeless and her training illusory. "If you go outside, you'll have line of sight. Enter the international code, the three digit prefix, and the number of the phone you're calling."

"Line of sight to what?" she demanded.

"To the satellite," he explained. "Also, Enderby must have seen the phone in your shooting hand and the lantern in your left hand. Don't make the same mistake. Put the phone in a pocket, undo the holster strap, and switch off the safety on the M9. Leave the lantern, too."

He added a final piece of advice. "Turn around your vehicle, so you can depart fast."

Before leaving the room, she snapped, "You've always thought you're smarter than me, but you're the one shackled to the floor, and I'm the one with the Beretta."

He counted seven minutes before she returned. "Did you connect?"

"I sent Felix my arrival text."

He welcomed the confirmation of his suspicions. "If Felix is alive, who was cremated in his place?"

"His body double. Felix used him for years."

He remembered Westbrook's file. "What was his name?"

"I don't know," she replied. "I never met him. Felix never told anyone except me that he existed."

"Having a doppelgänger must have made his treason easier."

"I came to kill you, Nathan, not chat with you. I need to get back to the White House, so stop wasting my time."

Monsarrat pointed at the Beretta. "Can you do it, Abby? Shoot me, see my blood, live with the knowledge that you ended my life?"

"With as much emotion as flushing a toilet."

He had taught her to shoot and knew she could place a round through the heart of a paper target, but firing a bullet into a living person was a different game. "How many mags do you have?"

"I only need two bullets, the first to kill you and the second to make sure you stay dead."

"I'm wondering about your plan to take out Enderby before he double taps you with his own two bullets."

She pulled the M9 from its holster. "You have ten seconds to pray."

He hoped that Chaggai arrived before she tired of his voice. "Enderby accepted a second contract to kill you from a man who didn't offer a name, just as you hired him anonymously. He doesn't care about your final payment, since that money was factored into his second payment. He'll send proof of our deaths and receive his cash."

"No one knew I hired Enderby, and no one knew I'd be in the Sinai. There's no second contract."

"Not no one, Abby. Felix told you to hire Enderby, and he sent you to kill me," he replied. "He gave Enderby the second contract, to kill you after you kill me. No loose ends. Pure Sanhedrin."

"If you're right, Enderby is also a loose end. Who kills him?"

Once, he had loved her innocence. "Felix kills him and his team."

She dismissed his claims. "Felix loves me."

"Felix loves Felix. Everyone else is just a dalliance."

"He would never hurt me."

"Probably not," Monsarrat admitted, "but he will kill you."

She pointed the barrel of the M9 at his chest. "You think Felix followed me here to kill me?"

"Pay attention to my words, Abby. Felix sent you to kill me, he hired Enderby to kill you, and he bought a third contract, maybe someone local, maybe something more dependable, like a cruise missile, to kill Enderby."

"Felix loves me," she insisted. "He loves me so much, he agreed to allow me to kill you, even though he wanted to pull the trigger himself. He knows how badly I want to end your life."

"He sent you here to die."

"He sent me here to get rid of you in a place where your corpse would never be discovered, but before I do it, I want you to know that right now Felix is in Greylock to kill your girlfriend."

He wanted to believe that she lied but knew in his heart that he had made a fatal mistake, not wanting to further frighten Sylvie, already fraught after the conversation with her father, with a warning for her own safety. He blamed himself for withholding the danger from her, for not protecting her. In his desire to shield her, he condemned her.

His soul passed into darkness, replaced by a brutal strength. "Felix never forgave you for loving me."

"I never loved you. I only fucked you," she taunted, "and you'll never have the chance to mourn Sylvie, because you're going to die here, in the Sinai."

He encouraged her cruelty, a small cost to buy more time for Chaggai to arrive. "Who else does Felix plan to kill?"

"The parents of your girlfriend are already dead. Felix paid someone to behead them," she said.

Prepared by Chaggai, her announcement failed to surprise him. "The Libyan, Bin Nafe. I heard him on the sat phone call."

She continued, "On his way home from Greylock, Felix will stop in Manhattan to eliminate your Jewish friends."

He trusted Goldman and Shackowitz to protect Grinnell. "Good luck to him"

"I'm all the luck Felix needs," she declared. "I love him, and he loves me. He's my husband. We married last year."

Monsarrat hid his surprise. "Was your first anniversary gift a wood coffin instead of a paper box?"

"You're the only one dying here, Nathan."

His anger was primal. "You and me, we're going to spend eternity together, Abby. Enderby and his team, too. You shoot me, Enderby kills you, and Felix buries all of us beneath a sand dune."

She responded with her own measured fury. "My only regret is not killing your girlfriend myself, but Felix promised to film her death for me, so I can watch her die over and over again. When I'm finally bored, I'll upload it to the internet with a catchy title so the rest of the world can laugh at you. Strong, tough, handsome Nathan Monsarrat, who couldn't keep his girlfriend alive."

"It's a video you'll never watch."

"Why not? You think I'm too squeamish?"

He flung his words at her. "I think Felix is the devil and you sold your soul to him. When he comes to collect, right after you shoot me, he's going to bury you so far beneath a sand dune, you'll spend eternity trying to connect to the internet."

In Trebuchet, the Sacrifice of a Pawn Saves a More Valuable Piece

Monsarrat experienced the slow strangulation of hope. His former lover was a cat tiring of tormenting a mouse. He watched her finger stroke the trigger of the Beretta. "Shoot me outside, Abby, so I can see the sky before I die."

"I'm not a DJ, Nathan. I don't take requests."

Desperate to buy time, he yelled, "Harper! Get in here!"

Watching Enderby step into the room, he felt a surge of hope. "Tell her that Sanhedrin hired you to kill her. Tell her how much he paid you. She needs know her husband betrayed her with pocket change."

Enderby exuded innocence. "I don't understand."

"All my money, everything I own, it's yours. Tell her about Sanhedrin and shoot her in the head."

"I never though I'd see you beg. Academia made you soft."

Monsarrat hurled pleas to fix the attention of his captors as three figures garbed in black glided across the main room. Each held a Heckler & Koch MP5K in gloved hands. The suppressed weapons fired silently. Anderson and Lee pirouetted like dancers before collapsing. The lead assassin entered the room, killing Enderby with a single bullet into his neck. Two shots, one into his chest, the other into his eye, completed the signature triple tap of a Mossad assassin.

"Don't kill her, Amos! I need her to talk!"

Blood erupted from Houghton's right thigh, and the Beretta fell from her hand. The assassin kicked it beyond her reach. He removed his balaclava and spoke a rapid Hebrew to his companions. "Move quickly. Apply a hemostatic pressure dressing and bandage her. Bag the intel from the bodies, plus the laptops, tablets, and commo gear. You have five minutes. Leave no calling cards. We were never here."

Amos Chaggai turned to Monsarrat and said, in his accented English, "*Shalom*, my friend. It is good to see you alive."

"I'm happy to be alive."

"I count seven dead, one wounded. Are there others?"

"You took them all."

In his mid-thirties, two inches shorter than Monsarrat, Chaggai bore the compact physique of a gymnast. His skin was tanned, his muscles granite, his hair black with flecks of silver. He clasped Monsarrat by the neck, a sign of affection. "Your instincts are sharp, my friend, although you have looked better. Did your hosts offer you the wrong sort of Middle Eastern hospitality?"

"I feel better than him," Monsarrat said, gesturing at Enderby. "The key is in his pocket."

Chaggai unlocked the padlock. "We must fast march to our rendezvous. The helicopter pilot is a very impatient man. We are on top of the clock."

Monsarrat rubbed his wrists and ankles. He slowly stood, his smile large. "On the clock."

Chaggai accepted the correction. "Can you walk?"

"I'm good, but how did you find me?"

"My former Mossad colleagues in Jerusalem coordinated with the Mukhabarat in Cairo to obtain the intelligence we needed. My Jerusalem friends also provided the equipment for the mission."

"The other two are Mossad?"

"Like me, they are retired assassins, but you understand why I will not introduce them," Chaggai said. "Tell me. Who is the woman?"

Monsarrat provided a brief explanation. "She's the wife of Felix Sanhedrin. She works for Augustus Haverhill. She sent an arrival message to Sanhedrin. He'll expect a departure message. If he doesn't send it, he'll know the mission failed. If he receives it, he'll think I'm dead. I'll have a head start to find him."

"I thought Sanhedrin died in Georgetown?"

"If only it was true."

"If Sanhedrin trained her, she will send a wrong word code, if she is under duress," Chaggai noted.

"It's why I have to interrogate her."

An assassin finished bandaging to her thigh. "The wound is clean, no visible bone or muscle damage. She's unconscious, but I can administer morphine."

"No drugs," Monsarrat stated. "I need her focused."

The floor swayed as he crossed the room. He took the sat phone from her pocket and slapped her hard across her face. "Wake up, Abby. I want the password and the departure message for Felix."

She pawed at his eyes, but shock weakened her, and blood loss exhausted her. "He'll kill you."

He slapped her harder. "Tell me, and I'll stop the pain."

Like a recording, she repeated, "He'll kill you."

He banished memories. She was his enemy, not the woman he once loved. Selecting the middle finger on her left hand, he bent it backward until the knuckle snapped. Above her screams, he demanded, "Tell me the password and the departure message."

"Go fuck yourself, in upper case letters," she sobbed.

He snapped two additional fingers before receiving the information. Turning to Chaggai, he said, "We need space between us and the compound. Is your team ready to leave?"

The Israeli nodded."I suggest you wear clothes from a dead man."

Monsarrat stripped, checked the clothes for identification, and dropped them onto the floor. Hollinger's outfit fit him like castoffs from an older brother. He gathered his Sig Sauer P226, M-4, and a five inch boot dagger in a leather sheath. He transferred the Sanger identity from the overnight bag to his pockets before hauling Houghton upright. "We're moving."

The Israeli examined her. "She is not strong enough. End her life."

"I can't kill her."

"Then I will do it for you."

"You don't understand," Monsarrat insisted. "I can shoot her in the heart, but first I have to extract the intel she holds in her head."

Supporting her, he followed Chaggai and his two companions from the building. Beneath a brilliant firmament of stars, he counted four corpses in the compound and outside the walls. He noted the late model Range Rover next to the beam gate. Beyond the Gulfstream on the landing strip rose a ridge of squat dunes. He dragged Houghton to the crest and dropped her on the other side.

Chaggai motioned for his colleagues to halt. "Why do we stop?"

"It's time to send the departure message."

He activated the phone, typed the words, and sent the message to the last number called. "Five minutes. If nothing happens, we go."

"If we miss the rendezvous, we must cross into Israel on foot, but the *mechablim*, the terrorists, prowl the Sinai."

The tearing of the sky smothered Monsarrat's reply. He cradled Abby's head as the first high explosive missile slammed into the center of the compound, pulverizing the buildings. A second missile followed, exploding the fuel tanks of the Range Rover and Gulfstream. Twin fireballs rose from the desert like the destruction of Sodom and Gomorrah.

Monsarrat pressed his face close to her. "The missiles weren't for me. Felix launched them to kill you, Enderby, and his team."

"You're lying," she insisted. "Your friends launched the missiles."

Chaggai interrupted him. "We must leave now, Nathan, before unwanted guests arrive."

"I need to ask her questions. She knows the location of Sanhedrin."

Chaggai spoke again to his colleagues. "Leave now for the rendezvous. Return to Israel. Do not wait for us."

He led Monsarrat away from Houghton. "Only we will enter Israel. Not the woman. I will kill her, if you are not able."

"Once I have her intel, I have no reason to keep her alive."

"Less than two klicks distant, there is a cave in the cliffs above the wadi. You can question her and leave her body there."

Monsarrat disagreed. "I do it now, while she's in shock, and I do it here. I want her body found."

Chaggai surrendered. "You are stubborn like an Israeli."

"Flattery from the master," Monsarrat replied

Advanced Pawn Placement May Offer a Pyrrhic Advantage

Despite the betrayals of Houghton, Monsarrat pitied her, puffing on her broken fingers, stroking the bandage on her thigh, wiping sweat from her face. He doubted she possessed the strength to withstand torture, just as he was unsure that he maintained the will to apply it. "Abby, help yourself. Tell me where I can find Felix."

She spat into the sand. "I have five fingers, two thumbs, ten toes, and dozens of bones. Which will you break next?"

"I don't want to hurt you, Abby."

"Too late, asshole."

"I just want you to tell me the location of Felix."

"Fuck off."

He broke a fourth finger and waited for her sobs to subside. "Where is he?"

"Break them all, Nathan! Break everything!"

He had not expected the strength of her resistance. "Why the loyalty, Abby? He tried to kill you."

Chaggai again led him away from Houghton. "I suggest we use a lollipop. In five minutes, she will tell everything she knows. Are you familiar with it?"

An eight hundred microgram lozenge of fentanyl secured to the end of a plastic stick, placed beneath the tongue, the lollipop provided relief for traumatic battlefield injuries. A gentle loquacity was a side effect. "I've never used it."

"Give her too much of the drug, she will undergo respiratory shock. Give her too little, the fentanyl is as useless as candy. Even if you administer the exact dose, extracting her intelligence will depend upon your skills as an interrogator. If you make her angry, you will lose her cooperation."

"You've administered the fentanyl?"

"I have experience."

Opening the first aid kit, Chaggai kneeled next to Houghton. He placed a foam and steel field splint over her broken fingers, wrapping it with surgical tape. "The breaks are clean. They will knit."

He examined her wounded thigh. "The damage appears minimal, but you will need a doctor."

"You're his friend. Why are you helping me?"

As a young man, before joining the special operations unit of the Israeli Defense Forces, and later Mossad, Chaggai had studied for the rabbinate. Knowing her life would soon end, he sought to comfort her, offering the words of Nahum Gam Zu from the Talmud. "This too is for the good."

He removed the lollipop from its sterile package. "Place this lozenge beneath your tongue."

He held her hand until her eyes glazed. Removing the lollipop, he waved for Monsarrat to join him. "Do not upset her. If she feels threatened, she will withdraw, and you will lose her cooperation."

Monsarrat kneeled next to her. "I'm sorry I hurt you, Abby."

"Your friend shot me," she replied, "and you broke my fingers."

He cradled her bandaged hand. "I'd like to take away your pain."

"You need to be like Felix, think less about them, more about you."

"I should speak with him," he agreed. "Is he in Georgetown?"

"Oh, no, not the townhouse," she replied in a singsong cadence. "He can't live there, even with his surgery. He can't risk anyone knowing he's alive. We moved to Fermanagh House in Ashby Gap."

He noted the information. "Why did Felix have surgery?"

"He changed his appearance," she replied. "New body. New face. New house. New name. François Salamanca. Sexy, isn't it?"

He tried to connect Sanhedrin the American traitor to Sanhedrin the Russian asset. "Was if difficult for Felix to pass his intelligence to the *Rezidentura*?"

"You discovered his secret," she complimented. "Selling intel to the Russians made Felix rich."

"Tell me everything, just between us. No one will ever know."

Her words defined the limitations of her knowledge. "Moscow Centre provided Felix a code name, Pavlik, and a handler, Cairstine Fergusson. She lives on Dumbarton Street in Georgetown. Her cover is the owner of an antiquities gallery. She came to the manor. She's dishy. Felix is jealous of her. I fucked her. Does that shock you? I'm a killer who goes both ways? I'm spying on Haverhill, too. Are you shocked again, Nathan?"

"You're the best, Abby," he replied, "but Moscow Centre must be upset with Felix, enjoying the Virginia horse country but not providing intel from the White House."

"They think he's dead," she explained patiently. "Don't forget the body double Felix used."

Instincts again spurred his questions. "Was the body double Russian? Did Russian doctors and dentists treat him?"

"I know nothing about the body double," she repeated. "I only know that Felix spied for the Russians, but his doctor and dentist worked in Georgetown."

He stroked her hair. "Not Felix. His body double."

"I told you. I don't know anything about him," she insisted. "Felix never told the Russians about him, either. He didn't want them to interfere. He said they were a sewing circle of old ladies."

A flash of insight, like a heavenly ray of light, prompted his question. "Abby, you can tell me. Is Felix a Russian?"

"Pay attention, Nathan," she chided. "The Russians paid Felix to work for them, just like they're going to pay me. Why do you keep asking about Felix? Why don't you ask questions about me?"

He saw Chaggai shake his head in warning. "Okay, Abby, I will. Tell me. Are you part of Felix's network?"

"Felix didn't need a network. He was the National Security Adviser," she replied. "He worked alone, just like me. I already passed a transcript of Haverhill's conversation with the Chinese premier to Cairstine, just before I fucked her, but I'm not giving away the intel. The Russians will pay for it."

"You've come far, Abby," he agreed. "Tell me about your new friend, Cairstine."

"She has a butler, Rupert Marlowe, who reports on her to Anton Maximovich Dovlatov. He's the top Russian spy in their embassy. His title is *Rezident*. In fact, all three of them are Russian assassins."

"Do you have cell phone numbers for them?"

She provided the information for Fergusson. "I only know hers."

"Did Felix use the Russians to kill Westbrook, Zeigarnik, and Datura? Or did he do it himself?"

"I don't know any of those people."

"I guess Felix didn't tell you about them."

"He tells me everything," she said, "but he never mentioned them."

He believed Sanhedrin kept a separate life from her, but he

continued to ask his slow questions. "Did Felix send the Russians to kill me in Manhattan?"

The question confused her. "He wants you to die in the Sinai."

"What are his plans, after he kills my friends?"

"He has to return home right away to take of Robespierre," she replied, her voice drifting.

"Is Robespierre your son?"

"He's our puppy," she said, her face tilted. "Look at the sky, Nathan. The stars are popping."

Despite her betrayals, the thought of ending her life saddened him. He drew the dagger, dropped the sheath onto the sand, and tested the sharpness of its blade. Listening to her slow breathing, he turned her head gently, exposing her throat. He pressed the tip of the blade against her carotid artery, placed the palm of his hand against the pommel, and pressed the sharpened point into her flesh. As her warm blood surged, she opened her mouth but spoke no words. She raised her hands but lacked the strength to push him away. Her body thrashed for a moment before she sank into the sand, the dagger protruding from her throat.

He gazed at her, feeling affection, pity, and disgust. "You should have left me alone, Abby."

Chaggai gestured toward the dead woman. "The knife, Nathan?"

Monsarrat cleaned his hands with sand before releasing the safeties on the Sig Sauer and the M-4. "Leave it. I don't want to deal with the mess, if I pull it out."

A trek across hard shale led to the serpentine path of the wadi. Chaggai pointed to the ridge line. "A goat track follows the crest, but the shale is loose, the footing is dangerous, and the progress is slow.

Also, the sun sets quickly in the desert, and in the dark, in your physical condition, I suspect you will break your neck."

"Do we have options?"

"We continue on the floor of the wadi, but we will be exposed to ambush from above."

"What do you suggest?"

Chaggai observed him carefully. "We will risk the floor."

Hiking through the wadi, sweat drenched Monsarrat, the too large clothes chafing his skin, the oversized boots rubbing his feet raw. Struggling to maintain pace, he followed the Israeli, who navigated the route as if it was a childhood shortcut, atop a rise. He accepted a pair of night vision binoculars. Holding them to his eyes, he noted a clearing seventy-five feet long and fifty feet wide in the wadi. In the midst of the open space, the two assassins flanked a Black Hawk helicopter, its rotors drooped above its fuselage.

Chaggai activated his commo gear. "Two friendlies approaching from the south."

The answer arrived immediately. "Come in."

Moments later, Chaggai chided his colleagues. "Why have you disobeyed my order?"

"We decided it was stupid, so we chose not to follow it, a perk of retirement," answered the first.

"Stop arguing," advised the second. "It's time to go home."

On benches in the hold, the four men secured their harnesses. In the cockpit, the pilot engaged the rotors, the blades roiling the desert. Nose down like an angry wasp, navigational lights darkened, the Black Hawk rose from the wadi, cleared the cliffs, and raced low over the sand. Crossing the border, the pilot switched on the lights. Above the noise of the wind and the engines, Chaggai yelled, "Welcome back to Israel, Nathan."

Beyond the ancient city of Be'er Sheva, the helicopter banked toward the Mediterranean Sea, the lights of Tel Aviv bright, and approached Ben Gurion Airport. It hovered before setting down on a helipad. Chaggai removed his weapons, collected the Sig Sauer and the M-4 from Monsarrat, and passed them to his Mossad colleagues.

The Israeli led Monsarrat from the helicopter, jogging beneath the rotors. A four-wheel drive Storm with government license plates was parked at a safe distance. Taking the driver's seat, he motioned Monsarrat next to him. He opened the center console, removed a key ring and an envelope, and started the engine before passing the envelope to Monsarrat. "From my former employers, with their appreciation. They are very particular about sharing the Sinai with uninvited guests. You have cash to buy clothes, a pass for the King David Lounge, and a First Class seat on the late night flight to Frankfurt. In Germany, their assistance ends. Also, they do not wish to know your final destination."

Monsarrat opened the envelope. "Thank them for me. They're very generous."

"Do not use your cell phone and credit cards until you are in Germany. There must be no evidence that you or any of your cover identities entered Israel. About this, they insist."

Monsarrat read the boarding pass. "My name is Yonaton Levy?"

"Do not worry. No one will ask for your passport."

Across the tarmac, an emergency exit led to the basement of Terminal Three. They stepped from the Storm, and Chaggai pushed open the door. "The alarms have been deactivated. I will escort you to your concourse. You can purchase clothes in the duty free stores."

Chaggai led Monsarrat through silent halls. At a service elevator, he inserted a second key from the ring. The doors slid open, and he punched a button. "In the King David Lounge, you can shower and change into new clothes."

"I owe you, Amos."

"A friend never owes a friend, Nathan."

Inside the departure terminal, a circular waiting lounge ringed by coffee shops and stand bars anchored the spokes of corridors bristling with boarding gates. Travelers stared at the two men, one garbed in black, and the other dragging sand encrusted military fatigues like a bridal train. "The King David Lounge is fifty feet ahead on the left. Sleeping chairs are available. Tell the staff your new name, and they will make sure you board your flight."

Monsarrat understood the message. He thanked the Israeli. "I'll be first in line at the gate."

Chaggai offered a promise. "If you need my help, I will come."

Monsarrat bought clothes, a shoulder bag to replace the one abandoned in the Sinai, sunglasses, and a black baseball cap. In the bathroom of the King David Lounge, he threw Anderson's clothes into a trash bin and used the complimentary toiletries to carefully shave and brush his teeth. After showering, he felt better but still looked like the victim of a violent mugging.

In the dining area, he ate a light meal of orange juice and toast. Despite Chaggai's warning, he called Sylvie, but her cell phone did not engage. He sent a text. Her office phone requested that he leave a message. He tapped a memorized number into the cell phone. The call connected, and he issued instructions. "Don't use names. The *farshtinkener* intends to kill you very soon. Keep your friends close and go somewhere safe until you hear from me."

Grinnell responded, drier than sand. "Where is the bad guy now?"

"I suspect he's close to you," he replied, ending the call.

He pocketed the cell phone at the approach of an airline steward. "Is the flight ready to board?"

"If you would follow me, Mr. Levy, I'll take you to the gate."

"I can find it myself."

"I understand, but I will escort you."

At the gate, the steward held out his hand. "Could I have your ticket and boarding pass?"

"Won't I need them?"

"Not at all."

A mocha skinned stewardess with a gleaming bald skull placed his bag into an overhead bin. The seat beside him remained empty. He closed his eyes. A moment later, he felt a hand squeeze his shoulder.

He fumbled for the belt. "It's already secure."

The stewardess stood over him, his bag in her elegant hand. "We've landed, Mr. Levy. If you would follow me? I'll escort you to the customer service desk."

He declined her offer. "I can find it."

"I have my orders, Mr. Levy."

He took the bag from her. "Just tell Amos that I left Frankfurt on the first available flight."

A Pawn Breakthrough Disrupts the Opposing Defense

Inside the terminal, Monsarrat stood before the departure board. He opened the Canadian cell phone to find that Sylvie had not answered his text. He again called her but received the same result as in Tel Aviv. He considered the reasons she did not answer his calls and return his messages. She lost the phone. It was broken. It had been stolen. He did not want to consider the most likely reason, that Sanhedrin had reached Greylock, and she could not answer.

He closed his phone and studied the departure board. The earliest flight, to Washington, departed seven hours prior to the first Boston and New York flights. As Mark Sanger, he approached a customer service representative. "I just arrived for meetings in Germany, but my company wants me in Washington immediately, so I need to buy a one-way ticket to Dulles on the Lufthansa flight departing in forty minutes. First class, if available."

Eight hours after leaving Frankfurt, he cleared airport formalities at Dulles and exited the terminal. After the heat of the Sinai, the early morning Virginia sunshine chilled him. His head ached, and he felt slow and thick. Despite the cap and sunglasses, his bruised face attracted attention. He reached the head of the taxi queue and provided the dispatcher with an address. Inside the taxi, he failed again to reach Sylvie but connected with Grinnell on the first ring.

"Everything okay?"

"So far, so good."

"Stay sharp," Monsarrat advised.

He paid the cabbie in Dupont Circle. He entered stores and

stopped on the sidewalk to check cell phone messages, checking for tails. He walked to the corner of New Hampshire Avenue and Riggs Place. Customers filled the tables inside Bread and Freedom, sipping coffee and tapping keyboards, Carlyle not among them. He approached the cashier, a young woman wearing overalls with pink hair, the physique of a bodybuilder, and a one word neck tattoo, Pinkie. "I'm looking for Brenda."

She frowned and removed a photograph from her overalls. Her eyes flicked between the image and Monsarrat. "Lose the sunglasses."

He did as she asked. "Is this better?"

"You win the fight?"

"Last man standing."

Turning over the picture, she said, "Two questions. First, on what street did you first met your friend?"

"Novinskiy Boulevard."

"Second, which shirt did she wear?"

His photographic memory supplied the answer. "A white University of New Hampshire sweatshirt."

The cashier returned the photograph to her overalls. "Brenda's my friend. I don't know your name, but I have your photo, and if you hurt her, I'll fuck you up even worse than you are now. I'm the third ranked MMA fighter in the city, women and men."

He suppressed a smile. "I understand."

She whispered the information. "Rosslyn, Fort Myer Drive, number 1209, apartment 3C. One long ring, then three short rings and a final long ring. Introduce yourself as the schizo guy from the book, *Crime and Punishment*. Also, pull the battery from your cell phone. Don't ask why. Just do it."

He departed Bread and Freedom. On the sidewalk, he slipped on the sunglasses and dismantled the Sanger cell phone. He walked to the Dupont Circle Metro Station, rode the escalator toward the tracks, bought a fare card from the machine, and waited for a Red Line train. The floor lights flickered, he boarded a middle car, and grasped an overhead strap until the train reached Metro Center. Crossing to the Vienna-bound platform of the Orange Line, he entered a waiting train. At the fourth stop, he stepped from the car and rode the escalator into Rosslyn Station plaza.

He followed North Moore Street to the Iwo Jima Memorial. He gained Fort Myer Drive, walked up the hill, and entered the lobby of a three story brown brick building. Apartment 3C offered an androgynous name, M. Smith. He pressed the buzzer and spoke into the intercom. "My name is Raskolnikov."

The lock clicked, and he opened the door. He climbed the stairs to the third floor. Knocking on the door of the apartment, he said, "It's the guy from Novinskiy Boulevard."

Carlyle greeted him with the muzzle of a Glock 42 centered on his chest. Scratches marred her face. She lowered the .380 pistol. With her free hand, she pulled off his sunglasses. "Nice look, Nathan. You try to kiss an orangutan?"

He stepped into the apartment, closing the door. "What happened, Brenda, and why are you hiding in Rosslyn?"

Dormitory furnishings and a jungle of plants filled the apartment. "Second question first. It belongs to a friend from the Agency. He's in Prague on a temporary assignment. I have the key, so I can water the plants while he's gone. I used it to drop off the grid until you returned from wherever you went."

"Tell me what happened to you."

"Come into the kitchen. I'm brewing coffee."

A French press, its plunger extended, and two ceramic mugs occupied a small table. She set the Glock next to it and pressed the plunger. "Pinkie told me you were coming."

The water in the press turned the color of chocolate. She sat at the table and filled the mugs with coffee. "Hungry?"

He dropped his bag onto the floor and accepted the mug. "Not food, just information, so start at the beginning."

Carlyle spoke in a rush. "Our talk in Bread and Freedom blipped my radar, so I dressed in my Baghdad business suit to see my client. I left his office at my usual time, walked down "K" Street, and passed the St. Regis. I didn't hear a sound, but I felt three slugs smash into the Kevlar vest I wore beneath my blouse. I hit the sidewalk with my face, but I was lucky. The shooter was lazy. A bullet to the back of the head would have finished me."

"What do you know about the shooter?"

"Absolutely nothing."

"What did you tell the cops?"

"I didn't talk to them. It took a while to get off the sidewalk but I heard sirens and knew I had to move. The good news is that it was dark, I was alone, and no one saw my face."

"Who knows you're here?"

"Only Pinkie. She's brought me food and clothes. I haven't gone outside since I arrived."

"I'm sorry, Brenda. I underestimated the opposition."

"Pay your debt now. Full disclosure. Who shot me and why?"

He tried to make sense of her story. "Whoever hired the Russians to kill me probably went after you, but I don't know how you made it onto their radar."

She grasped onto the Russian connection. "I'll tell you how in a minute, but a lot has happened since you left, so pay attention."

"I'm listening."

She began with Prince Jasper Adumu. "You said that you were off to meet a contact who owned Luxor. He was garroted in his office. Did you kill him?"

Monsarrat considered the Libyan package Adumu had arranged on short notice. "He worked in a nasty business with even nastier clients. Dozens of people could have wanted him dead."

"Do you think it's an innocent coincidence? Adumu was murdered after you saw him? Someone tried to whack me after you visited Bread and Freedom?"

"Like unicorns and pink bunny rabbits, there's no such animal as a coincidence, especially innocent," he stated.

"I don't believe in coincidences, either, but I believe you're the link between the murder of Datura, the execution of Adumu, and the botched hit on me, so stop playing Saint Nate and give me a brief."

He surrendered, taking her from the voice message of Westbrook to the demands of Bin Nafe, the killings in Manhattan, the duplicity of Enderby, the death of Houghton, the resurrection of Sanhedrin, and his fears for Sylvie. "I have to return to Greylock fast. She's not answering my calls or texts. I'm afraid Sanhedrin reached her."

"Before you leave, you need to hear the rest of my intel."

"Go ahead."

"At the same time Adumu's neck was separated from his shoulders, a fire in Georgetown gutted an antiquities gallery named Fergus &

Son. The fire marshal found accelerant and determined arson."

He recalled the confession of Houghton. "Was the name of the owner Cairstine Fergusson?"

"Been busy, haven't you, Nathan?" she asked. "Fergusson is missing, and you're linked to her."

"How?"

"The fourth call to Datura. My NSA contact said the call was made from a cell phone in the system of the *Rezidentura*. He doesn't know who placed the call, but it originated on Dumbarton Street."

He again recalled the words of Houghton. "The call to Datura came from the home of Fergusson?"

"A gold star," she applauded. "Can you tell me why she called your friend the night he was murdered?"

"I wish I knew."

She handed him a file. "The call was made on a Russian spook phone, so the person who made the call is a Russian spook. My NSA contact also told me that Cairstine Fergusson and her butler, Rupert Marlowe, lived at the Dumbarton Street address. He sent me copies of their driver licenses. For the *Rezident*, Anton Maximovich Dovlatov, too. He also gave me copies of their passport data pages, American for Marlowe and Fergusson, Russian for Dovlatov."

Monsarrat memorized the features of the three Russians. "I need to find them, right after I return from Greylock."

"I hope Sylvie is fine, but you need to resolve this situation fast. I can't run two businesses from this apartment."

"I understand, Brenda, but I need more time."

"Saint Nate, patron of stupid impulses and suicidal causes."

He spoke with an empty confidence. "It'll be over soon, Brenda."

Her anger faded. "Do you want someone to watch your back?"

"You're safer here, but you can still help, if I can borrow your car."

She walked to the bedroom, returning with a fob and an envelope. "Garage address, access card, stall number, insurance and registration for my Aston Martin DB11. Use premium gas. You get a speeding ticket, you pay it."

He whistled softly. "You're doing well."

"Be careful, Nathan. The news reported shots fired on "K" Street but nothing about a dead woman, so whoever hit me knows I walked away. My car may be under observation. Also, you're exhausted, your radar is down, and your instincts suck."

"You know something specific?"

"Remember what I promised to tell you?" she asked. "Whoever hit me is tracking your cell phone. It's how I was connected to you."

He showed her the dismantled device. "Pinkie had good reason when she told me to remove the battery. I should soak it in acid."

"Lose it. Take a burner from my friend. It's a low tech flip phone, domestic and Canada only, fully charged."

He accepted a phone and charger. "Your friend is prepared."

"My friend is paranoid," she admitted. "I'll contact you from a burner, a different SIM card and number each time. You won't recognize the caller, but it'll be me. No one else knows your number."

He pointed to the Glock. "Keep it close. If the people who tried to kill you learn that you're here, they won't ring the bell. They'll knock the door off its hinges and spray the apartment with bullets."

"Chipper, aren't you, Nathan?"

"Better to be grumpy and alive than cheerful and dead," he replied.

In Opposition, a Pawn Forces the King to Retreat

Before leaving the apartment, Monsarrat opened the flip phone and tapped Mendel Shackowitz's number onto the keypad. The call connected, and he issued a warning. "The cell phone your boss uses is compromised. Pull the battery, snap the SIM card, and drop everything into the river."

"I understand. Anything else?"

"Our next conversation will be soon and in person."

Carrying the bag, he walked through Rosslyn, pausing to check his back in the reflections offered by store windows. Lacking a weapon, he felt light, as if poorly dressed for a date. Aware of Moscow Centre's fondness for dispatching enemies on bridges, he stepped carefully onto Key Bridge, the spires of Georgetown in the distance. Midway between Rosslyn and Georgetown, he dropped the Sanger cell phone into the Potomac River.

Despite his desire to reach Greylock, he detoured in Georgetown, stopping before the residence of Felix Sanhedrin. Neglect cloaked the townhouse, its windows dark, security cameras disabled, and the black Suburbans that had once idled before the entrance absent. He climbed the steps to the door, bending close to examine the lock. The keyway appeared crusted with dirt.

From a garage across from Kalorama Park, he retrieved the silver Aston Martin and locked the bag in the trunk. He stopped at a convenience store to buy a flashlight, work gloves, and light bulbs. He crossed Arlington Memorial Bridge and gained Route Fifty, surveying the road for unwanted company. His calls to Sylvie went unanswered.

At Ashby Gap, he followed the turnoff to Fermanagh House. He steered the Aston Martin between the matching red brick pillars. Before the manor, he reversed the car for a fast departure. The fob activated the security system. He pulled on the gloves, removed the light bulbs from their sleeves, and climbed the staircase to the portico. In the beam of the flashlight, he studied the doorway for wires, pushed open the door, and stepped into the foyer.

Faded yellow roses curled upon a plastic chair. The walls were empty of hangings, the wooden floors bare of rugs. He crushed the bulbs and spread the shards across the empty hallway, Hansel strewing crumbs of glass. He followed the hallway toward a room with floor to ceiling windows. An overturned card table, collapsed folding chairs, and a ladder blocked the entrance.

Pushing aside the barricade, he entered the room. The stench of old death assaulted him. Before the far wall, a cloud of flies swarmed over a tarp, their buzzing a chainsaw assault. Crossing the floor, he fought the urge to gag. He waved off the flies and lifted the tarp to find a Golden Retriever puppy, its throat sliced and fur gummed, forever settled into a pool of congealed blood.

He explored the remainder of the manor but found no further evidence of Sanhedrin. The broken glass crunched beneath his feet as he crossed the hallway. He unlocked the Aston Martin and drove between the pillars. Regaining the road, the sun low on the horizon, he retraced his earlier route, driving toward the Beltway fast, his calls to Sylvie still unanswered.

Night fell as he entered Maryland. He stopped to fill the gas tank in Delaware. In southern New Jersey, he pulled into a rest area and closed his eyes, waking hours later. He drove through New York, entered Connecticut as the sun rose, and crossed into Massachusetts. Approaching Springfield, he exited the interstate. In the parking lot of a shopping mall, he waited for the stores to open to purchase clothes and toiletries. Returning to the car, he opened the trunk and placed the items into the bag.

Entering the college town in the late morning, he felt less a prodigal son than a fugitive. He parked before an express delivery store. Before leaving the car, he again called Sylvie, with the same results. He dropped the flip phone into the pocket of his new blazer. Entering the store, he recognized the clerk, a former student at the college. "Are you holding a package for me, Jimmy?"

The clerk brimmed with enthusiasm. "Dean Monsarrat! What happened to your face?"

Monsarrat evaded the question. "Can you check on my package?"

Excitement animated the clerk. "What did the cops say?"

"The police want to speak to me?"

"They want to talk to you about all the crap that just went down."

"What crap, Jimmy?"

"About your house."

A cold fear gripped him. "What about my house?"

"You don't know?"

"I've been away."

The clerk leaned forward, as if divulging a confidence. "Your house burned to the ground."

The destruction of his home formed the start of a pattern, following the burning of the gallery in Georgetown. "What happened?"

"People say the fire must have been set, since the cops shot a guy about two miles from your house," the clerk replied. "He was fixing a flat tire, they pulled over to help, long story short, he tried to steal their cruiser. They shot him. They searched his car and found arson materials. Now he's in the urgent care clinic on Cumberland Road."

Playing to expectations, Monsarrat said, "I'll contact the police."

The clerk whispered, "Really, Dean, how did you get those bruises?"

Monsarrat flashed anger. "The package, Jimmy?"

The clerk slapped his forehead. "Of course! Lemme get it."

Monsarrat signed the receipt. At the Aston Martin, he retrieved his bag, placing his house keys and the Westbrook file into it. He again called Sylvie, with the same results. He drove to Cartwright Road, despite the risk that watchers awaited him. Parking the car beyond the yellow police tape, he walked to his property, bag in his hand.

He pulled on the work gloves and ducked beneath the tape. He surveyed the charred remains of the garage before switching on the flashlight and stepping through the blackened doorway. The stench of melted rubber hung in the air. From the garage, he crossed to the ruined house, picking a careful path through the foyer to the staircase.

Swinging the beam of the flashlight, he tested each step as he climbed to the second floor. The Class 5 safe was scorched, but the heavy door swung open when he entered the combination, and the interior was pristine. He transferred the original section of Westbrook's file, his wallet, personal papers, cell phone, and laptop into his bag. Retrieving the engagement ring, he experienced a profound sense of foreboding.

He exited the house and drove the Aston Martin to the college campus. Parking in the visitor lot, he made his final call to Sylvie, as if proximity might bring success. Carrying the bag, he walked to Denham Hall and climbed the stairs to the Department of English.

On the third floor corridor, the sounds of hushed advisements leaked through open doors. Outside Sylvie's office, flowers and wreaths formed a neat mound.

Wrapping his hand in a handkerchief, he rattled the knob, but the door was locked. He stepped into an adjoining office, where a graduate assistant graded essays. He did not recognize her. "When did Professor Epstein die?"

The intrusion startled her. "A day ago? Maybe two? Three? The cleaning crew discovered her."

"She passed away in her office?"

She stared at him suspiciously before answering. "Precisely, no. Suicide implies choice, so she didn't actually pass away."

Nerves strained, he snapped, "Exactly how did she die?"

She hesitated before answering. "She slashed her wrists."

"Did she write a note?"

"She printed it and pinned it to her shirt."

"What did the note say?"

"I didn't see it, but I heard that Professor Epstein confessed she was too sad to continue living. I also heard that the college failed to contact her parents, so they arranged the funeral without them. People said the ceremony was very nice," she explained.

He returned to Sylvie's office. Guilt assailed him. His desire to spare her pain sentenced her to death. He should have shared the dangers with her. He had botched his most important assignment, and the woman he had hoped to marry was dead, as if he had killed her with his own hands.

His apology to Datura had torn his heart. His words to Sylvie shredded his soul. "I failed you."

He placed the engagement ring atop the flowers and wreaths, offering a silent prayer and an oath to avenge her. Exiting Denham Hall, his flip phone vibrated. Carlyle's first message announced that her NSA contact had pinpointed Dovlatov's cell phone inside the *Rezidentura*. Her second message jolted him. The cell phone that had called Datura from Dumbarton Street was in Greylock.

He sent a curt reply. "Who? Where?"

She replied immediately. "Who, don't know. Where, 47 Cumberland Road."

He texted a warning. "Greylock friend dead. Be extra careful."

Her reply pressed hard the limited emotions of a text. "Very very sorry. Be careful, too."

"The time for careful is gone," he muttered.

Triangulation of the King in the Endgame is a Stalling Tactic

Monsarrat reached 47 Cumberland Road shortly after the urgent
care clinic closed for the day. Parking the Aston Martin, he noted a
dented Volkswagen van with a pizza delivery sign strapped to its roof
glide to a stop across the road. He dropped his bag onto the floor of
the Aston Martin and draped his blazer over it. He removed his
sunglasses, stepped from the car, set the alarms, and sprinted to the
Volkswagen as the driver, a thin young man with a billy goat beard,
exited the van. He wore the red vest of the pizza company, and a
white cap covered his hair.

Monsarrat applied pressure to the driver's carotid artery until he
passed out. He settled him into a driver's seat patched with strips of
duct tape, checked his pulse, and stripped off his hat and vest.
Reaching into the glove box, he removed a thick roll of the tape,
secured the young man's ankles, crossed his wrists, and fastened them
to the steering wheel. He cut a hole in a strip of tape and placed it
over the driver's mouth. From the passenger seat, he lifted a warming
bag and placed the tape inside.

At the entrance to the clinic, the cap low on his face, he pressed the
buzzer. A moment passed before a nurse opened the door. He
removed the pizza from the bag and handed her the box. "Can I use
your toilet? It's an emergency."

Following her into the clinic, he lifted the box from her hands,
placing it and the warming bag behind the reception desk. Like the
driver, she succumbed to the pressure against her throat. Propping
her against the desk, he retrieved the tape, secured her wrists and

ankles, sliced a hole in a strip, and gagged her. Stuffing the roll of tape into his waistband, he checked the log book. A recent notation listed Rupert Marlowe and the number of an examination room.

At the end of a hallway, an elderly man in the uniform of a local security company dozed in a metal folding chair, his sole weapon a ring of keys hanging from a loop in his belt. Monsarrat rubbed his shoulder gently. "Sir? Can you wake up, please?"

The elderly man opened his eyes. He adjusted his glasses. "You looking for someone to pay for your pizza, son?"

Monsarrat tossed the vest and hat onto the floor. "I need to talk to you about the prisoner."

"Only the doctors, nurses, and police are allowed into the room."

"The doctors are gone, the nurse is sleeping, and you're not a cop."

"The police force is too small for an officer to sit here full-time, so they hired me. I'm moonlighting to stretch my pension check."

Monsarrat asked his first question. "Is the prisoner manacled?"

"Right wrist and ankle to the bed frame."

"Where's the key, in case of an emergency?"

"With the nurse," the elderly man replied. "Excuse me, son, but who are you, and what happened to your face?"

"It's better if you don't know."

"So it's that way?"

"It is," Monsarrat agreed, showing him the roll of tape. "I need you stay here and keep quiet, but I don't want to restrain you."

The elderly man wagged a finger. "I can't accept a paycheck and not do my job. Use the tape."

Monsarrat loosely secured his ankles and wrists. "Let me know if the pressure's too tight."

"I'm okay, given the circumstances."

"Don't try to stand. You'll fall and hurt yourself."

"You've got that right, son. I'd break a hip."

"How often do you check with your supervisor?"

The elderly man considered the question. "I sign in at the start of my shift, and I sign out twelve hours later. I take a five minute break every hour and a thirty minute break for meals. I don't call the main office, but every once in a while someone checks in on me. I take short walks up and down the hallway for my circulation, and I use the bathroom often. Don't tell anyone, but I nap sometimes."

Monsarrat sliced a hole in the final strip of tape. "I won't be long."

He pressed the gag across the old man's mouth and tossed the roll onto the floor. Pushing down the door lever, he stepped inside the room. A bed, its wheels locked, occupied the middle of the room. A sink, a supply cabinet, and a folding chair lined the far wall. A bald, middle-aged man with a beer barrel chest and a trimmed goatee lay beneath a sheet, a pair of black plastic glasses on his nose, reading a paperback novel. A bedside stand to his left held a plastic cup half-filled with water and a straw. Metal handcuffs secured his right wrist and ankle to the bed frame.

Monsarrat used the Russian slur for prison sex slave. "Reading time is over. Put down the book, *petukh*."

The prisoner folded the corner of a page and placed the paperback onto the stand. His plummy accent rang. "As I live and breathe, if it isn't Nathan Monsarrat himself."

"You're the butler."

"Rupert Marlowe in the wounded flesh, so to speak, but you look much worse than me. To what do I owe the pleasure of this visit?"

Successful interrogations were languid seductions, but Monsarrat needed to quickly receive answers to his questions. He pulled back the sheet, exposing a bandage on a thigh as thick as a tree stump. He crossed the room to the supply cabinet, found a box of surgical gloves, and pulled on a pair. Returning to the bed, he removed the bandage and thrust his fingers into the wound. Ignoring the butler's screams, he demanded, "What's your birth name?"

Sweat soaked Marlowe's face. "I'm a *mokroye delo* assassin, so you won't break me, but I want to help, so I'll answer your questions. My name is Arkady Alexeevich Limonov."

"Who sent you to execute me and burn down my house?"

Breathing hard, the butler replied, "Anton Maximovich Dovlatov. You may know him as our *Rezident*."

"Who terminated Sylvie Epstein?"

"I know she's your girlfriend, but she wasn't my mission. If she's dead, someone else ended her."

His belief that Houghton had spoken the truth, that Sanhedrin had killed Sylvie, grew stronger. "Tell me about Cairstine Fergusson."

"She's a bitch Leningrader, a bleeding black widow spider with an appetite for bad boys."

"What's her birth name?"

"Yulia Lazarevna Belyakova."

"Where is she now?"

"Dovlatov told Fergusson that Moscow Centre recalled her, but it was a ruse. She was never supposed to board a plane to Moscow. He ordered me to dispose of her on the way to the airport, but she bested me, and she took out my back-up at Dulles. Nobody knows her location now. She's in the wind."

Monsarrat broke his nose with the heel of his palm. "You know the drill. I snap small bones first, graduate to your tibia and fibula, break your kneecaps, crush your balls, and end by snapping your neck. If you don't want to die in agony, tell me something useful."

Blood poured from the butler's nostrils, and pain deadened his voice. "Pavlik, Dovlatov's great White House asset, died last January in Georgetown, but something happened recently to force the *Rezident* to launch an operation to erase his existence and the lives of anyone associated with him."

"What something?"

"Fuck me if I know."

Monsarrat punched him hard in the face. "Wrong answer."

Marlowe wiped blood from his face with his free hand and spat blood onto the floor. "You don't need to use Lubyanka methods. I said I'll cooperate."

"Talk now, or I'll start breaking bones."

"Dovlatov years ago recruited a Navy captain, an oral surgeon with a lust for things she couldn't afford on her government salary. She's a rear admiral now, serving at the military hospital in Bethesda. She told Dovlatov that two of her officers submitted a report that accused the National Security Adviser of having Soviet dentistry in his mouth. She passed the original report to him and destroyed all the copies."

"Pavlik was the National Security Adviser? Pavlik was Dovlatov's White House asset?"

"You're not stupid, Monsarrat. You know Pavlik was Sanhedrin and the two navy officers were Westbrook and Zeigarnik."

Monsarrat did not explain that the Soviet dentistry belonged to Sanhedrin's body double. "Where is he now?"

"You have to be specific. My brain is overwhelmed with pain."

"Where is Pavlik?"

"Are you having me on, mate?" the butler replied. "Pavlik was cremated. His ashes are in an urn."

A primal instinct launched his question. "What's his birth name?"

Marlowe again spat blood onto the floor. "You mean the middle name between Felix and Sanhedrin? If he has one, I can't recall it."

"I mean his patronymic, the name between the given and the family that all you Russians carry."

"You think Pavlik is Russian? You're mad. He's a Yank traitor."

Monsarrat changed his approach. "Why did Dovlatov send you here to kill me?"

"The same reason he destroyed every copy of the report. The same reason he terminated the rear admiral with an overdose of oxycodone. The same reason he ordered Fergusson to eliminate Zeigarnik and Westbrook. The same reason he wants me and Fergusson dead. He's a careful son of a whore. He knows no one can hurt him if no one knows what the report said about Pavlik."

"How did I come to his attention?"

Marlowe offered grudging praise. "Westbrook told Fergusson about your lunch date in Hyannis. She told Dovlatov. The *Rezident* ordered me to terminate you, but you're a hard man to kill. I fucked up, too, renting the pair of clowns that Fergusson used to help her take out Westbrook."

"The same two thugs who murdered my friend in Cambridge?"

"Their orders were simple, kill you and kill the kid you talked to in the coffee shop, do the hits clean, no witnesses. They screwed up both jobs. They killed the kid in front of witnesses, and they let you kill them in Manhattan."

Monsarrat looked forward to the pleasure of ending the life of the Russian. "Who killed the owner of Luxor in Washington?"

"I garroted your African friend at his club after you visited him, by order of Dovlatov, but you pissed off the *Rezident* when you took down the minivan crew. They weren't clowns. They were Moscow Centre trained."

Monsarrat ignored the compliment. "Who hit the woman on "K" Street in Washington?"

"Dovlatov said he would do the job himself, but there's no body, so I suspect the son of a whore fucked up the hit, just as he lost your friend from the restaurant in Dupont Circle. He's still tough but he's too old for wet work."

Monsarrat hoped he was right. "What else did he order you to do?"

"I torched Fergusson's gallery, and I burned your house to the ground, but I don't like my odds of killing you. It's poetic justice. I came here to waste you, but you're going to end me."

Monsarrat again c hanged his approach. "You fucked up the hit on my friend in Cambridge in more ways than you know."

"How do you mean?"

He explained the analyst's use of two cell phones. "Your thugs found one, but you called the phone they left behind. I used it to track your location."

"When I saw the number of the cell phone they took didn't match the device you called, I ordered them to return and find the second cell phone, but you already took it. They were *zalupov*, fucking idiots. You did me a favor, killing them, so now I'll do you one now."

"What favor would I need from you?"

Marlowe confirmed Carlyle's diagnosis. "I hacked both your cell phones, the one in your own name and the Canadian cell phone owned by Mark Sanger."

"How did you find the Sanger phone?"

"Westbrook gave us your Massachusetts number when he called you from Boston. You gave me the Canadian number when you used your own phone to call the Sanger phone. I looked into him. It took about a minute to realize he was a cover identity."

"Did you give the Sanger identity to Dovlatov and Fergusson?"

"Maybe your service is filled with do-gooders, but in Moscow Centre intelligence is kept in your pocket to be sold or traded but never given away," Marlowe sneered.

"I want an answer, not an explanation."

"I informed neither Dovlatov nor Fergusson that you and Mark Sanger are the same person."

Monsarrat wanted to erase the smirk from his face. "Last question, *petukh*. Where are Fergusson and Dovlatov?"

"I told you, Fergusson's in the wind. If I knew her location, I'd give it to you. I want the bitch dead. As for Dovlatov, he's inside the *Rezidentura*, waiting to hear that you're a corpse, but I can deliver him to you. All you have to do is promise to end his life."

"Why not do it yourself? Hire a lawyer, get bail, and kill him."

"I wish I could, mate, but the *Rezident* is a nasty piece of work. Before he sent me here, he invited me for a pint in a Tenleytown pub. He held my hand in a way that Russian men of a certain age do when they want to play at *Dyadya* Vanya and explained that killing Fergusson was necessary to keep us both in the good graces of Moscow Centre. Next thing I knew, he had jabbed a fléchette into the vein on the back of my hand. The bastard injected me with a necrotic disease. I'm to have the antidote as soon as I kill you, but I know he lied to motivate me. A rash has already spread across my chest. It'll soon dissolve my flesh. I'll end up a puddle of bloody jelly."

Monsarrat recoiled. "Are you contagious?"

"It's victim specific. Dovlatov doesn't want to spread a pandemic. Like I said, he's a careful son of a whore."

Relief was a cold wash. "Don't worry, Marlowe. I'll kill you before the disease does its job."

"That's all I want, a fast death, no doctors making my final hours even worse, and your promise to send Dovlatov to hell. Fergusson, too, if you can find her."

Monsarrat almost felt sympathy for the butler. "You're sure you can deliver Dovlatov?"

"Of course, I can," he boasted. "In Moscow Centre, we say vengeance isn't an appetizer. It's a bleeding three course meal."

The Endgame is Won by Technique and Knowledge

Monsarrat listened to Marlowe, his respect for the butler's abilities increasing. The Russian glossed his savagery with English manners and a plummy accent, but he was a deadpan killer with the emotional range of a brick who bore responsibility for the death of Datura as if he had pulled the trigger himself. He waited until the butler concluded his plan for delivering Dovlatov before peppering him with questions. "What number do you use to contact him? What's your recognition code? Will he be suspicious if the message is sent from a cell phone number he won't recognize?"

Marlowe supplied the number. "He'll be wary, but the recognition code will allay his fears."

"Tell it to me."

"Reference the charity of a player on a New York sports team. Any player, any team, any charity. Send a text in Russian. Demand a crash meeting, somewhere you can both reach quickly, like New York City. Offer him an exchange, the antidote for your death. He'll believe I'll on the other end."

"Will he suspect a trap?"

"He knows I want to live," Marlowe replied. "Tell him to come alone but expect him to travel with his full team of bodyguards, six Group Alpha *Spetsnaz*, veterans of black operations in Chechnya."

Monsarrat felt the pressure of time. The interrogation had lasted too long. "I'll kill Dovlatov, but I want Fergusson, too. I have to know everything about her, so I can track her and find her. How does she spend her free time? How does she relax? Is she a true believer?"

"She has balls the size of grapefruits. She likes money, making and spending it, almost as much as she loves sex, men and women, young and old, single or with groups. She's also a chess savant who enjoys humiliating her opponents. If Moscow Centre hadn't conscripted her, she would have been a Grandmaster. In another age, she could have been Tsarina of all the Russias."

"Where would she go to play a match?"

"Just like sex. Anywhere she can find it."

Monsarrat asked his final question. "Would you like a moment?"

"I'm ready," the Russian replied, "but before I die, I'd like to hear my birth name one final time."

"You'll enjoy hell, Arkady Alexeevich Limonov," Monsarrat promised as he pulled the pillow from beneath his head.

He smothered the Russian until his struggles weakened and his manacled body stopped jerking. He held the pillow over his face for another moment. Removing it, he saw the bulging eyes and swollen tongue of the dead man. He took a towel from the supply cabinet, wiped his fingerprints from the surfaces he had touched, and dropped the towel and surgical gloves to the floor.

In the corridor, he released the elderly man. "How do you feel?"

The guard rubbed his hands. "Pretty well, considering."

"I won't ask you to lie, but I'd appreciate a bit of vagueness when you describe me," Monsarrat said. "I'd also like ten minutes before you call the cops. When they arrive, tell them the nurse is behind the counter and a pizza delivery guy is in a van outside the clinic."

"I heard the prisoner scream. Is he hurt bad?"

"He's dead."

"You killed him?"

"He was a very bad man."

"Just like that, in cold blood?"

"He murdered my friend," Monsarrat explained.

The old man pondered the information. "My eyesight is no longer so good, so I don't have to lie to the police, but my sense of smell is fine, so I will tell them about the smoke clinging to you."

Monsarrat thanked him. He checked the unconscious nurse, wrapped his handkerchief around his hand, and opened the clinic doors. The sun had set, and in the glare of the streetlights, he confirmed the driver of the van was alive. He stuffed fifty dollars into his shirt pocket. "To cover the cost of the pizza. And your tip."

In the Aston Martin, he pulled on the blazer and started the engine. He opened the bag, retrieved his own cell phone, removed the battery, and snapped the SIM card. Driving the dark back roads, the flip phone rang. "Are you good?"

"Better than good," Carlyle responded. "My NSA contact located Fergusson's car, a Ferrari Spider. She parked it in the long-term Economy Lot at Philadelphia International Airport."

"I need to search it."

She heard the request before he asked it. "Forget it, Nathan. I'm not breaking into her home to look for an extra fob. The best I can do is give you the license plate number and the VIN."

He took the information. "Did the contact provide anything else?"

"Before she drove to Philly, she checked into the Aeroflot flight departing Dulles for Moscow but never boarded the plane."

"She killed a pair of *Rezidentura* hit team by the departure gate."

"How did you know?"

"Her butler told me, just before he choked on a pillow," he

answered. "Did she go wheels up from Philly or just park her car?"

"She boarded a British Airways flight to London."

"Has she used a credit card or an ATM card in England?"

"No transactions. She may be spending cash."

"If she had a clean identity waiting for her or flew onward to another city, finding her will take a miracle, but I have to start my search in London."

"Do you want me to go with you?"

Like Datura, she was not an operative. "You're more help to me in Rosslyn. Also, I have bad news for you."

"What else is new?" she groused.

"The Russians believe you're alive."

"Like I told you," she reminded him before closing the connection.

He crossed into Connecticut and gained the interstate. South of Hartford, he called Shackowitz. "It's Nathan. The line is secure. Is Solomon safe?"

"Safe, yes. Happy, no."

"I'm on my way to you. Where can we meet?"

"Come to my apartment," Shackowitz said, providing the address.

He reached Manhattan before midnight, parking the Aston Martin in a valet garage on Washington Street. Carrying his bag, he walked to Perry Street, dropping the pieces of his cell phone into a series of trash cans. He climbed the stairs of an Italianate townhouse, entered the lobby, and pressed the buzzer marked MS. The door unlocked, and he climbed the stairs to the third floor. A door swung upon his knock, revealing a spacious apartment decorated with photographs, paintings, and memorabilia of Vilnius.

Shackowitz ushered him into the apartment, Grinnell and

Goldman standing behind him. "Welcome to my home, Nathan."

Monsarrat stepped into the foyer. "It's good to see you three."

"Look at your face! Who mugged you? You want help with the payback?" asked Goldman.

"I'm good, and they're dead."

"We are all very sorry for your loss, Nathan," Grinnell stated.

Monsarrat thanked them and offered a briefing on his actions since his exfiltration from the store. "I need your help, but if Moscow Centre learns what we did to its *Rezident*, we'll spend the remainder of our lives running from Russian hit squads."

"It's not like Dovlatov and his *Spetsnaz* bodyguards are free from sin," Goldman said.

"I agree with Moishe," Shackowitz stated.

"You have your answer, Nathan," Grinnell announced.

Monsarrat valued them immensely. Courageous and loyal, they would sacrifice to protect each other and him. "The snatch site and the surrounding area, including the shooting blind in the park opposite, are saturated with security cameras. If I can't negate them, I'll have to abort the plan."

"My cousin, who owes me many favors, is a supervisor in One Police Plaza. He may have a suggestion, if I was to consult him on a hypothetical situation," Grinnell offered.

"Do you trust him?"

"Is that a serious question?"

"Can you call him now? It's past midnight."

"Let me worry about my cousin's sleep habits."

"Where do we take Dovlatov after we snatch him?" Goldman asked.

"A secluded, secure location," Monsarrat replied. "Any ideas?"

"*Nit gidacht*! It should not happen," Shackowitz exclaimed, "but the perfect site is not ten minutes from here on foot."

"Will the Russian ambassador go public with accusations that someone kidnapped a senior diplomat?" asked Goldman.

"For a real diplomat, maybe, but Dovlatov is a high-level spook, and Moscow Centre hates publicity," Monsarrat replied.

Grinnell ended his phone call. Summarizing his conversation, he warned, "Five minutes will be all we have."

"It will have to be enough," Goldman said.

"Go over your plan once more, Nathan," Shackowitz requested. "We all need to understand it completely, because we won't have time to rehearse it."

"I also need to know if you prefer a .38 revolver or a a .45 pistol? If the pistol, with or without a suppressor?" Goldman asked.

"A .45 with a suppressor, a Beretta if possible," Monsarrat replied. "Take a suitcase with you, too. After we're done here, you and Mendel are going shopping for a weapon to hunt *Spetsnaz*."

A Winning Move Creates the Position to Achieve Victory

Despite the hour, Goldman and Shackowitz departed to purchase the items on their shopping list. Monsarrat and Grinnell remained in the apartment, studying maps and diagrams, lines of sight, access and egress routes, weather and wind reports, refining the plan and developing contingencies to eliminate the bodyguards and secure Dovlatov. Monsarrat rubbed his eyes. "In theory, everything works, but in real time, my confidence level is not high."

"I've never seen you so exhausted, Nathan."

"I'm good, Solomon."

Grinnell offered solicitude. "*Nisht gefloygen*, not so much, in my opinion. You blame yourself for the death of your young friend."

"I am responsible."

"You also suffer from the trauma of killing your former lover."

"Ending Abby was righteous."

"Finally, you return home to find the woman you love was murdered by the most evil man on the planet. You need to mourn her," Grinnell concluded.

"I'm responsible for Sylvie, too," Monsarrat insisted, "and I'll mourn her properly, as soon as I have time."

"Of course, you will. Until then, if you would like to talk, I'm here to listen."

"Thank you, Solomon, but I don't want to talk. I want to kill."

"It's not like you to speak so bitterly."

"Houghton is dead. Marlowe is dead. Dovlatov, Fergusson, and

Sanhedrin are next. After they're eliminated, I'll talk, and I'll mourn, but now I have another favor to ask."

"Of course, *habibi*."

He wrote two sets of numbers on a sheet of paper. "The first is the license plate for a Ferrari Spider registered in the District of Columbia to Cairstine Fergusson. The second is the VIN. It's parked in the long-term Economy Lot at Philadelphia International Airport. I don't have the ticket, but I need it moved to a private location, so I can search it, immediately after I finish Dovlatov."

"I have a cousin with a warehouse in New Jersey, not far from the airport. I'll call him."

Despite his tension, Monsarrat laughed. "Why am I not surprised?"

"Family is a blessing," Grinnell agreed. "What are your plans for the Ferrari? Will you keep it? Sell it?"

He recited a list of tools the cousin needed to supply. "Tell him that he can have the car, once I'm finished with it."

"In that case, I'm sure he'll help."

Shackowitz and Goldman returned at dawn, carrying a cello case and a backpack. "We bought everything from a Russian *mafya* contact in Brighton Beach," Goldman said.

"He lives by the *Vorovskoy Zakon*, the code of the thief," Shackowitz added. "He won't talk."

"We'll tool the bullets so they flatten upon impact, destroying any chance for the police finding forensic evidence," Goldman explained.

From the backpack, he took a .45 caliber Beretta Px4 Storm, a suppressor, a box of ammunition, and a leather paddle holster. "Also from the Russian."

Monsarrat inspected the weapon. "The condition is good, and the markings have been erased. Thank you."

Shackowitz removed the final items. "The tools you requested."

Monsarrat thanked them. "What do I owe you?"

"Our contribution," Grinnell said. "If there's no more to discuss, we need to prepare for work."

Monsarrat provided his flip phone number. "Call me with news."

Shackowitz gave him a set of keys to the apartment and passwords for the laptop and internet. "In the kitchen, eat whatever you like, just don't mix meat and milk, and don't bring *treif* food inside."

"Mendel is very observant," Goldman explained.

Alone in the apartment, Monsarrat showered, scrubbed the smell of smoke from his skin, and dressed in fresh clothes. He cleaned and reassembled the Beretta. He turned on the television, switching between local and cable news channels. He examined Shackowitz's collection of books in English, Hebrew, and Yiddish before closing his eyes, stretching out on the couch, and sleeping.

In his dreams, handcuffs bound Shackowitz and Goldman to prison bars. Sanhedrin stood upon a scaffold, holding an executioner's axe in one hand, the severed head of a puppy in the other. Behind him, a noose around his throat, Grinnell asked, Why use such a sloppy plan?

His woke to Grinnell shaking his shoulder, Shackowitz and Goldman standing behind him. He sat up and greeted them with a question. "What time is it?"

Grinnell told him. "We closed the store early, so we can go over the plan once more."

The dream was a fresh memory. "It's not too late to stand down."

"What are you talking about?" Goldman objected. "I'm looking forward to some fun."

"In that case, we review the plan, and I'll text Dovlatov."

They studied the plan again, testing its weaknesses and adding to its strengths. Their questions and objections satisfied, Monsarrat selected a virgin cell phone from the items provided by Shackowitz and Goldman, plugged it into the charger, and opened a text box. He switched to a Cyrillic keyboard and typed a message, starting with a reference to a relief pitcher for the Yankees and a Bronx food bank, finishing with instructions for the meeting.

He tapped the Send button. When the confirmation arrived, he removed the battery, snapped the SIM, and handed the pieces to Goldman. "Can you make sure they disappear?"

"I'll take care of it."

Monsarrat held up his own flip phone. "After you receive Solomon's final text, destroy your new cell phones. They're one time use only. We execute the op, exfiltrate the area, and rendezvous at the interrogation site. After we finish with Dovlatov, I drive south, and you get your lives back."

"The address of my cousin. I won't give you his name, and he doesn't know yours," Grinnell said, handing him a sheet of paper.

Monsarrat memorized the information and returned the paper. "In a perfect world, the Ferrari will bring me one step closer to finding Fergusson, and from her to Sanhedrin."

A Winning Position Ensures Defeat of the Opponent

Visitors arriving by car to Lincoln Center on the Upper West Side of Manhattan entered the sixteen acre campus from Columbus Avenue. Climbing steps illuminated with the word Welcome in multiple languages, they reached a crown of flattop bollards. Robertson Plaza stretched beyond the barrier. In the middle of the open area, the Revson Fountain spouted jets of pastel colored water into the night sky. At the far end of the plaza stood the Metropolitan Opera House. Following the conclusion of each night's performance, thousands of patrons exited the building into the plaza.

Before leaving the Perry Street apartment, Monsarrat issued instructions to Shackowitz and Goldman. "If you can't execute the plan exactly as designed, return here. No improvisations."

"We understand perfectly," Shackowitz confirmed.

"I replaced the license plates for the Audi and the Porsche with out of state tags. If cops stop you, you won't have the proper papers, so drive carefully," Goldman advised.

Grinnell drove uptown through the nighttime traffic. Reaching the corner of West 65th Street and Amsterdam Avenue, he pulled the Audi to the curb. "Manhattan drivers are the world's worst."

"If the cops tell you to move the car, remember that you're a tourist. Apologize, but not too much, or they'll be suspicious," Monsarrat advised. "Find a new spot to park but stay within your thirty second window to reach the pick-up point."

"Don't worry about me, *habibi*. I'm just the wheelman. You have the dangerous job."

The Beretta holstered against the small of his back, the suppressor in his pocket, Monsarrat walked along West 65th Street past a line of digital advertisements. He turned onto Broadway and crossed Columbus Avenue. In Dante Alighieri Park, ornamental gaslights illuminated the bronze statue of the poet. Shackowitz and Goldman sat on a bench, hiding in plain sight.

The older man wore a frayed brown overcoat, gray watch cap, and half gloves. His hands stroked the cello case between his thighs, as if rehearsing for a performance in the park. The younger man dressed similarly, save in black. He bounced the backpack on his knees like a baby. Passing them, Monsarrat tossed a question. "All good?"

"Affirmative," Goldman muttered.

At West 62nd Street, he followed the edge of the Lincoln Center campus past Damrosch Park, turning onto Amsterdam Avenue before reaching West 65th Street. At the corner, he noted Grinnell inside the Audi, his gaze on the side mirror. He completed the circuit on Columbus Avenue. Climbing the steps to Robertson Plaza, he assessed the extent of the surveillance, security cameras, undercover police, and drones overhead, praying that Grinnell's cousin in One Police Plaza would prove reliable.

Stepping between the bollards, he walked toward the Revson Fountain. He noted the Chagall murals visible through the arched windows of the Metropolitan Opera House. Passing the London Plane Trees and Barclays Grove, he circled the Milstein Pool and Henry Moore's Reclining Figure, confident Dovlatov's need for secrecy would have prevented him from dispatching *Rezidentura* assets to populate the rendezvous site.

He leaned against the circular rim of the Revson Fountain, flip phone in his hand, gazing toward Columbus Avenue until two black Mercedes-Benz G550s with darkly tinted windows and diplomatic license plates stopped before the steps. He entered a one word message into the text box, Go, and pressed the send key.

Four *Spetsnaz* bodyguards dressed in business suits formed a protective box as Anton Maximovich Dovlatov stepped from the second G550 onto the sidewalk. The *Rezident* projected the charm of an éminence grise, his silver mane swept off his forehead, his clothes chosen to accentuate his power. The Russians climbed the steps toward the plaza as the fifth and sixth bodyguards steered the two vehicles onto Columbus Avenue and the first wave of patrons exited the Metropolitan Opera House.

In the Audi, Grinnell read the one word message and sent a text consisting of a single question mark to his cousin in One Police Plaza. A smiling emoji arrived seconds later. He typed his own message, Offline, and sent the text. Dropping the phone into his jacket pocket, he rubbed his palms onto his pants and waited for a bus to pass before steering away from the curb.

Monsarrat read Grinnell's message, closed the flip phone, and dropped it into his pocket. He removed the Beretta from its holster and attached the suppressor. Holding the weapon against his thigh, his finger light against the trigger guard, he allowed the throng to sweep him toward the approaching bodyguards, resisting the urge to bull forward, afraid to alert the four *Spetsnaz.*

Shackowitz read Grinnell's text, rose from the bench, and walked quickly beyond the arc of the gaslight to a space between two oak trees. From the case, he removed a Chukavin sniper rifle with a Schmidt & Bender night scope and a sound suppressor. Goldman followed him, a laser designator from the NPZ factory in Novosibirsk in his hand. He took sightings and whispered data.

Shackowitz sighted the trailing bodyguard. Exhaling, he squeezed the trigger of the Russian rifle. The .338 Lapua Magnum round exploded the skull of the bodyguard. He fired again, killing the *Spetsnaz* on the left with a head shot. He fired a third bullet into the head of the *Spetsnaz* on the right, leaving only Dovlatov and the forward bodyguard alive.

He placed the sniper rifle into the cello case as Goldman acquired the three casings, dropping the spent brass and the designator into the backpack. They exited the park and walked briskly to Central Park West. They retrieved the Porsche, Goldman destroyed their cell phones as Shackowitz drove. "Go slow, Mendel. I don't want the cops to ask us for a cello performance."

In the plaza, Monsarrat saw the three bodyguards fall. He watched the remaining *Spetsnaz* draw a nine millimeter MP-443 Grach pistol and lead Dovlatov through the patrons toward Stanton Way, the passage to West 65th Street. The crowd yielded slowly until the bodyguard fired two rounds from the Grach into the air.

Monsarrat closed the distance to the Russians quickly. The throng surrounded them, and as he came aside his targets, he stepped forward, executing the bodyguard with two suppressed rounds into his skull. The force of the bullets hurled him into the *Rezident*, knocking Dovlatov to his knees. Lifting the *Rezident* upright, Monsarrat gripped his shoulder as if supporting an inebriated friend and jammed the suppressor against his ribs. "Greetings, Anton Maximovich Dovlatov. Rupert Marlowe sends his very best regards."

He marched the Russian along Stanton Way. Approaching the

steps leading to West 65th Street, Dovlatov grabbed his arm and launched his body forward, but Monsarrat anticipated the movement and rolled his hip, throwing the *Rezident* onto his back. He yanked him upright and struck the bridge of his nose with the butt of the Beretta, sending a cascade of blood over his lower face. "Act stupid again, and I'll split your skull."

At their approach, Grinnell unlocked the Audi. He waited until Monsarrat propelled Dovlatov onto the rear bench before handing him a roll of duct tape. "Good timing, *habibi*. You have eighteen seconds until the security cameras come online."

"Any problems with the cops?"

"Not a one."

Monsarrat secured the wrists and ankles of Dovlatov before gagging his mouth with tape. He found the Russian's cell phone, removed the battery, snapped the SIM card, and dropped the pieces into his own pocket. Leaning against the door, he pointed the suppressed Beretta at the chest of the *Rezident*. "Drive slowly, Solomon. We don't want to attract attention."

Grinnell secured the locks. "This from the man who orchestrated the assassination of six *Spetsnaz* in the middle of Lincoln Center?"

"Only four. The two drivers are active."

Sirens screamed across the Upper West Side as Grinnell drove an indirect route, turning onto West 59th Street at Columbus Circle. Reaching Fifth Avenue, he drove south before turning again toward the East River. He changed direction, driving south toward Gramercy Park before steering the Audi west toward the Hudson River. In Greenwich Village, Charles Street was dark and quiet. Across from a 19th century brownstone, the Audi's headlights illuminated Goldman standing in an open space behind the Porsche.

Grinnell lowered the window. "Everything go according to plan?"

"One hundred percent," Goldman reported. "What about you?"

"We're also good."

"Mendel is waiting for you," Goldman continued. "You and Nathan take the Russian inside. I'll join you after I exchange the license plates on the Audi."

As Grinnell parked the car, Monsarrat slapped the *Rezident*. "Let's go, Dovlatov. It's time for us to chat."

Winning Exchange Swaps a Minor Piece for a Piece of Greater Value

A date, September 14, 1897, was chiseled into the cornice of the Charles Street Synagogue. Above the cornice of the brownstone, two Hebrew letters representing life, a *chai* and *yod*, crowned a menorah. Rusted bars protected stained glass windows, each inlaid with a golden Star of David. For over a century, the synagogue had served the spiritual needs of its congregants, but as its members aged, its numbers shrank. When the rabbi passed away, the synagogue lacked the funds to hire his replacement and maintain the building. The Jewish Community Council shuttered the synagogue and removed its books, Judaica, and Torah scrolls.

Monsarrat and Grinnell dragged Dovlatov toward the brownstone. Muscles aching from the weight of the Russian, he said, "You're eating too much, Dovlatov. You could die from a heart attack before I interrogate you."

Shackowitz stepped from the shadowed entrance of the synagogue. "Let me help."

"Excellent work in the park, Mendel," Monsarrat said.

Plucking the Russian from the grasp of Grinnell, Shackowitz nodded his head. "Did the fourth *Spetsnaz* give you any problems?"

"He cooperated. He died."

Grinnell opened the door to the synagogue. From a musty vestibule, a wooden corridor led to the rear of the building. They followed a second corridor into an empty sanctum. The paint on the walls and ceiling was faded and cracked, and spots of mold like mange scarred the rug on the floor. The odor of disuse was strong. A metal chair with a lopsided leg occupied the middle of the room. On the *bimah*, where the rabbi once led the service, a battery lantern provided light.

Shackowitz shoved Dovlatov onto the chair. "*A shvartz tog far ir*. A black day for you."

Goldman entered the sanctum, carrying a bag and a bucket. He placed them onto the rug. From the bag, he removed a roll of duct tape, a double edged boot knife with a narrow blade in a hard plastic scabbard. From the bucket, he withdrew sponges, towels, and a bottle of bleach. "Everything you ordered."

Monsarrat secured the Russian to the chair with the tape. He tore the old strip from his lips. "Do you know who I am?"

"I hope a Russian beat you, Monsarrat," Dovlatov replied.

"You're going to die here," Monsarrat stated. "If you cooperate, it'll be fast and easy. If you annoy me, it'll be painful and slow, so you can truly regret killing my friends and burning down my house."

Despite his situation, Dovlatov appeared to enjoy their conversation. "I received a text from Arkady Alexeevich Limonov. Did he turn against me or did you kill him?"

"Both."

"Then I hope he suffered before he died, just as you and your friends will suffer for what you have done tonight."

Monsarrat slapped his face, first with the palm of his right hand, and again with the back of the same hand, a fast, blurred movement. "I can keep this up all night, Dovlatov. Can you?"

"Oh, yes, for much longer."

Monsarrat saw condescension in his eyes. Cursing his own stupidity, he took the pieces of the Russian's cell phone from his pocket, inspected them, but did not find a tracking device. "He must have a tracer. The two *Spetsnaz* drivers are coming. Moishe, cover the front entrance and watch the street. Mendel, take the rear. Let them enter the building. I don't want a firefight on Charles Street."

Grinnell frisked the Russian. He removed his shoes and tried to pry off the heels. He pulled off his belt and pressed the leather. "I can't find it, Nathan."

Dovlatov laughed. "You couldn't find your own Jewish *khuy* with a magnifying glass."

Grinnell drove his right fist into his jaw. The force of the blow toppled the chair, and the Russian's head bounced off the floor. "What have I done?"

Monsarrat kneeled, pressed fingers against Dovlatov's jugular, worked his jaw, and felt his skull. "He'll be fine."

Hauling the chair upright, he reapplied the tape to the mouth of the *Rezident*. Using the boot knife, he sliced the Russian's shirt. "Moscow Centre embed tracers into their people. I'll work his left side. You take the right. It'll feel like a hard, oblong bump beneath the skin the size of a caplet."

After a minute, Grinnell exclaimed, "There is something in his right forearm."

Monsarrat pressed the tip of the blade into the Russian's skin. He worked the point into the flesh and made three small incisions, ignoring the flow of blood. He peeled back the skin and freed the tracer, dropping it into Grinnell's palm. Bandaging the wound with duct tape, he said, "It's virtually indestructible but will function only within a ten degree heat band of normal body temperature, so keep it warm. I want the *Spetsnaz* to follow the signal to us."

"You want them to find us?"

Monsarrat confirmed the objective. "On my signal, toss the tracer across the room."

Grinnell grasped the plan. "Do you think it will work?"

"We're in the House of the Lord, Solomon. Everything is possible."

From the vestibule, Goldman called, "Two black G550s just drove by slowly, turned around, and drove by again."

Grinnell turned off the lantern on the *bimah*. "Better for our eyes adjust to the dark."

In the stillness, the labored breathing of Dovlatov sounded like a dirge. Monsarrat slapped him awake. Pressing the flat of the blade against his cheek, he whispered, "Stay quiet."

Shackowitz returned to the sanctum. "One Russian bodyguard approaching the back entrance."

Goldman entered seconds later. "One Russian bodyguard advancing toward the front entrance."

Monsarrat placed the two men prone on opposite sides of the sanctum. He tipped the chair holding Dovlatov onto the rug, kneeled next to the Russian, and pulled Grinnell next to him. "Take head shots. They'll have body armor."

He tapped Grinnell as the *Spetsnaz* entered the darkened sanctum, saw his arm arc as if launching a hook shot, and imagined the flight of the tracer across the room. He yanked the tape from Dovlatov's mouth, pressed the sharp edge of the knife against the joint of his index finger, and pushed the blade deep into the flesh and bone as the Russian screamed.

Dropping the knife, he drew the Beretta, exhaled, and squeezed the trigger, firing two shots into the face of the first bodyguard. A volley of suppressed bullets from Grinnell, Shackowitz, and Goldman dropped the second bodyguard. Rising from the rug, he asked, "Everyone whole?"

Receiving three affirmative replies, he issued instructions. "Solomon, turn on the light. Moishe, collect the casings, then step outside to see if we disturbed anyone in the neighborhood. Mendel, search the bodies for intel, then drag them into the vestibule."

He prodded the two *Spetsnaz* with his foot, feeling the body armor, as Grinnell switched on the lantern. He checked for pulses, found none, and fired a *coup de grâce* into the forehead of each Russian. Turning to Grinnell, he said, "Solomon, the *Spetsnaz* arrived in two black Mercedes-Benz G550s. Take their keys, find the vehicles, and search them for intel. Be careful. Don't leave your DNA."

Alone with the *Rezident*, he said, "You thought killing me and my friends would protect Pavlik. You were wrong."

Dovlatov tossed the fig leaf of denial. "Pavlik was our most successful asset. I will die before I tell you anything."

He hauled the chair upright. "You'll die, and you'll talk, Dovlatov, easy or hard. It's your choice. Personally, I'm hoping for the latter."

A Trap Exploits an Opponent's Neglect of Strategy and Tactics

Monsarrat flicked blood from the blade, placed the knife onto the rug, and set the Beretta next to it. A scent of burnt almonds leaked from the suppressor. He tore a strip of duct tape and wrapped it like as bandage around Dovlatov's bleeding finger, repeating his final words to Houghton in the Sinai. "You should have left me alone."

The *Rezident* spoke as if addressing a recalcitrant child. "Remain calm, Monsarrat, and remember that professionals don't kill each other. Let me go now, and neither my government nor I will pursue you. You have my word."

"Your promises are worthless."

Monsarrat retrieved the knife, grasped the Russian's left ear, and severed the lobe. Tearing a strip of tape, he pressed it against the wound to stanch the flow of blood. Above the screams of the Russian, he said, "A glimpse into your future, if you continue to piss me off. For now, we'll skip the part where I ask questions, you supply bullshit answers, I break your fingers, you bleed and bullshit again. We'll go straight to the part where you spill your guts, the fat lady sings, and I put a bullet in your head."

"*Nyet.* Start at the beginning. I want the entire performance."

"Fine with me, Dovlatov. First question. Where is Cairstine Fergusson?"

"I don't know the name."

Monsarrat rotated his wrist to increase the torque of his punch, driving his fist into the Russian's chest. He fell backwards, his skull bounced off the floor, and his eyelids fluttered. "You won't die until

I'm ready to kill you, so you might want to change your answer. Where is Fergusson?"

Dovlatov gasped, "Was that your best punch?"

Monsarrat set him upright. "Fergusson escaped your killers and flew to London from Philadelphia."

"You are better informed than me."

"Does she have a new identity waiting for her in London? Is she transiting on her way to another location? Give her to me and save your own life."

"Take me to a hospital, Monsarrat. After the doctors fix me, I'll tell you everything you need."

Monsarrat pressed his thumb against the knuckle of Dovlatov's undamaged index finger, slipped his own fingers underneath, applied leveraged pressure, and snapped the bone. He waited until the Russian ceased shaking before demanding, "Where is Fergusson?"

"Take me to the hospital."

Monsarrat repeated the procedure on his middle finger. The spasms stopped, and he again posed his question "Where is she?"

"I don't know," Dovlatov moaned.

Monsarrat broke his ring finger. He asked his question, received the same answer, and snapped the Russian's little finger. "Your thumb is next. Would you rather I break it or slice it off?"

The Russian moaned again. "If I knew, I would tell you!"

Monsarrat didn't believe him. Shifting his questioning, he asked, "What's her back-up identity?"

Dovlatov answered as if trying to make amends for earlier failures. "Officially, she has none. If she created a cover, it is her secret."

Monsarrat lifted the knife. "I don't like vague answers."

The Russian eyed the blade, wet with his own blood. "You're a good operative. Take advantage of what I can do for you."

"I'm listening."

"Bring me to a hospital, and I'll tell you something about Fergusson that Marlowe never knew."

Monsarrat stepped behind the chair, grabbed a fistful of his silver hair, and yanked his head back. He pulled the tip of the blade across the soft curve of his throat, carving a shallow arc in the flesh. Blood seeped from the wound. "I don't negotiate."

He slowly traced the bloody tip of the blade around the healthy ear of the Russian. "Most people slice off an ear starting at the pinna, but I cleave it at the tympanic membrane."

"I'm an old man," Dovlatov moaned. "Torture me and your soul will burn in hell until the end of time."

"You're concerned for my soul?" Monsarrat mocked, twisting the knife into the ear canal.

Dovlatov bucked against the bonds as his blood flowed. "Bring me to a hospital! I will tell you everything you want to know!"

Monsarrat inserted the knife deeper into the ear. "Tell me the location of Fergusson. Where would she hide?"

"Take it out!" the Russian pleaded. "I will tell you, I swear."

Monsarrat paused the slow twisting of the blade. "I'm listening."

Despite his promise, the Russian only repeated his demand. "Bring me to a hospital."

Monsarrat stepped in front of the chair, the knife balanced in his palm. "You know nothing about Ferguson, so you have no value to me, but I have one more question, and if I like your answer, I'll take you to the hospital. If I don't, you'll die in that chair."

"Ask me anything!"

"Where is Sanhedrin? Where is Pavlik?"

Confused, the Russian asked, "What do you mean? Pavlik is dead."

"We both know Pavlik is alive. Where is he?"

"Pavlik died in Georgetown. I am the *Rezident*! I know!"

"Pavlik is alive, but if you don't know he survived the bombing, and if you don't know Fergusson's location, you're wasting my time."

"Pavlik is dead!"

"If so," Monsarrat replied, "he'll be happy for your company."

"You promised to bring me to the hospital!"

"I didn't like your answers, but I'll give you one more chance."

"Ask me anything!"

He repeated the question he asked Marlowe. "Tell me the full Russian birth name of Pavlik."

The question confused the *Rezident*. "Why do you think that Moscow Centre gave Sanhedrin a Russian name? He was given a code name, like all American traitors."

"Sanhedrin was a born and bred Russian."

Dovlatov snorted. "If you think so, you are a fool."

"Is that your final answer?"

"It is the truth!"

Monsarrat stared into the eyes of Dovlatov and saw the soul of a *mokroye delo* MD assassin. He understood that the Russian would lead him through twisting lies and layered evasions. Dovlatov would die before he broke. He sliced a strip of tape and pressed it across the mouth of the Russian. He pushed forced the blade through the outer and middle ears, twisting it into the inner ear, slicing through the labyrinth of nerves as the *Rezident* thrashed and animal sounds leaked from his sealed mouth. The blade entered the brain stem, sending him arching against the restraints. His body spasmed, his eyes bulged, and his mouth worked against the tape until his head sagged, his bowels and bladder released their foul contents, and the stench of death rose like a noxious spirit from his body.

He removed the knife, flicking away the blood. "For my friends."

He placed the knife, suppressed Beretta, and the holster onto the rug. He added the pieces of the Russian's cell phone for disposal as Grinnell entered the sanctum. "Any problems outside?"

"The neighborhood is quiet," Grinnell replied." I found nothing inside their vehicles. Mendel and Moishe are preparing to make the deaths of our Russians look like a *mafiya* hit. They'll wrap the bodies with chains and toss them into the Henry Street Basin in Red Hook, along with the sniper rifle. They'll also strip the two G550s of identification and abandon them."

Remembering the Lexus, Monsarrat shuddered. "It's a good plan."

Grinnell pointed at the dead Russian. "First Marlowe, now Dovlatov. When you find Fergusson, what will you do to her?"

Monsarrat saw the course of his plan clearly. "I'll use her to locate Sanhedrin. Then I'll kill her."

"What will you do if she won't help you?"

"I'll just kill her."

"At least, you'll have closure," Grinnell agreed. "When do you leave to meet my cousin?"

"As soon as possible."

"We'll clean up here. Go to Mendel's apartment, take a shower, change your clothes. How you look now, you'd scare a ghost."

CHECKMATE

An Attack on a King that Cannot be Repulsed

A Passed Pawn in the Eighth Rank May Turn Defeat into Victory

As the dawn broke, Nathan Monsarrat drove the Aston Martin fast, heading south on the New Jersey Turnpike, cursing his impatience to end the life of Dovlatov. His desire for vengeance and fervor to locate Fergusson had blinded his ability to parse the oniony layers of the Russian's lies. A *mokroye delo* assassin, the *Rezident* should have perished denying the existence of Pavlik but had ended his life in an auto-da-fé of confession, insisting that Pavlik was an American traitor. He suspected Dovlatov would betray Sanhedrin only to protect the existence of an even more valuable asset inside the White House.

Two hours after leaving Manhattan, he exited the Turnpike. In East Camden, a chain-link fence crowned with concertina wire protected a warehouse and a lot, empty save for a lone Ford F-150, its bumpers adorned with stickers of Philadelphia sports teams. A gate retracted at his approach. At the far end of the lot, a metal bay door in the warehouse clanked upward. He drove into the empty interior. The bay door descended behind him, as if the warehouse had swallowed the Aston Martin whole.

He killed the engine. Stepping from the car, stand lights burst brightly, illuminating a floor the size of a football field. Affixed to ceiling beams, security cameras monitored the interior. A Ferrari Spider occupied the middle of the space, and a work table next to it held the tools he had requested, a strong flashlight, a handheld vacuum cleaner, cotton towels, slot and Phillips screwdrivers, coveralls, safety goggles, work gloves, and hand cleaner.

Standing by the car, Grinnell's cousin wore a green Philadelphia

Eagles jacket, blue jeans, and work boots. He resembled his relative but stood two inches taller, carried twenty fewer pounds, and appeared ten years younger. He wore his black hair in a ponytail without a *yarmulke*. "It's a beautiful machine."

"Any trouble removing it from the airport?"

"If you look competent, busy, and official, people tend to leave you alone," replied the cousin. "I understand the Ferrari belongs to me after you finish your inspection, so please work carefully."

Monsarrat gestured toward the cameras. "They're recording us?"

"I disabled the system. I don't want evidence of our meeting."

"You're alone?

"My cousin said he trusts you, so I trust you. He also told me not to ask you questions, like your name and about your face."

"If your cousin was here," Monsarrat agreed. "he'd tell you to have breakfast and come back in a few hours."

"There's a diner down the road. You want me to bring something back for you? A bagel and cream cheese? Coffee?"

"Two sesame bagels with cream cheese and lox, plus an extra large black coffee, no sugar."

The cousin pointed to an entrance portal next to the bay door. "I heard you like spy games. I'll knock there times, then twice, then three times again."

Alone in the warehouse, Monsarrat donned the coveralls. With the flashlight, he searched the front section of the Ferrari, probing seats, lifting mats and rugs, unscrewing door and ceiling panels, shining the torch into nooks and crannies. He vacuumed hard and soft surfaces, emptied the bin onto the table, and sifted through the sparse contents, discovering nothing more important than lint.

A mid-engine vehicle lacking a spare tire, the Ferrari offered two storage spaces. The rear boot was pristine, as if the car had only rolled off its assembly line. In the equally clean front boot, leather straps secured two leather pouches, one to each sidewall. Adhered to the rear of the left pouch, he discovered a scrap of yellow paper the shape of a pennant stapled to a streamer of thin plastic. Beneath the heat of the stand lights, it fluttered like a warning flag.

He memorized the contents of the fragment before carrying it to the Aston Martin and placing it inside the glove box. He returned to the Ferrari and examined the contents of the two pouches but discovered nothing. A search beneath the chassis and into the wheel mounts produced identical results. Satisfied with the inspection, he removed the grime from his skin with the hand cleaner and towels.

A series of knocks boomed. Opening the door, he offered a greeting. "Good timing. I just finished with the car."

The cousin stepped through the entrance portal, holding a paper bag. "My treat. Not worth as much as a Ferrari Spider, but the bagels are really good."

Monsarrat ate the food and drank the coffee quickly. "Solomon warned you that some nasty people might look for the car?"

"By sunset, it won't exist. I'll retail the parts. My profit margin are bigger than if I sell it whole."

Shortly before noon, Monsarrat slipped on his sunglasses and reversed the Aston Martin from the warehouse. Returning to the Turnpike, he continued driving south. He quickly passed through Delaware. In Maryland, he paid cash to fill the fuel tank. North of Washington, he exited onto the Beltway, driving toward Virginia. Crossing the Potomac River, he entered Old Town in Alexandria, locking the car in the parking lot of a private equity bank where he held a fifty year lease on the rental of a biometric safe deposit box.

Thirty minutes prior to its closing, he carried his bag into the bank lobby. Removing his sunglasses, he approached a clerk. After providing identification, he followed the clerk to a protected area. He tapped an alphanumeric password onto a touch screen before pressing the tip of his right index finger against an optical reader. Diodes flashed green, and a dispenser released a digital fob, dual deadbolts withdrew from the mortise, and the gate swung open. He stepped into the secure zone, activated the fob, and entered its twelve digit one-time code into a wall keypad, followed by his personal eight digit security code. He pressed his right eye against an iris scanner. The hatch of his biometric safety deposit box swung open.

He withdrew the box from the wall, entered a privacy room, closed the door, and locked it. To block any hidden cameras, he hunched over the box before removing a Beretta .380 Pico, a leather holster, two extra magazines, a box of bullets, a five inch boot knife in a hard plastic scabbard, and packets of cash. He placed the Westbrook documents, his own wallet, personal papers, and laptop into the box, returned the original contents minus the cash, exited the privacy room, and returned the box to the wall slot. He passed the fob to the clerk and departed the bank.

He drove the Aston Martin across the Arlington Memorial Bridge. Circling the Lincoln Memorial, he continued to Kalorama Park. At the garage, he removed the yellow scrap of paper from the glove box and placed it into his bag. He walked toward Connecticut Avenue, flagged a taxi, and directed the cabbie to Rosslyn. He walked up the hill to the three story brick building on Fort Myer Drive. In the lobby, he pressed the buzzer of M. Smith and climbed the stairs to the apartment. Knocking on the door, he announced, "It's Raskolnikov."

Carlyle opened the door, her expression sharp. "Welcome back, Saint Nate."

In the kitchen, he placed the Aston Martin fob onto the table. "I returned the car to the garage. Other than the miles added and the faint smell of smoke, it's none the worse for the trip."

"Tell me everything," she ordered.

He briefed her on his actions since they last spoke and his next steps. "I'll start by looking for Fergusson in London."

"What will you do if she's not in London?"

"I'll follow her trail."

"She may not leave one."

"She's flesh and blood, Brenda. She'll leave a trail."

"What will you do when you find her?"

"Extract the location of Sanhedrin from her."

"What if she doesn't know?"

"Then she's no use to me. I'll kill her."

"How do you go forward if she gives you the intel?"

"I'll kill her, find Sanhedrin, and exterminate him," he replied in a burst of passion. "Bottom line? No matter how long it takes, they're both going to die. You'll be safe. Sylvie, Datura, and the others will have their vengeance."

"About time," she said. "How can I help?"

He placed the scrap of yellow paper onto the table. "It may be a lead to Fergusson. I found it in the front boot of her Ferrari."

She examined the pennant. "It's recent. The date is this year."

Opening her laptop, she tapped commands onto the keyboard.

"We know she flew to London. The word "Peckham" on the masthead could refer to the street in South London, and the initial digits of the phone number match a neighborhood exchange."

He pointed to the Dr, without a following period. "Maybe it's a receipt from a doctor?"

"It's possible," she conceded, "given its location on the paper, though, more likely it's the start of a business description, like drugstore, but the Brits usually use chemist or pharmacy, so it could be dry cleaner or drapery store."

"It looks like a receipt, and dry cleaners use the kind of plastic that was attached to the paper."

"Look at the digit on the next line," she ordered. "The 3 most likely is part of a street address. The first of the two boxes below is followed by To Call. The second box, with a check inside, is followed by To D, probably To Deliver."

"Stores usually deliver within a limited area. We confirm the address of the business, we narrow the search radius for her address."

Carlyle continued to the next line. "The three letters, Fio, probably start the first name of the customer. Since Cairstine doesn't match, it could indicate she's switched identities. Or it could be a receipt that belonged to a friend, they ran errands or went shopping together, placed the items into the boot, and we're tracking an innocent Brit."

"Everything's possible," he admitted, "but let's stay positive. Can you search for names that start with those letters?"

She typed an inquiry into laptop. "Not many, which helps us. It could be Fio, it could be Fiorenza. Both are Latinate. It could be Celtic, Fiora or Fiona."

"Fergusson is a Scot. She might want to stay with the familiar."

"Like you and your Canadians," she grunted, typing a new inquiry. "Five dry cleaners operate in the area. Three have "Peckham" in their names, but only one has an address that starts with a "3," Peckham Dry Cleaner on 31 Peckham Road. Also, the initial digits on the paper scrap match the start of the phone number."

"You've found it, haven't you?"

"I think so," she agreed,."You want to search for drapery stores?"

"Let's stay with the dry cleaner. Is there a website?"

She found the link and opened it. "They offer a delivery service within a two kilometer area."

"Can you show it?"

She opened an interactive map. "My confidence is high that Fergusson lives inside the yellow circle. Should I print it?"

"I've memorized it."

"Showing off, Nathan?"

"All glory to you, Brenda. Your skills are outstanding."

"I won't argue," she said. "When do you leave for London?"

"I need to reserve a seat on the next flight."

On the Eighth Rank a Pawn Becomes a Queen

Monsarrat remained inside the apartment until night fell. Prior to departing for the airport, he handed Carlyle the domestic use flip phone. "It won't work where I'm going."

"You want me to just sit here and worry about you?" she asked.

"Until I kill Fergusson and Sanhedrin, you have to hibernate. I know it's not pleasant, but I don't want to lose you."

"A romantic tough guy. You continue to intrigue me, Saint Nate," she said. "Watch your own back. I don't want to lose you, either."

He walked through the dark night into Rosslyn. At the metro station, he hailed a taxi. The roads leading to Dulles International Airport were old friends. As Mark Sanger, he checked in for the British Airways redeye flight to London, received his First Class boarding pass, and cleared formalities. At a book kiosk by the departure gate, he bought a chess magazine, a book of famous twentieth century chess matches, and a tourist guidebook to London.

During the eight hour flight, he studied chess strategies and games. He perused the guidebook for information on hotels and landmarks. Landing in Heathrow the next morning, he stuffed his purchases into the seat pocket. In the arrival hall of Terminal Five, he joined weary travelers shuffling through Immigration and Customs. At a money exchange before the exit doors, he converted dollars to pounds.

Outside the terminal, he hailed a black cab, providing the cabbie with the name of a hotel in Belgravia, in central London. He loitered in the lobby, returned to the street, and hailed a second cab for the trip across the River Thames. On Peckham Road, he directed the cabbie to the Lucas Inn. Mark Sanger provided his passport and credit card to the receptionist. In his room, he placed cash into the safe. Before leaving the Inn, he plucked a copy of the Daily Mail from a lobby stand.

On Peckham Road, he entered a coffee shop, choosing a stool at a counter next to a window offering a view of the Peckham Dry Cleaner shop. Placing his order with the waitress, he noted her smile. "Have I offended you?"

"Oh, no," she insisted, "but you must be a Yank, matching a blueberry scone with coffee, not tea."

"Canadian, actually."

He sipped the coffee, pecked at the scone, and flipped through the tabloid. Drinking his second cup of coffee, he watched a windowless yellow panel van with the words Peckham Dry Cleaner – We Deliver painted in black on the doors drive into the lot next to the store. He noted the time, shortly before noon, and the driver, a thin young man with shoulder length brown hair, a scraggly beard, and an elfin face wearing blue jeans, orange running shoes, and a long sleeved white tee shirt. Wireless headphone buds protruded from his ears, and he carried a tablet in his hand. He locked the van and entered the store through a service entrance.

Five minutes passed before the driver reappeared. Monsarrat paid his bill, exited the coffee shop, and followed the young man on his determined march to Benhill Road. The driver entered a corner pub, The Willow Grouse. He lingered by the entrance until a trio of workmen approached. Following them inside the pub, he spotted the driver in the main room, eating a toasted cheese sandwich and drinking a pint of bitters.

Sitting at a round table with a clear line of sight to the young man, Monsarrat ordered the same. He perused the tabloid for the better part of an hour, until the driver exited the pub. He followed him until the young man returned to the dry cleaner shop. He continued walking to the Lucas Inn. At the entrance, he hailed an idling cab. Sliding onto the rear bench, he said, "Thebes, on Dean Street."

The cabbie approved. "I appreciate the high end talent, myself."

Situated between an avant-garde theater and a Moroccan restaurant, Thebes was a subdued bookend to Luxor, lacking the Great Sphinx, Tutankhamen, and a bouncer in the costume of a harem guard. He settled the fare and surveyed the street before entering the club. Paying the cover fee, he stepped into a dark room redolent with perfume. The afternoon clientele was sparse, but the hostesses were attentive. He waved off the offer of a table and approached the bartender. Pressing a ten pound note into a thick hand adorned with prison tattoos, he said, "Tell Prince Joshua that Nathan from Warri would like to speak with him."

The bartender wore a pugilist's mask, cauliflower ears, and a flattened nose. Scars spread across his knuckles. He glanced at the money. "Sure thing."

Only the pin waving the dual flags of the United Kingdom and Nigeria on the lapel of his brown suit differed Prince Joshua Adumu from his deceased twin brother. The Nigerian held Monsarrat for a long minute in a bone crushing embrace. His voice mimicked the falsetto of Prince Jasper. "Welcome to Thebes, my dear friend. Too many years have passed since we last spoke."

Speaking with the Nigerian was conversing with a ghost. "You're looking robust, Prince Joshua."

Adumu led Monsarrat to a table in the rear of the room. He summoned a scantily clad waitress. "Your pleasure, Nathan?"

"A double espresso, with a lemon rind, if you have it."

The Nigerian held up a pair of stubby fingers. "Two espressos, Cleo, both with rinds."

Turning to his guest, Adumu declared, "My brother was my heart and my soul. Have you information on who took his life?"

Monsarrat began his deception at a disadvantage, not knowing if the brothers had spoken before Prince Jasper died.. "Your brother has passed? When? Was it his heart?"

"He was executed gangland style, by garrote. My brother had many competitors and many enemies. Soon I will know who ordered his death and who wielded the weapon. My brother will be avenged."

"It must have happened shortly after I met with him," Monsarrat said, unwilling to reveal the deathbed confession of Marlowe.

Adumu showed surprise, "Of what did you speak?"

"I asked for his help obtaining a visa to Libya. When I picked it up at Luxor, he was well."

The Nigerian spoke directly. "Are the bruises on your face related to the death of my brother?"

"I was mugged in Boston," Monsarrat lied.

Adumu began to reply but stopped at the approach of the waitress. He waited until she withdrew before speaking again. "I am sorry for your misfortune."

"As am I for your loss, Prince Joshua, and I am at your service, if I may be of help to you."

The Nigerian rubbed the rind around the lip of the cup before swallowing the coffee. "Thank you, Nathan. You know that my brother loved you, as do I. He considered you a brother, as do I still. We owe our successes to you. Without your assistance, we would have perished in Warri, but let us not dwell on sadness. You have come to me for assistance? I will help you, if I am able."

Monsarrat drank his espresso in a series of small sips assessing the man. Like his dead brother, Prince Joshua's loyalty was suspect and his greed profound. "I need a clean weapon, ammunition, and an expedited delivery this afternoon."

All is possible, but tell me if your request is related to the death of my brother. Do you seek your own vengeance?"

"I'm afraid it's a private matter, Prince Joshua."

Disappointment laced Adumu's reply. "Then I only need to know your preference of weapon."

"A Smith & Wesson .38 Special with a two inch barrel."

"You shall have it. Where would you like it delivered?"

"Fifty meters from here, toward Oxford Street, is a coffee shop with a blue awning," Monsarrat answered. "I'll wait inside and pay upon delivery, in cash."

"I will do my best to provide swift service, Nathan."

"I know you will, Prince Joshua."

Adumu squeezed Monsarrat's arm. With his free hand, he pulled their foreheads together. "I love you as if we shared the same blood, Nathan. Whenever you need me, I shall always support you."

Exiting the club, Monsarrat walked to the coffee shop. The door trilled as he entered. He took a table at the rear, ordered an Americano, and opened the tabloid, but his attention focused upon the entrance. Two hours passed before the door trilled again and bartender from Thebes entered, carrying a pastry box adorned with blue ribbons from a Frith Street bakery.

He motioned at a chair. "Have a seat."

The bartender placed the box onto the table but remained standing. "A gift from Prince Joshua. No payment necessary."

Monsarrat waited ten minutes before departing the coffee shop. Carrying the box, he walked to Oxford Street and flagged a cab. He provided the cabbie his destination and sat silently on the rear bench, the box on his lap. He paid the fare before an all-hour convenience shop on Peckham Road. Inside the shop, he purchased an electric razor, a pair of scissors, aspirin, and bandages.

He returned to his room in the Lucas Inn. In the bathroom, he spread the purchases across the counter and charged the electric razor in the outlet. From the box, he withdrew a brushed nickel Smith & Wesson .38 Special with a two inch barrel and a synthetic hand grip wrapped in a chamois towel. He inspected its mechanisms, counted the five bullets in the cylinder, sighted the weapon, and confirmed the identification markings had been removed.

Stripping off his clothes, he stood naked before the mirror. He sheared his hair with the scissors until a stranger stared at him. The razor removed the stubble. He scooped the hair from the sink and dropped it into the trash can. He shaved his face carefully. In the shower, hot water soothed his muscles and his nerves.

He toweled dry and dressed, the jacket covering the revolver held against the small of his back by the pressure of his belt. In a secondhand clothes store on Shenley Road, mindful of Marlowe's claim of Fergusson's fondness for bad boys, he selected a black ensemble of jeans, tee shirt, harness boots, leather jacket, and watch cap. He carried the items to the cash register next to a jewelry case.

A woman with purple hair and a pair of neck tattoos, Chelsea for football, Saracens for rugby, tabulated the items. "What else, lovey?"

He glanced at the case. "Give me two silver and turquoise bands to fit my middle fingers and a pair of the studded leather bracelets."

She placed the items atop the glass case. "Is it a costume party?"

"More like a midlife crisis," he replied. "Do you pierce ears?"

"I do," she agreed. "Which one?"

"A silver and turquoise stud in each ear, to match the rings."

She removed a selection from the case. "Will these two do for you?"

"Perfectly."

She inserted the studs into his lobes with a piercing gun and swabbed the areas with hydrogen peroxide. "You're a new man, aren't you, lovey?"

He paid in cash, returned to the Lucas Inn, and immediately slept. The following morning, dressed in his new purchases, the revolver again against his back, he picked up the morning tabloid in the lobby. Returning to the coffee shop, he chose a different stool but ordered the scone and coffee combination from the same waitress.

He noted her expression. "Is there a problem?"

"It's not common, black coffee and a blueberry scone," she replied, "but yesterday another tourist ordered the same."

The success of his disguise pleased him. He read the tabloid until the driver parked the yellow panel van next to the service entrance. He waited for the young man to depart the dry cleaner shop, paid the bill and followed him to The Willow Grouse. Instead of entering the pub, he returned to the dry cleaner shop and waited next to the yellow van. An hour passed before he again saw the young man. "I like the color of your truck."

The driver considered the size and appearance of Monsarrat. "What did you say?"

"I need to speak with one of your female customers."

"Try a dating app."

Monsarrat showed him three 50 pound notes. "The first is for her name, the second for her address, and the third for her cell number."

"Not worth my job."

He added a fourth note. "For your fast service."

The driver took the money. "Meet me at The Willow Grouse in two hours with four more of these notes, and I'll help you find her."

To upset the confidence of the young man, Monsarrat entered The Willow Grouse five minutes late. He found the driver at a table in the rear of the pub, nursing a bottle of brown beer and staring into his tablet. He took the opposite chair and placed 200 pounds onto the table. "Give me the information."

The driver covered the money with the tablet. "Flashing quid in this pub begs for trouble."

Monsarrat ignored his warning. "The customer is six feet tall, middle aged, weighs about 125 pounds. She takes home delivery."

"I deliver to dozens of women who fit that description. Give me something more specific."

Monsarrat trusted his instincts. "She has a Scots accent."

"I know who you want," the driver claimed. "Fiona Murray. A real looker, for an older woman. Hands like cinder blocks."

He swiped the tablet and scribbled the name, address, and cell phone number onto a napkin. "We're done. I forget about you, and you forget about me."

Monsarrat grabbed his wrist, taking no pleasure from his grimace of pain. "I'll tell you when we're done. Describe her building, size, color, fence, wall, number of windows, how many apartments, what kind of dogs, sophistication of the security systems."

The young man struggled in his grip. "I don't want any part of it."

"Either you talk to me," Monsarrat warned, squeezing the wrist harder, "or I'll break it."

He listened to the young man, glanced at the napkin, and forced the paper into his beer bottle. "If you tell anyone about me, I won't bother with your wrist. I'll break your neck."

Perpetual Check Never Leads to Mate

Monsarrat waited until the young man departed The Willow
Grouse before leaving the pub. He experienced the familiar emotions
of launching an operation, anticipation, trepidation, exhilaration,
topped by the prospect of vengeance. He wanted to look into the eyes
of Fergusson as she died, and he wanted to enjoy the slow death of
Sanhedrin. He walked along Peckham Road until he reached Essex
House, a pub on the corner of Crofton Road. He stepped into a well
lit room. Choosing a bar stool next to the front window, he ordered
black coffee.

The window offered a clear view of number fourteen, the London
home of Fiona Murray. As the afternoon faded into evening, a cab
stopped before the low concrete wall. A woman holding brown and
gold Harrods shopping bags exited. Her straight auburn hair reached
her shoulders. Gold-flecked green eyes rested above an askew nose.
Her eyebrows were thick, her full lips, skin pale, and ears small.
Approaching middle age, her weight trim, she stood six feet tall. Her
knuckles resembled knobs of gnarled oak. Despite her disguise, he
recognized her as Cairstine Fergusson.

He watched her walk toward her home like a runway model on a
sidewalk, but her bags hampered the quick draw of a weapon, her
stiletto heels impeded escape on foot, and her eyes not once surveilled
the area. Admiring her confidence, he disdained her fieldwork. He
watched her insert a key into the door lock of number fourteen.
Minutes passed before lights inside the second floor flat brightened
the edges of the shuttered windows. He ordered another cup of black

coffee, hoping she would soon reemerge from the flat.

Forty-five minutes passed before she reappeared, wearing a mustard colored calf length leather coat with a rainbow hued silk scarf over her shoulders. He paid his tab and followed her onto Peckham Road, walking toward the Surrey Rifles War Memorial. She turned onto Camberwell Grove and pushed open the gate to the Church of St. Christopher. Carefully maintained flower gardens framed the manicured churchyard, and the gravestones of the parish cemetery stood in neat rows. Before the entrance to the building, a spotlight illuminated a signboard of community announcements. Pulling open a wooden door, she stepped into the building.

Monsarrat waited a moment before following her. At the signboard, he read an announcement for a chess friendly, players of all levels welcome. Checking his watch, he saw five minutes remained before the friendly commenced. He stepped into the church. Inside the nave, white columns with foliated capitals flanked rows of wooden pews lining both sides of a central aisle. A neoclassical pipe organ rose from an altar, and leaded stained glass panels depicting New Testament struggles crowned the space above the chancel. Balanced on a music stand beneath a Pietà, a paper arrow with the words Chess Friendly pointed toward a staircase.

Incandescent bulbs lit the passageway. He descended a flight of wooden steps into a basement. A second arrow directed him to a card table. Dehumidifiers hummed in the corners of the room. A placard requested a two pound donation. He dropped a coin into a basket and signed the register as Mark Sanger.

A woman with hair tinted blue asked, "How do you describe your level of expertise, Mr. Sanger?"

"I haven't played since high school."

She handed him a name tag. "Tell Father Bernard. He'll partner your first game with a player at your level."

Monsarrat glanced about the room, set with a dozen square card tables, each with two chairs, a plastic chessboard with pieces, and a clock. Pensioners and teenagers stood by the tables, their attention to Fergusson obvious. A teenage boy approached her but turned away at the sound of a bell, announcing the start of the friendly.

In his first match, Monsarrat mated the same teenage boy in four minutes. His second match resulted in a pensioner tipping his king onto the board after seven minutes. A teenage girl surrendered the third match after ten moves. "Well played," he offered.

"You would have won faster if you paid more attention to the board, instead of the beautiful Fiona Murray."

He feigned ignorance. "Who is she?"

The teenager pointed at Fergusson. "If you play with her, she'll kill you. She never loses."

Monsarrat drew her in the fourth match. He examined her, absorbing strengths, seeking weaknesses, and shook her strong hand. "Good luck, Fiona."

"You hold an unfair advantage, laddie. You're anonymous."

He pressed the name tag onto his jacket. "I'm Mark Sanger, from Halifax. Canada, not England. I'm a travel writer."

Releasing his hand, she said, "After the friendly, you'll have to tell me about your journeys."

"As long as you let me buy you a drink."

She offered her fists. He tapped the left, and she revealed the pawn. "You play white. Good luck to you."

Monsarrat chose the 1924 match between Capablanca and Tartakower at the International Chess Masters Tournament in New York. He played the Cuban's opening and second moves, but the strength of her hand checked his third attempt. "What's wrong?"

"Do you plan to repeat each move Capablanca made? I came for the human interaction. If I wanted a classic match, I would have remained with my laptop in the comfort of my living room."

Ten minutes later, he tipped his king onto the board. "You've defeated me."

"After your silly start, you played well, but a softness in your middle game led to the inevitable."

He heard her disdain for weakness. Stripping the name tag from his jacket, he balled and dropped it onto the board. "Let me buy you a few drinks to celebrate your victory. Later, I'll show you there's no softness in my endgame."

She offered a Scottish reprimand. "You're the wee hen that never laid away, coming on to me in a church like a choir boy in black leather. What is it that you want from me?"

His reply offered aggression. "Nothing from you, Fiona. Just you."

She placed her strong hand onto his chest. "If it's your game, I know a fine place for a few drinks."

She led him from the room. They climbed the stairs and exited the church. "What brought you to my neighborhood, aside from your pursuit of virginal chess players?"

Monsarrat appreciated her skills, using her sexual aura to cadge intelligence. "A Toronto magazine commissioned me to write a piece on the gallery scene in South London."

"We share the same interests. I acquire fine arts for private clients."

"I knew we were simpatico as soon as I shook your hand," he claimed. "I felt your energy."

She nipped his earlobe with her teeth. "Tell me, Mark. How did you learn of our friendly?"

"Just my good luck."

"Oh, no,' she replied. "The good luck is all mine."

Approaching Essex House, he ran his fingers over her scarf. "It's exquisite, like you."

"Keep up with the flattery. I enjoy it."

"Where do you live, Fiona? Somewhere close?"

"Are you wishing for an invitation to my flat?"

"If you prefer, we can step into a pub for drinks."

She pointed at the signpost. "I live on Crofton Road. The service is very personal. I'll show you my collection of silk scarves, too."

Outside number fourteen, she kissed him, more assault than seduction. "I can't decide whether to have you before, after, or during our first drink. Maybe all three."

She unlocked the door and ushered him inside the building. On the second floor, she led him into the flat before securing the alarm and engaging the deadbolts. She stepped behind him, grabbed the collar of his jacket, and pressed her face close to his ear, whispering, "We're going to have fun, laddie, so make yourself comfortable. I only need a moment for myself."

She released him and, as he shrugged off his jacket, smashed the back of his head with the butt of her Walther. Bleeding from a gash in his skull, he dropped unconscious onto the floor. She removed his revolver, examined his wallet, and stripped him naked, tossing his clothes and jewelry into a pile on the floor. She walked to the kitchen, took plastic restraints and duct tape from a drawer, and returned to her unconscious guest. A set of restraints secured his wrists behind his back. A second set bound his ankles. She covered his mouth with tape, wiped blood from the Walther with his tee shirt, and dragged him into the living room.

She hung her coat in the bedroom closet, removed her shoes, shed her wig and contact lenses. In the living room, she poured a single malt into a crystal cordial glass, swallowing the whisky neat, the thick taste of peat fueling her anger. The pain of abandoning Cairstine Fergusson had been eased by the knowledge that Fiona Murray awaited her. Discarding Murray meant creating a new identity, moving to a new city, embarking on a new start. The alternative, remaining on Crofton Road, would be a mistake as blatant as sending her address to Moscow Centre, but before she abandoned London, she would learn how Fiona Murray had been discovered.

She tapped the screen of her cell phone. The call connected on the first ring. "Come home now."

Closing the phone, she heaved the naked man onto a spindle chair. She adjusted his legs, so that his scrotum swung beyond the rim of the wooden chair. "How did you find me? Your answer will intrigue me."

She settled into an armchair, attached the suppressor to the pistol, and considered Pavlik, her lover, an epochal man, more demigod than mortal. Once, she would have killed for him, and she would have died for him, but he had kept his resurrection from her for many months, and he secretly married another woman. Her eyes fixed on the unconscious man in the chair. Despite her analytic brilliance, she could not understand how Nathan Monsarrat had found her, when only she and Pavlik knew the existence of the flat.

A Rook and a Knight Deliver the Arabian Mate

The longer Fergusson gazed at Monsarrat, the more deeply she questioned the loyalty of Pavlik, her lover, and her suspicions sharpened, as bitter as hemlock. She rose from the armchair and again prodded Monsarrat's exposed scrotum with her toes. "It's a pity, truly a waste. I would have spent hours enjoying all that you offer."

Monsarrat jolted awake as the tape tore his lips. He spat blood onto the porcelain tiles. His eyes focused, and he saw Fergusson. "You look different, Fiona, but maybe my vision's just blurred."

She lifted her foot again, prodding his scrotum with additional force. "Welcome back, laddie. You've been gone quite a while."

He recoiled from her toes. "I like naked, and I'm into rough sex, but I don't like blood, especially my own."

She ground her heel against the arch of his foot. "I can't begin to express my pleasure at finally making your acquaintance, **Nathan**."

The pain transformed his words into a hiss. "It's not my name."

She provided a summary of his career and personal life, concluding with a declaration. "You're not Mark Sanger from Halifax. You're Nathan Monsarrat from Greylock, by way of Langley."

"You're confusing me with another guy."

Her toes returned to his scrotum. "I made you as soon as you left the pub to follow me. It's not that you were sloppy, only you're not in my league, but I would like to know how you found me."

Nausea surged from his stomach. "I don't like this game, Fiona."

"We need to have a wee chat, Nathan. There's no time like now."

Despite the pain in his foot and the aching in his groin, his mind sharpened, and his Agency training controlled his response. When accused, the instructors at The Farm had counseled, deny, deny, deny until the interrogators doubted themselves. "I'm Mark Sanger. I'm here to write an article on the gallery scene in South London."

She exchanged the Walther for his revolver. "How does a travel writer from Halifax earn a face full of bruises?"

"I was mugged."

"Are you afraid of being mugged a second time, or do you always carry a weapon on assignment?"

"London is a dangerous city."

She bounced his scrotum again. "Have you come to avenge the death of Daniel Westbrook?"

Waves of nausea spread from his groin. "I don't know anyone by that name."

Her foot bounced his scrotum until he gagged from the pain. "Tell me how you found me."

The instructors at The Farm had also preached offense over defense, the value of taking the fight to the interrogators. Using her Georgetown name, he responded. "Work with me, Cairstine. I'll share the intel I took from Dovlatov. It'll save your life."

Pleased she had broken his resistance, she replied, "You're all bum and parsley, Nathan, a true blowhard. The *Rezident* would not have shared intelligence with you over a friendly cuppa tea."

"We didn't drink tea, and it wasn't friendly. I interrogated him. When he had nothing more to give me, I killed him, just like I ended the life of your butler."

"Yer bum's oot the windae. You're talking tripe," she accused, but her eyes betrayed her interest.

"Call the *Rezidentura*. Ask if they've found the corpse of Dovlatov. Ask if they've discovered his six missing bodyguards. Ask if they've recovered the body of Marlowe. I killed him in Greylock."

"If true, I am appreciative, but I'll not make that call. Since you're naked and bound with my toes bouncing your manhood, give me the intel you took from Dovlatov, and I'll decide its worth."

He countered with his own offer. "I'll give you the first half the intel, we'll walk to the pub, you'll answer my questions, I'll pass you the second half, and we'll go our separate ways."

She bounced his scrotum again, taking pleasure in his pain. "Save yourself the suffering. We both understand that you'll tell me what I want to know. The question is how much agony you'll endure before your need to survive replaces your desire to persevere."

He used her eagerness against her, blending the intelligence taken from Marlowe and Dovlatov with his own fiction to achieve his own goal. "Your name is Yulia Lazarevna Belyakova, born in Leningrad."

"You have my attention."

He drew from the confession of Marlowe. "Moscow Centre didn't recall you. Dovlatov set you up. He ordered your butler to kill you before you reached the airport, but Marlowe fucked up. The back-up team in Dulles fucked up, too."

"They were amateurs."

He expanded his fiction. "Dovlatov ordered a snatch team to acquire you. Since he's dead, he won't call them off. They're coming for you, and if you keep wasting time, they'll kick down the door and shoot both of us in the back of our heads."

She bounced his scrotum harder. "Even if you speak the truth, there's no connection between Cairstine Fergusson and Fiona

Murray, nor between Dumbarton Street and Compton Road. No one will find me."

He fought the rising waves of nausea. "I found you."

She removed her toes. "That you did, laddie, so tell me how you located me, and I'll dispatch you quickly. Lie to me, and I'll shoot your manhood and allow you to bleed to death."

The absence of her foot was a joy. "Dovlatov told me."

Her punch, a smooth and fast cross to his jaw, knocked him to the floor. She placed her foot on his throat and demanded, "I want a serious answer. How did you find me?"

Like a gaffed fish, he writhed on the tiled floor. His voice rasping, he said, "You're half right about why I'm here, Cairstine. I want to avenge Westbrook, but I'm also here for Felix Sanhedrin. You know him as Pavlik."

His knowledge impressed her. "In that case, you're on the fool's own errand. He died in the Georgetown bombing."

He recognized the tics of the professional liar, the almost too fast twitch of the eye, the tiniest curling of the lips, the flash of blood tinting the cheeks. "We both know he's alive. Give him to me, and I'll explain how I found you."

"You're badly mistaken," she claimed as she kicked the side of his head. "Neither are you in a position to make demands, so tell me. How did you find me? Dovlatov knows nothing of this flat."

His vision clouded, and pain hammered his skull. Counting down from ten, he continued his story. "Before she died, Abby Houghton told me that Felix Sanhedrin is Pavlik."

"The woman is dead?"

He steeled himself for another kick. "I stuck a knife into her neck."

Remembering her humiliation in Ashby Gap, Fergusson experienced vindication. "A pity. I enjoyed our time together."

The lack of punishment emboldened Monsarrat. "She boasted about sex with you, too. It's something we have something in common, Cairstine. We both liked fucking her."

"What else did she tell you?"

"She said that Sanhedrin faked his death with a body double."

She confirmed Houghton's story. "Since you're soon to be dead, I'll tell you that Pavlik is Sanhedrin, he's alive, and he kept the fact of the body double from Dovlatov and Moscow Centre."

"Where did Sanhedrin find him?"

"He was a low-level member of a Soviet trade delegation to Rome. Pavlik saw him in the hotel bar, chatting with an Italian hooker. The resemblance shocked him, and they struck a deal. Pavlik smuggled him into the United States, provided him with a deep identity, and the rest you know."

He probed to discover her knowledge of Haverhill. "Houghton also told me about the transcript and her plan to replace Sanhedrin as your asset in the White House, but you didn't need her, did you?"

Fergusson hauled him upright and shoved him onto the chair. "I'm done discussing the woman. It's time that you answered my question. How did you find me?"

Monsarrat continued to probe her knowledge of Haverhill. "Both Marlowe and Dovlatov confirmed that Pavlik is Sanhedrin, but the *Rezident* also confessed to a more important fact."

Her toes pressed hard against his scrotum. "You might want to answer my question."

"Stop tickling me and pay attention," he gasped. "Moscow Centre owns another asset inside the White House."

"We both know about Houghton."

"She was a wannabe. The real second asset is the most powerful man in the country, and he's supplied Moscow Centre with the highest levels of intelligence for a long time."

"Who is it that you think you're describing?"

He prayed she would confirm his suspicion. "Augustus Haverhill."

Fergusson drew back her foot and kicked his scrotum, like an old style field goal kicker. "You possess a vivid imagination, but your stories are a waste of my time. Tell me how you found me!"

The pain was a molten skewer into his brain. Its intensity froze his muscles. Moments passed before he could speak again, his voice a whisper. "You didn't have the need to know."

She kicked him again, and he passed out. She slapped his face until he lurched back into consciousness. "How did you find me?"

He spat onto the floor before replying. "Give me Sanhedrin, and I'll tell you."

Fergusson again bounced his scrotum with her toes. "Since you only have a few moments of life remaining, I will tell you the truth of Pavlik. He is coming to us now. He did not betray his country, because he's an American like I'm a Scot. Pavlik is a hero of the *Rodina*, born Fyodor Stepanovich Shchedrin in Yaroslavl, trained since boyhood by Moscow Centre. He is our most illustrious deep penetration agent. He is also my lover."

Monsarrat welcomed the confirmation of his suspicions. He gazed at her through eyes blurred with pain. "Why did he marry Houghton? Did the thought of them fucking upset you?"

She pressed the barrel of the revolver against his temple. "A clean shirt will do you. You're not long for this world, Nathan Monsarrat. I haven't shot you yet only so Pavlik can kill you himself."

He flung a warning at her. "He'll kill you, too, Cairstine. He doesn't feel love. He has no loyalty."

"Tell me now, and I'll tell Pavlik to kill you quickly, so you won't suffer. How did you find me?"

His eyes shifted between her face and the revolver. "Like you said, you won't kill me, so why should I talk?"

She cocked the hammer. "I'm apt to change my mind."

He believed her. "Dovlatov gave your address to the snatch team, and he gave it to me, but who gave it to him? Who possessed the information other than you and your lover?"

"You're very good, laddie," she admitted. "Pavlik always said you lie with the soul of a poet."

"You're not just his lover, though," he continued. "You're his loose end, and he wants you dead."

The opening of the door prevented her response. A voice sang her childhood nickname. "Yulechka! I'm home!"

Emotions passed across the face of Fergusson, joy, doubt, anger, and fear. "In here, Fedyenka!"

Felix Sanhedrin entered the living room like the return of the Sun King. He wore a blue suit, cordovan Venetian loafers, and a white shirt with buttons of amber. His regimental tie bore the blue and maroon colors of the Royal Welsh Fusiliers. A watch encrusted with emeralds and a platinum ring capped with a diamond baguette enriched him. His voice whipped like a flail. "As I live and breathe, it's Nathan Monsarrat. You should have died in the Sinai, old buddy. How did you survive?"

Monsarrat absorbed the man before him. His once skeletal body was packed with muscle. His weak jaw appeared square and firm. His thin and bloodless lips now resembled ripe, red fruit. A thick pelt of sandy hair adorned his previously bald head, and his muddy brown eyes burned with a cobalt intensity. "Your wife let me go. She said she loved me too much to kill me."

"You're lying," Sanhedrin replied. "Somehow, you pulled one of your Houdini acts and escaped."

"Obviously, you didn't love her enough. You killed her."

"She was useful, until she wasn't," Sanhedrin admitted.

Turning to Fergusson, he kissed her, more fondly than with passion. "Where did you find him?"

"In the Church of St. Christopher," she began.

"Tell me later," he interrupted. "I want to chat with our guest."

"Enjoying your second coming, Felix?" Monsarrat asked. "Can I still call you Felix? Fyodor Stepanovich Shchedrin seems so formal."

Sanhedrin turned to Fergusson. "Someone's been talking out of turn, Yulechka."

"Before he died, I wanted him to fully understand your genius."

Sanhedrin studied the naked man before him. "Call me François Salamanca. Felix Sanhedrin was cremated along with the bones of another man, and Fyodor Shchedrin died a long time ago in Russia."

He turned again to Fergusson. "Could you cover him with a large towel? I don't fancy a conversation with his virility glaring at me like a bruised Cyclops."

She handed him the revolver. Returning from the bathroom, she dropped a towel onto Monsarrat's lap, smoothing it with her hand. "Too bad for me."

Sanhedrin watched her, his jaw clenched. "I would give you the name of my plastic surgeon, Nathan, except he died an hour after my bandages were removed, and you can always be buried in a closed casket, if your body is ever found."

"Did you find your wife's body after your missiles killed her and destroyed the rendition site?"

Sanhedrin glanced at Fergusson, unsure of the extent of her knowledge. "Dead is dead."

Monsarrat prayed Fergusson understood his message. "Good news for you, though, being such a miser. You didn't have to bury her. You saved the cost of a funeral."

Sanhedrin took the Walther from Fergusson, holding it in his right hand, the revolver in his left. "I wanted to kill you myself, but Abby insisted. She wanted to prove her loyalty to me. Still, all's well that ends well, and your life ends now."

Monsarrat tugged against the restraints. "What's your plan for my body, Felix? Weigh it with chains and drop me into the Thames, like I dropped Dovlatov into the Henry Street Basin?"

"Dovlatov is dead?"

"I killed him with a knife into his brain stem," Monsarrat said, launching his final gambit. "I told Cairstine to confirm with the *Rezidentura*, but she can't, since before Dovlatov died, he ordered a *Rezidentura* snatch team to come here. I also told her that Dovlatov gave me the address of the flat, but she doesn't want to believe me."

The butt of the revolver struck Monsarrat above his ear. His vision blurred, and blood dripped from a second gash in his skull, but he continued, his words slurred. "She asked how Dovlatov knew the address. I explained that you gave it to him, but she thinks I'm lying."

"Is it true, Fedyenka?" Fergusson demanded. "Did you give Dovlatov the address to our flat?"

"Monsarrat lies like other men breathe, Yulechka."

"He isn't lying. He's inside our flat. If you can't explain how he found us, I have to believe him."

"He's smart, and he's devious, and he lives inside your head."

"He waited at the pub. He followed me to the church."

Impatience laced his voice. "It's time to interrogate our guest. When I'm done, we'll discuss your lack of trust."

She stared at her hands, realizing she no longer held a weapon. "Did you betray me, Fedyenka?"

"How can you ask me that question, Yulechka?"

"Answer me."

Sanhedrin reached for her cheek, but his palm cradled the butt of the suppressed Walther, and his index finger pressed against its trigger. The silent bullet drilled a neat circle into her forehead, exiting through the top of her skull in a bloody geyser of bone fragments and brain matter. As she dropped onto the floor, he pointed the revolver at Monsarrat's nose. "Stay very still."

Monsarrat gazed at Fergusson, his slimmest, wasted chance for survival. Her eyes were wide with shock, and blood pooled beneath her head. "You lack people skills, Felix. First you kill Abby."

"Still jealous that she left you for me?" Sanhedrin interrupted.

"Now you murder Cairstine."

"Despite her accent, Yulechka was pure Leningrader, and Russian women are incredibly difficult."

Sanhedrin sat in the armchair Fergusson had vacated, both weapons aimed at the chest of his prisoner. "A good day. Yulechka's dead. You'll soon join her."

"It's a nice thought, but it probably won't happen."

"Do you know something I don't?"

"I know Fergusson thought you led me to her. In truth, she led me to you."

"Go on, old buddy. The longer you keep my attention, the longer you live," Sanhedrin encouraged.

In Direct Opposition, Only One Square Separates Both Kings

Monsarrat pulled against the plastic restraints, with the same empty results. Blood dripped from his skull, and the pain in his head jackhammered. With the death of Fergusson, his sole hope to survive rested in his ability to manipulate the massive ego of Sanhedrin. "You fooled everyone, the Agency, the White House, even me. No one suspected you're a Yaroslavl born hero of the *Rodina*."

Sanhedrin dipped his head in recognition of the compliments. "It's not like Yulechka to talk so much. What else did she tell you?"

"She said you're the most illustrious deep penetration agent Moscow Centre ever produced, in addition to being her lover."

Sanhedrin replied magnanimously. "The story about Dovlatov giving you this address was brilliant, except I haven't spoken with him since my supposed death in Georgetown."

"You forgot to mention that fact to her."

"I wanted to judge the extent of her suspicions, but I'm curious. How did she lead you to me? Be careful of your answer. If you say Dovlatov, I'll shoot you in the face."

Monsarrat modified the facts of his discovery. "I stole her Ferrari. In the boot, I found a dry cleaner receipt. It listed her new name and this address in London. I made sure that Dovlatov received the intel before I kidnapped him, so he could dispatch a snatch team from the *Rezidentura*. Still, your situation is even worse than you imagine."

"How so, old buddy?"

"I also gave the address to Solomon Grinnell, who passed it to one of his Russian clients, the *Rezident* at the Manhattan consulate.

Grinnell swore that Fergusson abducted Dovlatov and killed his
bodyguards at Lincoln Center before escaping to London."

"Did the Russian ask how he came to possess this information?"

"There's nothing more convincing than a corpse, and Grinnell told
his client that Dovlatov was at the bottom of the Henry Street Basin.
I expect the Manhattan *Rezident* forwarded the intel to Moscow
Centre. Crunch the numbers, Felix, and come up with the sums."

Sanhedrin provided the conclusion. "If you're telling the truth,
which is difficult for operatives like us, two snatch teams are heading
here. One from Dovlatov. The other from Moscow Centre."

"I've never been allergic to the truth. Not like you."

"I've always said that your pretty face hid a steel trap brain. I'd like
to continue our chat, but as you noted, I may be pressed for time."

Monsarrat needed him to keep talking as he formulated his plan to
escape. "Where will you go?"

"The world is my oyster, but before I eat it, I need to wrap up my
final loose ends. I should be in Manhattan as we speak, taking out
your Jewish friends, but Yulechka was acting like a Leningrad bitch,
as usual, so I flew here to take care of her. I have to return to New
York, directly after you die."

Bolts of pain shot through his skull, but Monsarrat refused to
surrender. "You think you have a problem with two snatch teams? If
you approach Grinnell, Shackowitz and Goldman will kill you. You
won't have the opportunity to enjoy your new face."

"You're just mad that I terminated your girlfriend in Greylock."

"Killing her parents was gratuitous, but murdering Sylvie was cruel,
even by your sadistic standards," Monsarrat declared. "I will make
you suffer horribly for ending her life."

"Your girlfriend was a pain in my ass, just like Abby and Yulechka. Like you, too, ever since the first day you arrived at Langley. You were smug then, you're smug now, and I will take great pleasure in shooting the self-satisfied expression off your face."

"Personally, I hope Shackowitz and Goldman find you, not the snatch teams," Monsarrat interrupted. "My eternity will be pleasant, knowing my friends ended your life."

"Nobody's coming close to me, not my Russian brothers and not your Jewish playmates," Sanhedrin scoffed. "I'm too rich, and I'm too powerful. I embezzled millions from the Agency and Moscow Centre. My secret account at Baumuth and Gutzner Banquiers in Genève runneth over with stolen cash. Money buys security. It buys protection. It also buys privacy, like my own Greek island."

Monsarrat used flattery to irritate him. "You always planned well, Felix. To fool the Agency and Moscow Centre, you even played the role of the understudy, and you did it well."

"What are you talking about?"

As he did with Fergusson, Monsarrat probed the extent of Sanhedrin's knowledge. "You played back-up to Dovlatov's number one asset in the White House."

"I was Dovlatov's only asset in the White House."

"You really didn't know?"

"What didn't I know, old buddy?"

"After interrogating Dovlatov, I realized he didn't care about you. He only wanted to protect his real asset inside the White House. You were Dovlatov's sap, not his star. Your purpose was to take the fall in case there was too much heat on number one."

"Who in the White House was more important than me?"

"Augustus Haverhill," Monsarrat stated.

Sanhedrin's laugh was clear and true. "You're delusional."

"You didn't have the need to know."

Sanhedrin shifted the barrel of the Walther to Monsarrat's forehead. "I'd love to stay and discuss your fantasies, but I need to leave now, just in case there is a snatch team or two coming. Yulechka may be the target, but I'll make a nice consolation prize, and I don't feel like explaining my resurrection to Moscow Centre or the *Rezidentura*."

Monsarrat considered the odds of his success. He put them as suicidal, propelling himself forward with his arms and legs bound, knocking Sanhedrin to the floor, suffocating him beneath the weight of his body before bullets from the pistol, the revolver, or both ended his life. "You don't want to kill me, Felix. Explaining one corpse is difficult. Two will be a major headache."

"When your bodies are ripe, someone will complain to the Metropolitan Police, but I'll be tanning on my Greek beach."

"If you shoot me, you'll attract the attention of the neighbors."

"The Walther has a suppressor, and if I use your towel, it will baffle the noise of the revolver."

Monsarrat felt like a white belt on the wrong end of a *sensei*'s wrath. "The cops will connect Fergusson to you. They'll connect me to you. You don't want them hunting you."

Sanhedrin dismissed his logic. "I didn't put my name on the title or the utilities, and no one has ever seen me enter or exit the flat. So it's time for you to die and me to leave, old buddy."

Monsarrat refused to surrender his life to Sanhedrin, the ultimate ignominy. "Fuck you, Felix."

A brutal pleasure animated Sanhedrin. He stood, the pistol aimed at the forehead of his prisoner, the revolver steady on his center mass. "You'll only feel the first bullet, so I choose the Smith & Wesson. You'll feel more pain."

"You should rethink your plans. What about the noise?"

"Screw the noise," Sanhedrin replied. "This moment has been too long time coming to worry about the neighbors."

Monsarrat judged the distance between them, the angle to slide his body beneath the bullets. "Hurry up and shoot. I'd rather die than listen to you."

He watched the trigger press toward the point of initiation, the Smith & Wesson buck, and a flame leap away from the barrel. He felt a rush of heat scorch his face, and he heard a detonation followed by a scream as the revolver exploded. He saw Sanhedrin's hand and wrist disintegrate. Metal shards tore into his chest, face, and throat, and he collapsed onto the floor, blood gushing from his jugular.

At the Farm, Monsarrat had learned to rig the barrel of a revolver to backfire and explode in the hand of the shooter. Easier was faulting the ammunition in the cylinder. He suspected the latter, since he had inspected the weapon but not its bullets. He doubted Prince Joshua possessed the expertise to modify the Smith & Wesson, but the bartender with the prison tattoos seemed capable, and if the Nigerian had spoken with his brother before his death, he possessed motive for the action. Honor demanded the elimination of Prince Joshua, but he chose to serve the dish cold.

He slowly stood, staring at the corpse of Sanhedrin. "Your soul is a rat, and your body is a ship."

Deafened by the blast, hobbled by the restraints, his groin aching, he stumbled into the kitchen. A butcher block on the granite counter held knives. He leaned forward, the muscles of his stomach against the edge of the stone, and grasped a wooden handle in his teeth. Tilting his head, he lurched backward, pulled the knife from the slot, and dropped it onto the counter.

He grasped the dull edge of the blade between his fingertips, slowly rubbing the cutting edge against the wrist restraints until the plastic snapped. He sliced the restrains binding his ankles. Retrieving the towel, he gathered his clothes and jewelry and walked carefully to the bathroom. He rinsed his mouth and washed blood, his own and Sanhedrin's, from his body. In the bedroom, he dressed, found an empty Harrods shopping bag, wrapped his hand in the towel, wiped the surfaces he had touched, and flicked off the light switches.

He returned to the the living room. Standing once more over Sanhedrin, he said, "You killed Sylvie, and you killed yourself. Sometimes justice is poetic, but payback is always a bitch."

He cleaned his traces, dropped the towel into the bag, and exited the flat. On Peckham Road, he shoved the bag into a street bin. He walked slowly to the Lucas Inn. Inside his room, he drank a Scotch from the bar, followed by two more. After a fourth, he staggered into the bathroom and vomited. He rinsed his mouth and swallowed aspirin. Stripping off his clothes, he inspected them for identifiers before dropping them into a complimentary laundry sack.

A hot shower lessened the pain in his body. The ringing in his ears subsided, and his hearing returned. He toweled dry gingerly and pressed bandages over the wounds in his skull. He dressed slowly, emptied the safe, and packed his bag. Checkout required only a minute. Outside the Inn, he trudged toward the Peckham Fire Station. Shielding his face from the security cameras, he dropped the laundry sack into a charity bin.

A cab idled before a nearby pub, waiting for closing time patrons. He opened the door, slid onto the rear bench, and issued his destination. "The British Museum, main entrance."

Before the building, he paid the fare. Crossing Great Russell Street, he entered a hotel, waiting at the door to the business center until a patron exited the room. He stepped inside, sat before a computer, and opened a website. After a quick search, he cleared the cache and departed. A cab idled before the entrance. He gave the cabbie his destination and settled onto the bench.

At Heathrow Airport, he entered Terminal Two. Handing the Swiss Air Lines agent his Canadian passport and a wad of cash, he said, "I'd like a First Class ticket on the next flight to Larnaca."

The agent read the data page before printing the boarding passes and returning the documents. "They're nasty cuts, Mr. Sanger."

"I lost a bet and had to shave my head with a dull razor blade."

Clearing airport formalities, Monsarrat found a sundries store. He purchased a pay-per-call cell phone, loading it with one hundred pounds. In the First Class Lounge, he ordered a double espresso. Sitting at a table removed from other travelers, his first call found Grinnell. "Would you like to say *Kaddish* for the *farshtinkener* and his Scottish girlfriend?"

"Reciting the prayers for the dead is an honor," Grinnell replied. "Shall we say them together?"

"I have errands to run. I'll phone when I'm in your neighborhood."

His second call, to Carlyle, went to voice mail. He waited a minute before dialing again. The call connected on the first ring. "You're good to go, wherever you want to go."

"Thank you," she said. "You want to meet for coffee?"

Repeating the words he spoke to Grinnell, he added a request. "Give my best to your helpful friend."

The departure board announced the boarding of his flight. During the brief layover at Zurich Airport, he made a final call, listening to the accented greeting before asking a question. "Any blowback from your trip to the desert?"

"Not at all," Chaggai replied. "Are you satisfied with the results?"

"Getting there," he said before closing the connection.

He snapped the SIM card, broke the body of the cell phone, and dropped the pieces into a garbage bin. He carried his bag aboard the connecting flight, sleeping until the plane lurched onto the tarmac at Larnaca International Airport. The late afternoon sunshine warmed his face, and the soft Mediterranean breezes cooled his skin. Cyprus was the perfect locale to heal his body, mend his soul, and plan his confrontation with Augustus Haverhill.

TIPPING THE KING

A Player Surrenders the Game by Tipping the King onto the Board

Resigning Concedes the Game

The charter flight of Russian pilgrims departed Larnaca shortly
after dawn, landing two hours later at Ramon International Airport,
deep in the Negev Desert of Israel. With Christmas a week distant,
Israel's southern airport teemed with visitors. Some came to bask in
the balmy December breezes. Others arrived to tour the desert's
historic and religious sites. More than a few traveled to experience the
fleshpots of Eilat on the shores of the Red Sea.

The tour guide ushered the unruly group into the terminal. He
offered a stack of passports and a greeting in Hebrew to the
Immigration officer. "*Boker Tov*, good morning."

Nikolai Ivanovitch Kirsanov, a quiet man with a face marked by
faded bruises, a bald pate, intense eyes, a bulbous nose, puffed cheeks,
and a salt and pepper beard stood in the midst of his fellow pilgrims.
In his hemp pants, worn shirt, and rope shoes, he offered the haunted
appearance of a *starover*, an Old Believer. He communicated with
expressions and gestures, refused vodka, and ate sparingly. Beyond
the Bible he carried in his hand, he owned only a sackcloth haversack.

A bus drove the pilgrims across the barren landscape to a hostel in
the center of Eilat. In the confusion of the check-in, Kirsanov slipped
from the group. Crossing Arava Road, he entered a shopping mall.
At a money exchange, he bought shekels with dollars. In a drug store,
he purchased a bottle of witch hazel, a white baseball cap, a pair of
sunglasses, a bottle of water from a local spring, and an Israeli pay-
per-call cell phone, loading it with five hundred shekels.

He rode the escalator to the lower level of the mall. In a public bathroom, he removed his salt and pepper beard and bulbous nose, dissolving the glue with witch hazel. He washed the tint circling his eyes, plucked the cotton balls from his cheeks, and rinsed his mouth with spring water. From the haversack, he retrieved a pair of tactical pants, a white tee shirt, and leather sandals.

In Larnaca, Monsarrat had recovered from the physical beatings suffered inside the Crofton Road flat. His wounds healed and bruises faded, he became Nikolai Kirsanov, hiding in plain sight amongst the Russian pilgrims. Kirsanov was his protection against the dangers of Moscow Centre, if he had been connected to the deaths of Marlowe, Fergusson, and Dovlatov, and from the White House, if his actions had come to the attention of Augustus Haverhill.

To heal his soul, he needed to atone. Having missed Sylvie's funeral, he needed to find her grave, place flowers by her stone, and mourn her properly. He also needed to confront Haverhill. If the president was a traitor, an asset of Moscow Centre, he needed to remove the Russian asset from the Oval Office.

Nikolai Kirsanov ended his life in the bathroom trash can. Nathan Monsarrat emerged from the mall. He walked toward the center of the seaside city. At a street kiosk, he ate a *falafel* in pita bread sandwich and drank a cup of grainy *botz* coffee. Inside the Central Station, he fed shekels into a machine and received a one-way ticket to Tiberias, the holy city of the Galilee, on the western shores of Lake Kinneret in the north of the country.

He boarded a green and yellow bus, falling asleep as soon as he settled into his seat. Waking in Jerusalem, he transferred to a second bus. Passing through the Jordan Valley, he stared at the narrow blue ribbon of the Jordan River. In the late afternoon, the bus reached

Tiberias. He walked toward the southern end of a pedestrian promenade beside the shallow waters of the lake. He smelled sweet resin. In the shade of a tamarind tree, he entered a memorized number into the cell phone.

Amos Chaggai answered on the fourth ring. *"Hallo?"*

"Ma nishma? How are you?"

"I am better to hear your voice."

"Are you free for dinner tonight? I'm in the city across the lake."

"North end of the promenade. One hour, maybe less," Chaggai said, ending the call.

He walked along the promenade, listening to the animated conversations in Hebrew, Russian, and Arabic drifting in the air. Kiosks offered the cuisines of a dozen lands. Families picnicked on benches. Teenagers shared a *narghilla*, the tobacco smoke as thick as incense. At the northern end of the promenade, Chaggai stood like a stone statue before an old Land Rover Defender.

Monsarrat greeted him warmly. *"Shalom*, Amos."

The Israeli wore a gray tee shirt, faded jeans, and work boots. He clasped Monsarrat by the neck. "I am pleased to see you, Nathan. You appear almost healed from the Sinai, although your face is still bruised. You also look like an Israeli with your clothes, tan, and bald head. Tell me, are you here for business or pleasure?"

"I've come to ask for your help."

"Then we will first eat, and later we will talk."

Monsarrat pointed to the signs for the Kanaf Winery on the doors of the Defender. "Do many Mossad assassins retire to grow grapes?"

"Most do not live long enough to retire."

Chaggai drove north along the shore road into the Galilee, past sites revered by Christians, Jews, and Muslims. In the fading light, he crossed the Arik Bridge over the Jordan River, the white cap of Mount Hermon in the distance. Eucalyptus and jujube trees lined the riverbanks, and jasmine scented the air. On the darkening horizon, the escarpment of the Golan Heights towered. He turned onto a dirt road leading to the lake as the sun set beyond the waters and parked the Defender before a restaurant.

Inside the main room, oud music played in the background. He chose a table on the patio by the water. "If we are lucky, the loons will serenade us, also."

Monsarrat absorbed the view. "I knew the Galilee was beautiful, but I never expected to encounter such a profound sense of peace."

"My country is a land of surprises," Chaggai replied.

Summoning the waitress, he ordered a selection of *mezze* appetizers, green olives in red chili oil, *fattoush, tzatziki, hummus* and pita, *babaghanoush, dolmadakia*, and *tabbouleh*. He added two plates of St. Peter's fish and a bottle of local chardonnay to the order.

He turned back to his guest. "In Kanaf, I grow only grapes for Syrah, Merlot, and Cabernet Sauvignon, but the white wines of the Golan are very good, too."

Waiting for the food, Monsarrat offered a summary of his activities since the Sinai, including the murder of Sylvie, the duplicity of Prince Joshua, and the bloody end of Sanhedrin. "I'm glad he's dead, but not at the cost of losing her."

"I am very sad about Sylvie, my friend."

The waitress filled the table with the food, opened the bottle of chardonnay, and filled their flutes. "*B'teyavon*. A delicious meal."

Monsarrat ate with a rare pleasure. "You deserve a happy life."

Chaggai pointed toward the escarpment. "The small cluster of lights on the lower slope is Kanaf. My winery is 400 dunams. In a good season, one dunam yields two hundred cases of wine. Our summers are hot and dry, our winters brief and filled with rain, sometimes snow. The soil is volcanic with good drainage. Do you understand why I explain these facts to you?"

"Tell me."

"The harvesting is finished. Now the early grapes are fermenting before clarification. It is the time for destemming and crushing," Chaggai explained. "My vineyards need me. I need my vineyards."

"I understand."

"If so, stay here, work with me, start your life again. Sylvie is dead. I am sorry. Your home is gone. I am again sorry, but no one waits for you, no job needs you. Is there a reason to return to America?"

Monsarrat drained the flute. "Not a reason. A mission."

"My first mission, I studied in Jerusalem with the rabbis. My second mission, I killed for Israel in Europe and across the Middle East. Now my mission is to grow the best Syrah in the Golan."

"I need to finish what I started. Sanhedrin, Fergusson, Dovlatov, and Marlowe are all dead, but one more may need to join them."

"Who is this person?"

The name fell from his lips like a curse. "Augustus Haverhill."

His voice clinical, Chaggai said, "Killing your president is not a normal mission. It is a suicide mission."

Monsarrat did not argue. "I believe he is a Moscow Centre asset."

A rare display of emotion animated the Israeli. "You have proof?"

"I need to find proof, although part of me just wants to walk away."

"Listen to this voice. It is self-preservation speaking."

"I've tried to convince myself to let it alone, but I can't allow a traitor posing as president to sell my country to Moscow Centre," he explained. "I also believe that Dovlatov killed my friends to protect Haverhill. They deserve vengeance. I can't rest until I honor them."

"Do you honor them if you die trying to assassinate the president?"

Monsarrat offered a grim smile. "I'll try to avoid that ending."

Chaggai refilled their glasses. "Tell me. What is your plan?"

"When I killed Dovlatov, I cut the conduit for passing intelligence from the White House to Moscow Centre, but if I can discover the Russian end of the link, I can turn it and expose Haverhill."

"Moscow is a dangerous city. Why not wait for Dovlatov's replacement to arrive in Washington?"

Monsarrat elaborated on his suspicions. "I believe Dovlatov recruited Haverhill when he was a young diplomat with the State Department, prior to becoming a politician. Haverhill was one of the team who opened our Leningrad consulate in 1973, the same time Dovlatov served in the First Chief Directorate of the Leningrad KGB, watching foreign diplomats. I think they were partners for almost fifty years. Haverhill trusted Dovlatov, but he won't risk his position to pass intel to a new *Rezident*."

"On this suspicion you will wage war against the most well protected man in your country?"

"Killing Haverhill isn't only about patriotism and vengeance," Monsarrat said. "It's also for my own protection. I have to assume the *Rezident* warned him about me. When Dovlatov went missing, he probably concluded that I learned their secret and killed him. He may have already dispatched a black op team to terminate me."

"If so, returning to America will be your death."

"Which is why I need your help again."

Chaggai sighed. "Tell me."

Monsarrat listed his requirements. "A foreign identity with deep roots, passport, credit cards, driver's license, bank account, health insurance, and a cell phone. I also need to open a new account in the Moscow branch of Baumuth and Gutzner Banquiers."

"Why this specific bank and branch?"

"The headquarters of the bank in Genève holds Sanhedrin's money. I need the cash transferred to Moscow, so I can access the money and turn the Russian end of the link."

"Converting enemies into assets is your expertise. Eliminating enemies is mine."

Monsarrat recognized the offer. "I expect I will need your skills."

Chaggai offered logistical hurdles. "Do you possess the passwords and access codes for the account of Sanhedrin?"

"I'm still working on the details."

Waiting exacted tolls, physical and emotional. Stress ratcheted muscles, adrenaline pounded the heart. Movement offered release, survival vindication. Staring over the dark water, Monsarrat asked, "Have you ever lost someone, Amos? A special friend."

Mossad assassins, even retired, did not speak easily of themselves. A moment passed before Chaggai responded. His words revealed his own pains, but he addressed the future and the living, not the past and the dead. "Before Mossad, when I studied in the Jerusalem yeshiva, I found strength in religion. I learned that the Holy Land is a good place to seek solace. It is also a good place to discover closure. If you would like, I am willing."

Monsarrat watched brilliant stars emerge against the black

firmament, their reflections dancing upon the waters of the lake. He saw himself atop the granite summit in Greylock, contemplating his marriage proposal. He saw Sylvie standing proudly in her loft apartment before the framed poster of Stalin and Voroshilov. He saw her Titian hair, chestnut eyes, and pronounced cheekbones. He heard the whinnying of horses in her bedroom, and he heard her sobbing. "Does making wine absolve you from your past?"

"I have learned that the dead forgive more readily than the living."

Monsarrat envied his stoicism. "Who should I forgive?"

"If you are willing to forgive your enemies, perhaps you will also accept forgiveness from your friends. Perhaps you will also forgive yourself. Surely Sylvie wishes you to free yourself from your pain."

"Sometimes, I think it will last forever."

Another moment passed before Chaggai spoke. "In our tradition, we mourn intensively for seven days. Mourning consumes our lives. It is a passion, like a wildfire. For the next thirty days, we mourn but not with such ferocity. For the next eleven months, we reclaim our lives, but mourning remains with us."

Monsarrat recalled Grinnell urging him to mourn Sylvie in order to heal himself. "What happens after one year, Amos?"

"We no longer mourn," Chaggai replied. "We remember."

Monsarrat closed his eyes. He listened to the call of a loon across the dark water, a second, and a third. He opened his eyes as a comet streaked across the night sky, brighter than the stars, a flaming celestial message, if only he could find the wisdom to decipher it.

END

Made in the USA
Monee, IL
05 June 2022

97514438R10192